Curses didn't really exist…did they?

Adley reached back for the light switch. If the bulb still worked, the obscure image would disappear the moment the light when on. The bright flash relieved her sense of unease when she looked back at the corner but only for the briefest moment. As predicted, the shadow was no longer there.

Now it stood right in front of her.

A long string of bones whipped out the top of the obsidian mass, tethered on the end to a spidery hand. It whipped itself straight at her. Adley jerked to the side and the clawed limb smashed into the door and locked it. Adley couldn't scream but she ran to the other corner of the room, farthest from the door. She grabbed a frame off the dresser and threw it at the dark mass. The shadow dissolved. She willed every ounce of strength in a sprint for the door. From out of nowhere, the hand shot out in front of her and spread its fingers like a catcher's mitt ready to grab whatever came its way.

Adley slid beneath the bones and into the door as if she was sliding into home base. The spindly object grabbed her foot as she hit the door. Adley kicked at it and her foot crushed the bony hand. It broke into pieces that scattered across the floor, clattering like a bowl of marbles.

The creature cackled and whispered clearly into her ear, "Aaad—"

"Shut up," she shouted. "Don't say it! You have no right to say my name!"

She grabbed hold of the handle, ignoring the freezing burn on her skin. She yanked the door open and looked back.

Five skeletal fingers with deadly sharp tips flew directly at her face.

Adley must choose—
Save lives or save herself...

Fifteen year-old Adley doesn't know that something sinister haunts her grandmother's old mansion, or that it hides in a dark portal beneath her bed. The demonic being—born of a generational curse—kills the first born child in each succeeding family. And Adley will die on her sixteenth birthday unless she can find a way to end the evil curse. She meets seventeen year-old Victor Trumillo, a descendant of the original victim, and discovers that only he holds the key to destroying the hideous creature. Victor and Adley want to end the curse and save future lives, but will they succumb to fear just when they may have discovered real love?

KUDOS for *Death House*

"Avila has crafted a chilling and horrifying tale that's intense, yet still fun to read." ~ *Pepper O'Neal, author of the award-winning* Black Ops Chronicles *series*

In *Death House* by Carole Avila, Adley Lange is about to turn 16. She and her family move to her late grandmother's mansion in the high desert of Southwest New Mexico, and Adley soon discovers that not only is the mansion haunted, but the monster that inhabits her bedroom is destined to kill her on her sixteen birthday, thanks to an ancient curse. Adley soon befriends the neighbor boy, who turns out to be her only hope at surviving the curse. But time is running out as Adley turns 16 in two days. Avila really nailed her characters in this one. She does a brilliant job of portraying Adley as a troubled teen trying to convince her parents that there's really a monster under her bed when she is the only one that can see it. The plot is strong and will keep you turning pages from beginning to end. *Death House* will get your heart rate up and keep you riveted page after page. ~ *Taylor Jones, Reviewer*

While not a fan of horror for the most part, I really enjoyed *Death House*. Avila did such a good job of developing her characters, it was hard not to fall in love with them, from Adley and her befuddled parents—who can't figure out their strange, unhappy daughter—to Victor, the boy next door, who sees through Adley's angry façade to the vulnerable, lonely girl beneath. If you want a book that will pull you in and keep you there from the first paragraph to the last, you can't go wrong with *Death* House. ~ *Regan Murphy, Reviewer*

ACKNOWLEDGEMENTS

How grateful I am for the support of those who shared their input on earlier versions of *Death House*, including Jasmin Foegen, Laurena Foegen, Maya Porter, and Patti Vickers. I thank Jasmin Foegen, Laurena Foegen, Frank Haverkamp, and John Foegen for taking the time to read through the entire manuscript and share their valuable input. I thank my publisher, Black Opal Books, for their belief in me and my books, thanks to Lauri Wellington for all her kindness, Joyce and Faith for their sharp editing skills, and Jack the artist for his unfailing patience as he helped me with the cover.

~Carole Avila

DEATH

HOUSE

CAROLE AVILA

A Black Opal Books Publication

GENRE: YA/HORROR/PARANORMAL THRILLER/PARANORMAL RO-
MANCE

DEATH HOUSE
Copyright © 2014 by Carole Avila
Cover Design by Carole Avila
All cover art copyright © 2014
All Rights Reserved
Print ISBN: 978-1-626942-08-0

First Publication: NOVEMBER 2014

Published by Black Opal Books **http://www.blackopalbooks.com**

DEDICATION

For my lovely daughters,
Jasmin and Laurena
Girls, it was a pleasure exchanging nightmares!

In Memory of My Father,
George V. Rodriguez
I hope you're proud, Dad.

PREFACE

Never, ever sleep with your feet hanging over the edge of the mattress. It's far safer to scrunch your knees to your chest and tuck your arms and legs under a fortress of blankets. You'll want to cover every square inch of flesh, especially while you're sleeping, because the skeleton's hand creeps up from the farthest shadow under your bed, waiting to strike.

The second it knows you're lost in the world of dreams, spiny fingers dart like a spider and crawl straight to the bottom of your feet. At first you'll ignore the slow tickle of pointed bone, thinking the delicate touch too gentle to be anything wicked. But in the span of a single gasp, the feathered brushing becomes the hungry clawing of lacerating talons. Without a shred of mercy, razor sharp nails pierce the tender skin around your ankles. Anguished howls of terror are lodged in your throat, and no one can hear you scream for your life.

Smell the stench of decay grow stronger as an unseen creature hauls your squirming body closer to the edge of the mattress.

There is no hope of escaping the deadly grip, yet you struggle like a tiny mouse caught by its tail and desperately grab at thin air, trying to seize hold of anything that will prevent you from slipping nearer to death.

Finally, you crash to the floor and gnarled limbs drag you under the bed, into dark murky recesses, those rotting places where only evil can survive.

When you go to sleep tonight, look under your bed and see where the darkest spot lies. That's where it will come from when you're dreaming in the blackest hours, stretched comfortably under warm blankets with your feet just a little too close to the edge.

Don't think it won't come for you, because it will. But only when you think you're safe.

Chapter 1

I can't believe you didn't even ask what I wanted to do!" Fifteen-year-old Adley Lange crossed her arms hard against her chest. The New Mexico desert blurred past her window in a palette of camouflage colors, but Adley only saw red.

"We asked you what you thought about going to Grandma Aggie's for our vacation." her mother said.

"I thought you were just asking my opinion!"

Roger and Caroline Lange exchanged a glance across the front seat.

Adley's frustration level grew. Nothing she said could convince her parents to turn around in the baking desert and return to their Southern California home.

Her father kept his eyes forward on the road. "You told us you didn't care."

"That's because you didn't say you wanted to stay there for the entire summer."

The smooth drive over the highway flowed like a black river without a spec of road kill. Wavy lines rose ghost-like from the newly paved road, always staying just ahead of the vehicle. It might have been a pleasant trip through the Southwest desert but, in Adley's estimation, nothing could improve the lengthy ride.

"Grandma's house is in the middle of nowhere. There's nothing to do there."

Beyond the sagebrush a distant cactus held up its thorny arms, held hostage by its environment. Adley knew exactly how it felt.

"That's the point of a vacation," her father said. "We're getting away from it all."

Adley sighed and stared out the window at mounds of dried shrubs and grasses. She knew she was flying off the handle again but couldn't explain why. Over the last few months, maybe even the past year, her parents, teachers—everyone and everything—inexplicably irritated her to no end. She supposed that, with her friends avoiding her the past several months, it didn't matter where she spent her summer. Her friends had grown distant as Adley's temper grew volatile, but at least this time she had a really good reason to be upset. Her parents didn't care about her feelings, and that thought made her mad all over again.

"And you didn't even go back home for my cell phone," she blurted out.

"We were four hours into the drive before you realized you had forgotten it," her father said.

"Honey, please stop shouting," Caroline said. "My patience is dwindling, and you don't have to throw a fit every time Dad and I try to talk to you."

Adley ignored her mother. She pursed her lips until she thought of another argument in favor of returning home, remembering the creepy feelings that gave her goose bumps during their last visit to Grandma Aggie's mansion. "It's so gross living in a house that someone died in. It's probably haunted."

"Even if the house was haunted," Roger said, "I don't think my mother's ghost will hurt you."

"I'm sure you'll love it at Grandma Aggie's the same

way she did," Caroline added. "She didn't want to live anywhere else."

Adley continued to sneer at the breathtaking landscape covering Southern New Mexico and silently questioned her sour attitude even while letting loose another outburst. "I don't care who wanted to live in it. We've been driving for hours." Each time Adley told herself to be quiet, her parent's had only to say the smallest thing and it sent her back over the edge. The fits of anger had been going on for months, getting progressively worse, and she had no explanation for her outrageous behavior. And her foul mood didn't let up. "I want to stop at a mall before we're imprisoned for the whole summer!"

Roger looked at his wife. She placed her index finger over her lips and gave the slightest shake of her head.

"It's a shame Aggie fell down the stairs last year," Caroline said to him.

"That's what really started the decline in her health," he said. "I'm sorry I didn't see her before it happened."

Adley observed her father's glassy-eyed profile from the back seat as he quickly glanced out the driver's side window, unsmiling, and focused on nothing. She had never seen him without a cheerful mask in front of his family, and his regret looked foreign to her.

"You had no way of knowing, Roger. Your mother wasn't thinking clearly. After all, you couldn't believe all the crazy things she said—that she was pushed down the stairs while she was alone. I wonder just how much those disturbing letters played a role in her death."

"There can't be any truth to them. Those people are insane!" Roger snapped.

Curiosity brought Adley out of her foul mood. The girl leaned forward and set her hands on the back of her father's seat.

"Who, Dad? What letters, Mom?"

"Nothing you need to be concerned with, honey," Caroline said.

"You mean it's none of my business!" Adley crossed her arms and scowled, sliding back into her seat. She glared out the window. Her parents didn't say a word. "Ignored as usual," she griped under her breath, at the same time she wondered why she just didn't shut up.

Even she was getting sick of her own whining. It seemed the closer they got to the desert mansion, the more irritable Adley became. And she really wanted to know what letters her mother was talking about.

"It was strange how she lost her footing like that," Caroline said to Roger. "Didn't Aggie say she felt like she'd been poked by sticks? What on earth did she mean?"

"I don't know," Roger said. "But I wish she had let me get her some live-in help."

"But dear, she said she was happy to live her last days at Capilla Manor and didn't want anyone about."

"I know." He sighed. Adley saw the drop in his shoulders. "I had a lot of fond memories growing up there," he continued. "It's a beautiful place to live."

"Sure, Dad, for a corpse," Adley spat out, and venom saturated her cruel remark before she could take it back.

Roger flinched at the vicious response, and Caroline shouted over the seat behind her. "Adley! How dare you insult Grandma Aggie that way!"

"That was a very unkind thing to say, Deedee," Roger said.

"I keep telling you I hate that stupid name! Why don't you ever listen?" she snarled. "Why did you bother naming me 'Adley' at all?"

"That is quite enough, young lady!" Caroline said. "May I remind you that you gave yourself that nickname when you were four years old? And by the way, if you don't have anything nice to say—"

"—don't say anything at all!" Adley rudely recited in a sing-songy tone.

Caroline whipped her head around and narrowed her gaze at Adley. "Adley Rosalia Lange! That is enough!" she shrieked, her pitch raising several octaves.

It was always trouble on the rare occasion when Caroline resorted to using her daughter's full name and that formidable parental glare. Adley thought her mother was going to slap her, as angry as she was. And Adley wouldn't have blamed her. She felt bad for what she just said, but as she started to apologize something told her to keep quiet. The worst part was that Adley loved her grandmother. She didn't get to see her often but they e-mailed occasionally, and Grandma Aggie often sent Adley cards with a ten dollar bill tucked inside, twenty after she hit her teens.

A minute of silence passed and Adley caught a glimpse of her father looking at her in the rear view mirror. He started to speak to her mother. Adley looked back out the window, covertly sliding the headphones behind her ears so she could listen in on their conversation.

"Adley's grown more and more difficult these past few months," her father said.

"She did tell me a couple of weeks ago that it felt like her anger seemed to grow on its own."

In her peripheral vision, Adley saw her mother look at the back seat. Adley pouted and stared off at the distant mountains.

"She said she didn't know how to keep her bad moods at bay, but every time I give her suggestions for getting in touch with her feelings she gives me the brush-off," Caroline said.

Roger kept his voice low. "You'd think she'd be glad

to get away from home after having driven all her friends away. She's so damn belligerent!"

"I hope this trip to Aggie's makes a difference." Adley heard the futile wish and genuine sorrow in her mother's words.

"I hope my job transfer makes a difference. I'd hate to think I took advantage of my seniority and then have it be the wrong thing to have done."

Caroline patted his arm. "We're doing the right thing, Roger. I'm sure Adley will love spending more time with us now that you're telecommuting and I'm not working. Things can't help but get better when we spend more time together as a family."

Adley's daggered eyes nearly razed the scenery as her head rocked slightly to whatever tune came through on her iPad. Her parents kept speaking, but she clamped the headphones in place to shut out their conversation and disappointment.

Adley was the first to acknowledge that her parents gave her everything she ever needed and tried to spend quality time with her despite their busy schedules. Her mom had quit her teaching job, and her dad opted to move to another state to make their little family close again. And all Adley did was take her unwarranted anger and frustration out on them. She wished she could explain it, but *she* didn't even know what was going on.

At a special meeting, when her parents asked Adley's school counselor for some input, the man assured the Langes that their daughter was simply rebelling like any other teenager, but Adley knew another issue played into the mix. The problem was that not even she could define what kept her on edge. An underlying tension had showed itself months ago, a dark little voice that so easily convinced her to say mean things to people. She was as puzzled by its effect on her as her parents. Adley wondered if her inexplicable complaining and insensitivity would last through their stay at Capilla Manor.

The off-ramp to Grandma Aggie's home came into view, tucked in the southwest part of the state amid the foothills of the Little Hatchet Mountains. It took another twenty minutes of driving through desert vistas of mesquite and juniper that dotted the terrain to find the manor hidden behind rolling hills of drought resistant scrub. The weathered mansion sat at the end of a desolate, mile long road.

Adley pulled her headphones off and stared open mouth at the impressive Spanish oasis that opened up at the end of the lengthy driveway. She had seen it before, but the historical feel of the massive estate managed to take her breath away each time she visited. Adley heard her father's deep exhale. He had to be exhausted by the lengthy drive and frustrated by her outbursts.

"Why did Grandma Aggie build such a big house for just three people?" she asked.

"The original family that built the house had more children and a number of workers who lived on the property," her father said. "It was built in 1745."

"No wonder it looks like it's falling apart," Adley said.

She had only visited Capilla Manor a few times with her parents. Her father's busy work schedule made it difficult to see his own mother. Adley didn't enjoy their last visit, about four years back. Her grandmother was fine, but being in the house bothered her, especially at night. She chalked it up to being younger and less mature, not that she behaved more maturely now.

The vehicle drew closer to the lovely mansion, and its physical deterioration became more apparent.

"I may not know anything about home improvements, but this house is in need of some serious attention."

One side of Adley's lip curled up. She was disgusted by the unsightly home she was forced to live in.

"It does need some work," her mother agreed.

Roger pulled into the red brick circular drive. During Adley's last visit, the landscaping had been simple but well-manicured. Now the shabby front yard resembled a weed-choked lot, and the thick plastered walls begged for more stucco and paint.

"Dad, you said Grandpa left Grandma Aggie enough money to keep her comfortable and the house in good condition. Why didn't she take better care of it?"

Roger shut off the engine. "It's hard to keep up a big place, especially an old one that needs a lot of special care."

"Uh, yeah. That's why people with money hire people to take care of their homes."

"You've got a point. She used to do her best to get us to live here, but in the past few years she didn't seem to want us to come at all. Huh." Roger tilted his head as if he'd only just considered his mother's change of heart about his visits to Capilla Manor. "Maybe she was embarrassed about the condition of the house."

"Well, maybe we can fix it up," Caroline said. She squeezed her husband's hand and gave him a loving smile.

Adley slipped out of the back seat and spun in a circle, as if adrift in the sea and only seeing water from every vantage point.

"No sign of life for miles," she grumbled.

Her parents stretched in the warm sun. "My ancestors worked as miners and built the home with their only lucky strike," Roger said. "Ten or so years later the mines ran dry, and the town folded, but there was enough money to maintain the property as different families moved in. The house was always handed down to succeeding generations."

Caroline held her husband's arm and leaned against his

side, gazing at the historical home with an appreciative eye. "It's easy to understand why Aggie didn't want to leave. Just look at these mission style arches, recessed windows, and the terra cotta roof."

Adley saw stucco in need of repair, dirty panes of glass, and broken scalloped tiles overhead.

"Maybe everything will be different once we're a happy family again," Roger said.

"I'm sure that things will change for the better now that we're here." Caroline said.

Adley rolled her eyes. She thought her mother's weak smile held more doubt than hope. "Hello? Maybe you can't see the overgrown tumbleweeds and peeling paint on those broken-down flower boxes under the windows."

"Only things that need minor repair or cleaning up," her father said.

A vulture squawked in a nearby mesquite tree and drew the Langes' attention to the hunched bird. It flapped its wings and made a racket, as if laughing at the family.

Adley whispered to herself, "Welcome to hell."

She didn't know how close she was to being right.

Chapter 2

Adley stood on the adobe porch, a square no wider and deeper than a dozen crumbled tiles, forced to listen to more of the annoying history lesson as her father fumbled with the keys. He said that the current front doors of sturdy pine had been replaced a few times in the last two centuries. Adley ran her eyes up and down the distressed wood. Varnish peeled off in curly yellowed strips, and some of the iron hardware looked rusty.

"I don't know why Grandma didn't take care of the place," Adley said. "It looks like a dump."

Caroline pressed her lips together and shook her head at her husband.

Roger inhaled through his nostrils and ignored Adley's remark. "I still think my mother may have kept the property in near shambles as a guilt-based incentive to lure me back to Hachita," he said.

"Or maybe she kept this way to keep us from visiting," Adley said.

Both of her parents narrowed their eyes at her.

"What?" Adley said.

Roger shook his head and resumed working the antique brass key into the lock. They all heard the decisive click of the time-worn hardware. Roger pressed his thumb on the latch of the old-fashioned handle and pushed on the door. It creaked open and a rush of cold air greeted the family.

Caroline gasped and ducked behind her husband.

Shielded from the dark interior, Adley stood behind her parents and whispered, "And you want us to spend our vacation here?"

"Aside from a couple of housekeepers, no one's been here for a while, that's all," her father said.

Roger stepped over the threshold with the two others hunched behind him. He reached toward a switch and lit up the entryway. He pulled Caroline to his side so she could appreciate the impressive foyer.

"My mother always kept the interior of the mansion in far better condition than the outbuildings and the yards."

Caroline's eyes glowed like the crystal sconces mounted in the iron fixtures. "Oh, Roger! It's beautiful! You didn't tell me she did so much remodeling!"

"I didn't know she did so much either," Roger said.

Adley stepped past her mother and examined the large area, barely recognizing the entryway. The floor was covered in the same shiny adobe, but new colorful Mexican tiles faced outward between each adobe step of the stairwell, beautified by the addition of a decorative black iron banister. The stairs led straight up to a landing, then curved out of sight to the second floor.

"Thank goodness someone's been keeping it clean," Caroline said.

"The last housekeeper agreed to come in for a few hours," Roger said. "I'll bring the bags in while you two look around."

For a moment, Adley and her mother looked like they were both going to object, but when Adley saw her own apprehension reflected in her mother's eyes, she straightened up, led the way through an arched entry on her left, and flicked on a light switch in the formal dining room.

Caroline clapped her hands and sighed as if she'd just fallen in love. "Oh!"

Eight handsome hand-tooled chairs surrounded a thick wood table worn smooth from generations of use.

A wide door connected to a completely equipped kitchen. Adley pushed the dimmer switch on the wall and several fluorescent light fixtures brightened up the room. China, glassware, and cookware filled shelves and glass-fronted cupboards. Heavy pots and pans hung from a massive steel pot rack. The modern black appliances contrasted with the eighteenth-century, Spanish-style architecture but complemented the wrought-iron faucet, fixtures, and cabinet hardware.

"I don't remember Grandma being big on cooking."

"Your grandparents had a housekeeper who cooked for them," Caroline said. "Your father said Grandma Aggie wanted the woman to stay on after your grandfather died, and in addition to paying a very decent salary, she updated the kitchen for her, too."

Her mother pushed through another door and walked across a lengthy corridor leading back to the foyer. She passed through yet another door across the hallway. Adley looked up at the ceiling before she followed her mother out of the kitchen. Perhaps it was only the darkly stained wooden beams overhead that gave her the sensation of something slithering above her. She shook off the unnatural feeling and joined her mother across the hall in the well-furnished family room.

Caroline had switched on more lights, and Adley saw that the largest room in the manor extended from one side of the house nearly to the other. She thought it might have been a ballroom in another life. The room was partitioned by well-placed seating arrangements and beautiful wood framed screens. The fifteen foot ceiling had been crowned with modern recessed lighting and wood framed tiles.

Caroline nodded her head in approval. "I bet she paid a fortune for all of this."

A titanic entertainment center took up several feet of one wall. It held an impressive stereo, a big screen TV, and a generous surround-sound set up. And lots of old DVDs. The large overstuffed sofas and ottomans created an L-shape in the corner. Adley knew where she was going to be spending a lot of time.

"Please tell me Dad had the cable hooked up."

"We only have the landline connected so we can at least use the phone, but the cable company won't be here for another day or so before you can watch TV. It's such an out of the way place."

Adley smirked. "Yeah, I know."

Caroline started toward a set of French doors that led to a partially covered patio, but Adley stood still and kept her eyes on the door leading back to the kitchen.

"Did you hear that?" she asked.

"Hear what, honey?" Caroline said.

"I don't know." Adley looked up at the ceiling. "I thought I heard something knocking or tapping. It came from the kitchen but like...above it."

"It's probably your dad carrying the luggage up."

"Huh," Adley said.

The view outside the French doors claimed her attention. The breathtaking landscape she remembered as a child had served as a living watercolor, a masterpiece of flowers and shrubbery filled with cozy nooks for playing hide and seek. Now tall weeds, dead grass, and plenty of dried brush supplanted Adley's memory.

A few odd spatterings of wildflowers reminded the Lange's of the love that once thrived at the old manor.

Adley caught up to her mother who had walked farther across the expansive living area. She shivered and happened to notice her mother rubbing her arms.

"This place is pretty, but it always felt creepy to me."

"C'mon. Let's go over here," Caroline said, ignoring the remark.

Adley stayed close to her mother as they passed a table and four chairs centered before a huge bay window. Instead of turning right, back to the entry, they walked down an L shaped corridor at the end of the family room and found a spacious maid's quarters.

"If your grandmother wanted to entice a live-in helper this suite and bathroom would have done the trick," Caroline said. "It even has its own kitchenette."

"What are you talking about? I thought she didn't want to hire anybody."

"It's nothing, really. It's just that Grandma Aggie had a hard time finding a gardener and housekeeper after her accident."

Adley would have made a snide remark, but her nerves were on edge after walking through the house.

Caroline and Adley backtracked and meandered through the formal living room filled with impressive antique pieces.

They found themselves back in the foyer where Roger stood. Two straps of smaller cases crisscrossed his chest and a leather golf bag swung over his back. He held two of the largest bags in each hand. Suitcases flanked him on either side.

"Can I stay in the big room downstairs?" Adley asked.

Her parents glanced at each other. "The maid's room isn't furnished with more than a few odd pieces, and I don't want your dad to spend his summer moving furniture," Caroline said.

Adley quickly offered a suggestion to make the large suite her own. "I can move the furniture."

"Not these big antique pieces. Besides, there are plenty of rooms upstairs," her father said.

Adley stomped her foot and fisted her hands at her waist. "It's not like I'm a little kid. I'm almost sixteen years old!"

"End of discussion," Roger said. "Now everyone grab a box or a bag and follow me." He started up the stairs, his back to his wife and daughter. Adley opened her mouth and her father said, "Not another word, young lady."

Adley clamped her lips shut, yanked on a piece of luggage, and followed her parents up the stairs. The suitcase knocked against each of the steps. Roger paused at the midway landing and hefted one of the smaller suitcases to get a better hold.

"Dad, did you put anything upstairs yet?"

"Not yet. Follow me, girls."

Adley stole a glimpse at her mother, but Caroline showed no concern and trailed her husband with two small make-up bags.

Adley stayed close to the ornate iron handrails. A chipped tile provided a reminder that her grandmother had fallen down these very steps. The nearer she came to the top floor, the more uneasy she felt. Maybe this place really was haunted. Maybe Grandma Aggie's spirit cherished her home so much, she didn't want to leave. That wouldn't have bothered Adley if the mansion didn't feel so scary.

The alcove on the left of the stairwell marked the entry to the master suite on the east wing, Grandma Aggie's former quarters. From her last visit, Adley remembered that two of the four rooms on one side of the hall faced the back yard, with an immense bathroom between them. The other two rooms faced the front yard and were separated by yet another restroom. Adley looked down the long hallway of the west wing.

A lone window marked the farthest point of the house, and the area was slightly darkened in shadow.

"Roger, will you put Adley's bags in the room next to ours?" Caroline asked, startling Adley from her observation.

She and her parents set down the suitcases just inside the master bedroom.

"I don't need to take the room next to yours. I'm not a little kid. I'd rather have the big room at the end of the hall. Dad said it's been redecorated since our last visit."

The idea of being in a newly decorated room wasn't what made it Adley's choice. It was the farthest room from the master suite. Lately, her parents were constantly nagging and treated her like she was a burden. Adley wanted to be as far away from them as possible.

"I'm not sure about you having that room," Caroline said, and she looked at Roger for support.

"I'd feel better with you closer to our room, too," her dad said.

Adley argued her point. "I'm being forced to live in the middle of the high desert during my school vacation in a house someone died in. I should be able to pick the room I want."

"This is a big house, honey," her mother said. "I'm sure you'll feel more comfortable sleeping near Dad and me."

"That room is all the way on the other side of the house, Dee—I mean, Adley," Roger promptly corrected. "If there was a fire or worse—"

His daughter rudely interrupted. "If someone breaks in

or if my room catches fire I'll scream my lungs out."

"Believe me, we're well aware of your lung capacity, but—"

Adley's volume increased with the interruption. "I deserve to have that room in exchange for all the sacrifices I have to make by being here!"

"Now listen, Deedee," her father said in his soft voice, but Adley screeched her reply.

"My name is Adley! Why can't anyone respect what I want, like being called by my name? It's Adley!" she shouted again.

"You need to watch your tone, young lady," her father said.

Caroline closed her eyes for a brief moment. "Grandma Aggie didn't get around to buying a new bed for that room," she said evenly. "And even though she had the room refurnished, I don't think she wanted anyone to use it."

Adley felt her anger boil within. It shot into her balled up fists and tightened her facial muscles, a convincing sign of an impending outburst. She screeched every word of her upset.

"I'm not a little girl—I'm a teenager! And Grandma's not here anymore, so it's not like she'd care! There's no reason why I shouldn't have that room!"

"All right! All right!" Her mother raised her hands and relented. "Go ahead and take it!"

Roger shook his head and started to unpack a bag.

Adley lifted her nose above her haughty smile. Although it didn't feel good to shout at her parents, she still did a little victory dance along the carpet toward the other end of the hall, resembling a grade-schooler more than the teenager she claimed to be.

☣ ☣ ☣

Adley noticed that, unlike all the other doors in the house fitted with elaborate crystal knobs, a piece of old silver hardware embellished the door to her new room. She took a firm hold of the ornate L-shaped handle, and the metal chilled her fingers. She jerked back her hand.

Every part of her skin that touched the ice-cold handle looked practically frost-bitten. No wonder the knobs on all the other doors were different. Grandma Aggie must have forgotten to replace this one.

It didn't matter why the fixture was freezing to the touch. If Adley complained about it, her parents were sure to make a stink and use it as an excuse to keep her from taking the room. She tucked her hand into the cuff of her long sleeved T-shirt and pulled down on the handle. The fixture clicked, and the door slowly opened.

It felt like she stood in front of a freezer door. The burst of arctic air felt like the same icy breath as when her father first opened the front door. Adley shivered, chilled from head to toe, and hesitated. The room had been closed off for a long time and that had to be why she felt a sudden chill when she opened the door.

Adley looked back down the hall. Her parents stood at their bedroom door watching her, as if ready to change their minds about letting her have a room so far from theirs.

Maybe they also felt like she did in that moment, as if it was a big mistake for her to take a single step into the room.

Chapter 3

Her father called from the other side of the hallway. "Everything okay down there?"

Adley wasn't about to give up the fight for her room. She nodded, afraid her voice would crack, and entered.

"I'm going to get the groceries from the car," she heard her father call out. "Holler if you need anything."

Three tall windows, draped in striped pink and white organza with white sheer panels, faced the large circular drive out front. The same striped material that graced the windows also covered an easy chair and ottoman. A white antique six-drawer dresser matched a darling vanity table with a beveled mirror. The vanity chair was upholstered with a Victorian floral print.

Everything in the room was dainty and feminine, not the type of furniture that Adley pictured for herself, yet she was eager to become acquainted with this new, grown-up style. Just enough pieces outfitted the large room without feeling overcrowded. It was all perfect, except for the bed.

The bed sat in stark contrast to the glamour of the other furnishings in the room. The queen-sized headboard was composed of various lengths of rounded ivory colored strips. Some were short and horizontal. Others were lined vertically and curved slightly, reminding Adley of small antelope horns. The odd pattern was slightly familiar and almost primitive, as if the bed belonged in tribal surroundings. The white cotton comforter and lacy pillow shams appeared dull next to the ominous headboard. It detracted from the feminine touches decorating the rest of the room.

A light pink satin dust ruffle skirted the entire perimeter of the box spring, not quite touching the floor. Adley stared at the shadow beneath, and an intense uneasiness poured over her, similar to the eerie sensations of invisible snakes slithering above her when she and her mother inspected the kitchen, which happened to be located precisely below Adley's bedroom. Something wasn't right.

"Change your mind?"

Adley jumped. "Mom!" she shouted. "Why did you sneak up on me like that?"

"I didn't sneak up on you. Honestly, Adley!" Caroline set her hands on her hips. "It sounds like I spooked you."

"You did not!" Adley lied.

"Are you sure you don't want the room next to ours?"

Adley lifted her chin. "No, thank you. I'm not a baby," she declared as she stomped her foot on the floor. Her fingers curled into her palms and rested at her waist, and she unknowingly imitated her mother's peter-pan stance. "I love this room and it's perfect for me. I'm going to stay in it."

"Even so, I think I scared you," Caroline said. Adley made to protest but her mother added, "I'll have Dad bring the rest of your things, and if you need me, I'll be downstairs in the kitchen."

Her mother held securely onto the handle, not flinching at the temperature of the metal, and pulled the door closed. Adley heard the whistle of a happy tune as her mother walked down the hallway, as if she was glad to have scared

Adley. That proved all the more that she was right about her parents, especially her mom, who didn't demonstrate one bit of interest in the fact that her daughter was emotionally distraught. Obviously, her mother didn't love her anymore.

Adley heard a noise drift up behind her, like a quick but brief flapping of wings, and the disturbing feelings from moments before returned. She wanted to dash out of the room and escape whatever had made the sound, but her feet remained glued in place. She forced herself to pivot around and eye the dust ruffle at the foot of the bed.

The wavy bed skirt fluttered slightly, as if someone drew a finger across the fabric from one corner to the other.

Adley shuffled backward toward the door without removing her bulging eyes from the bottom of the bed. The retreat felt as if it took forever until the wintry silver handle poked into her back. With eyes still riveted on the dust ruffle, Adley slipped her hand inside the sleeve of her shirt and extended an arm behind her. The polar handle cooled her skin through the cotton fabric.

The ruffle fluttered again, only the wave flowed in the opposite direction. Panicked, Adley felt her shirt sleeve slide off the smooth surface. After repeated tries, she finally grabbed the fixture and gave a hard wrench. The door opened, and Adley backed out of the room, keeping the bed in sight. Once both her feet were on the carpet, she reached for the chilly hardware and pulled the door shut.

She paused a few seconds in front of her closed bedroom door, feeling safer in the hall. Her legs felt wobbly, and her heart thumped to a heavy techno beat. In a moment, her breathing steadied, and she willed herself to move.

Adley sprinted down the hallway before she had a chance to see or hear anything else.

☣ ☣ ☣

Caroline took the afternoon cooking duty while Adley gathered dishes in the kitchen and set the dining table. She returned to the hutch in the kitchen for three cobalt blue glasses and stopped at the door connecting to the dining room. Adley considered the possible outcomes if she told her mom and dad about the weird encounter in her bedroom.

Her parents might make fun of her for letting an overactive imagination get the best of her. Or worse, they'd use this as an excuse to make her take the room next to theirs. They could touch the handle and see for themselves how cold it was, but her mother hadn't commented on it at all when she left the room.

Adley wondered what the probability was of them believing that the fabric skirting the bed had moved on its own. She tried a different strategy.

"Mom, I'm pretty sure I heard a weird noise when we first walked through the kitchen. If Dad wasn't upstairs, what do you think made that sound?"

"I can't tell you," Caroline answered, sautéing vegetables in a skillet. "I didn't hear anything."

"What about those creepy feelings we got in the family room?"

Caroline shook a strainer of lettuce greens over the sink. "Honey, you said you had the creeps. I didn't say anything of the kind."

"Yeah, but I didn't hear you say otherwise. And the way you rubbed your arms—"

"Sweetheart, if this is about staying in the room down the hall—"

"It isn't!" Adley snapped. "Can't you admit that you had the shivers like I did?"

"I'm not going to argue with you, Adley." Caroline wiped her hands on her apron and pointed toward the dining room. "Please finish setting the table."

Adley pushed through the door. For whatever reason, her mother didn't want to acknowledge their shaky tour of the house.

Her father entered the dining room and smiled. "Great job on the table, sweetheart." She looked at the place mats askew, and the utensils crossed over each other. The glasses sat half off the mats.

Dinner was served under the well-lit chandelier, another wrought iron masterpiece. The pine table and sideboard enhanced the Spanish flavor of the interior, none of which impressed Adley. She pushed potatoes and squash around her plate as she contemplated various scenarios to explain the fluttering dust ruffle, none of which were believable.

Roger and Caroline discussed ideas for the yard.

"If a family was ever going to live here, a new gazebo out back might be a good idea," Caroline said. "Don't you think so, Adley?"

"What? Huh?" Her shoulders jerked as she snapped out of her reverie, distracted by her imaginings of what possibly shook the fabric skirting her bed.

"That's twice today I've managed to scare you out of your wits," Caroline commented.

Adley frowned at her mother. "You didn't scare me!"

That settled it. She knew any confession of how scary it felt to be in her room was a sure way to get herself treated like a child. Treated like a little kid named Deedee. She'd keep her mouth shut about what happened in her room. Right after dinner she'd try to resolve the dilemma on her own, starting with a peek under the bed.

Roger lifted his eyebrows at Adley's harsh response. He glanced across the serving platters at his wife who was especially bewildered by their daughter's vehement denial of having been shaken.

Roger and Caroline spoke exclusively to each other for the rest of the meal as Adley picked at her food.

Eventually, the meal was finished. Adley declined dessert and reluctantly pushed her chair back. Without a word, she picked up her plate and utensils and took them into the kitchen. She set them inside the sink and left through the back of the room. The hallway pointed the way to the foyer and staircase. Adley was ready to trudge back upstairs and face whatever lurked beneath her bed.

Too bad her parents didn't call the cable company in time, or she could have stayed up late to watch television, putting off her bedtime.

☣ ☣ ☣

Adley's parents enjoyed a cup of coffee and two servings each of plum cake before they cleaned up the spacious kitchen. Caroline rinsed a floral serving dish and handed it to her husband. Roger set it in the dishwasher.

"It's lovely here, but are you sure you feel comfortable staying in your mother's house?" Caroline said. "Not that Adley phrased it nicely, but last year's memories aren't very pleasant." Roger remained quiet and leaned against the counter. "I mean, it has to be difficult for you," she added.

He took a moment before answering. "My mother wanted to live her last days here because she loved Capilla Manor so much. That's why she had her bed carried downstairs instead of going to a nursing home. Not even that idiotic rumor of a family curse could put a damper on her living here."

Caroline dried her hands on a towel. "Other than those horrible letters, you've seemed reluctant to talk about it."

"I've already told you all that anyone knows," Roger said. "It's a ridiculous story. Some gypsy ancestor cursed a man but it backfired. Supposedly, the first born child from every generation was going to die before they turned sixteen years old."

"How did you survive? You didn't have any siblings."

"That's the proof of it being all a hoax," Roger said. "Either that curse is a bunch of hogwash, or I'm a powerful gypsy who can ward off the devil himself." They laughed and Roger said, "Don't you think Deedee seemed more uptight than usual this evening?"

"Don't let her hear you call her that," his wife jokingly warned. She rinsed out a dessert dish and sighed. "She doesn't realize how hard it is to love her when she's so difficult. Every time she acts up I can't help but feel responsible for her terrible behavior."

"That's exactly how I feel." Roger squeezed liquid dishwasher detergent into a cup inside the machine door. "But it's not like we spoil her. We don't give her everything she asks for." Caroline shrugged, as puzzled by Adley's behavior as her husband. "What did you mean tonight when you told—" He stealthily scanned the room and whispered, "Deedee," then spoke in a normal tone, "—that you scared her out of her wits twice today?"

Caroline chuckled. "Oh, you should have seen her face when I walked into her room this afternoon. It was like she turned to stone. Something really made her hair stand on end."

"I'm surprised you think it's funny that she was so scared," he said.

"What I meant was that Adley is afraid to be in a room so far from ours. What I think is funny is that she doesn't want to admit she's uncomfortable with the physical separation from us."

"Maybe she'll get some manners scared into her," Roger said.

"I agree." Worry flooded Caroline's face. "Where have we gone wrong in raising her? Haven't we tried everything we could to make Adley happy?"

Caroline dropped her head, and Roger pulled her into his arms. They both shared a sigh.

"If she didn't explode with those tantrums, it wouldn't be so bad," Roger said.

His wife agreed. "Or at least if she was a little quieter."

☣ ☣ ☣

Her parents couldn't have guessed that, at that very moment, Adley was as quiet as they had hoped.

She sat in the middle of her bed, completely paralyzed and unable to utter one word because of a constricting knot swelling in her throat. The blood had stopped flowing through her tightly clamped hands in a death grip on the comforter.

Adley couldn't have been quieter. Unless she was dead.

Chapter 4

After dinner, Adley went back to her room while Roger and Caroline finished the dishes. She summoned her courage and touched the handle.

It still felt like sub-zero ice.

She tucked her hand into her sleeve and opened the door. Thankfully, the atmosphere felt normal again. Neither odd shifting of fabric, glacial air, nor any eerie feelings crept up after five minutes of observation from the hallway. Adley felt ridiculous for letting her imagination go off the scale. How crazy to think the dust ruffle moved by itself!

She tiptoed to the bed, crouched on the floor beside it, and peeked beneath the box spring. The murky expanse underneath showed nothing unusual, only a few tiny dust balls and thin air occupied the shadowy space.

Adley unpacked her luggage and arranged her few favorite knick-knacks she brought from home. Some of her school photos and a couple of stuffed animals would at least make the room feel like her own during the long summer. Once again she admired the fabrics and colors that cheered up the walls and windows. She reexamined the charming vanity that gave the room the most feminine of touches. Soon, thoughts of frightening noises and unseemly movements disappeared. Even the foreboding headboard went unnoticed.

After changing into her pajamas, Adley sat on the comforter and kicked off her slippers. Her legs dangled over the edge of the mattress, and her feet swung back and forth as she conducted a meticulous inspection of her surroundings. Her confidence had been restored in the decision to occupy the room for the summer.

Adley's most important task involved deciding on the right spot for her latest school portrait. She concentrated heavily on the placement of the photo and barely noticed the tickle whisking along the bottom of her heel. She casually wiped one foot on top of the other, thinking the bed skirt created the light touch.

Adley considered displaying her tenth-grade picture above the dresser when she again felt the fragile touch, this time under the arch of her foot. It felt like a stroke from a sharp and chilled object, like the mechanical fork that lifts small toys out of vending machines. She shook off the unnatural sensation and tried to recall what she stored below the bed which might have rubbed uncomfortably on her sole.

Nothing had been stored underneath. What, then, stroked the bottom of her foot? She drew her legs up onto the bed and remained motionless, except for rubbing the cold spot on her heel. Adley dug up enough courage to lean over the edge of the bed and looked down. Nothing. Her head hung upside down, and her hair swept the floor. She lifted the dust ruffle like it was made of a volatile explosive, two fingers pinching the edge of the fabric.

Upside down, she squinted into the shadows where the gloomy darkness seemed to stretch for miles. A soft white blur skulked in the far corner and its white twig-like fingers crawled deeper into the black abyss.

Adley whipped her body upward and scooted to the center of the mattress, wiping off the needle-like tingling from her foot. Her ears labored to hear the slightest unnatural sound. She waited. Time had escaped her. Did ten seconds pass or ten minutes? At long last, a slight rattle drifted up from somewhere beneath her, a wisp of noise, so tiny, yet it roared violently in her ears and competed with the loud pounding of her heart. Adley became a living statue, cemented into position.

Unfortunately, she heard an equally terrifying sound. Fabric rustled against fabric. Something caught on the comforter and the material tugged slightly downward at the foot of the mattress. It was a small action with a huge impact.

Adley's mouth dropped open, and she willed herself to call out to her parents, but she couldn't emit a single syllable. She felt the blood drain from her face, and she paled like a ghost.

A loud knock sent her heart rushing out of her chest.

"Adley?" her father called. Roger pushed the door all the way open. His eyes grew wide the second he looked at his daughter. "Honey! What is it?" he said.

Adley succeeded in eking out a few words. "The—there's—some—something under my bed!"

Roger looked as if he wondered what could possibly have shaken her so badly. He stepped into the room, lowered himself onto the floor, and peeked under the bed.

"My gosh!"

Startled by her father's outcry, Adley lurched backward and fell on top of her pillows, her back pressing into the bumpy headboard.

"I've never seen so much dust!" Roger called up from the floor.

Adley felt all the tension drain from her body. Her fear and vivid imagination, nothing more, temporarily immobilized her. Her father stood up, brushing the dirt from his palms.

"What makes you think something was under the bed?"

"I saw the bed skirt flutter and something tugged on the comforter. I felt it move."

"These old houses aren't well insulated between floors. You probably have a crack in the floor or baseboard molding where an air current is flowing through," he explained. He looked about the floor, then back at his daughter. "And sitting on the comforter is probably what made it move. You were so panicked and focused at the end of the mattress, I'll bet you weren't paying any attention to what your feet were doing."

"I was rubbing them. Something underneath the bed tickled them," Adley said and wiped the bottom of her foot.

"It was probably one of those dust balls. The housekeeper must have missed your room."

"I saw something, Dad. It looked like a giant white spider."

Roger kept a straight face for all of a second then broke out in a grin, and his daughter couldn't help but join him after hearing herself say the ludicrous remark out loud.

"There's my beautiful daughter. Thought I'd lost her. Get some sleep, Deedee."

Just like that, her good mood vanished. "My name's Adley!" she said, plopping her arms across her chest and sinking into the pillows.

Put off by her tirade, her father shook his head at the floor and pressed his lips together. He turned out the light just before he shut the door.

Although she didn't feel any cool streams of air, Adley tucked herself into the warmth of the comforter. She didn't know what made her speak rudely to her father when he was being so kind.

He looked at her with a heart filled with pure love, and she did nothing but throw a wet rag on it, dampening his spirits as well as her own.

Sapped of energy by the frights of the day, sleep easily alleviated any residual fears. Fast asleep, her back to the closet door, the exhausted girl never saw the hulking black shadow against the wall pulse in time with her heartbeat.

The onyx figure swayed to and fro, dripping blobs of gooey sludge from its black, elongated fingers. The image collapsed into a thick mass, and dark slime poured slowly onto the floor. It coagulated into a viscous puddle, and its edges wormed in and out.

The oozing muck stretched into a curvy stream and snaked its way underneath her bed.

☣ ☣ ☣

"Adley!" Caroline nudged her daughter. "Get up! It's nearly ten o'clock!"

"I'm sleeping in. I'm on vacation," she groused and angled her head the other way.

"It's a family vacation. Come on down for breakfast. Your dad made crispy French toast, just the way you like it."

Adley lifted her head. "That's an unfair bribe."

Caroline laughed. "Yeah, but it worked."

Adley hadn't had cornflake fried French toast in ages. After dipping triangular cuts of sweetened bread into a cinnamon egg batter, Roger rubbed the bread in corn flake crumbs and cooked it in hot oil and butter. Adley didn't know if she liked it more because it was a tasty alternative from regular French toast, or if she relished the breakfast treat because her father made it only for her.

Caroline jostled Adley on the shoulder.

"I'm getting up!"

Adley plodded downstairs in pajamas behind her mother and into the dining room. She shuffled in pink fuzzy slippers like an aged convalescent, her tangled hair poking out in different directions.

"How about a drive into Minero after breakfast?" Roger said.

"Do they have a mall or a Starbucks?" Adley asked and folded into a chair.

"Probably not, but it's a great old mining town," he said.

"Maybe later," Adley said, "when I'm desperate."

Roger placed a hand on Caroline's arm before she had a chance to object to Adley's rude comment. Without another word, Adley finished her meal. She stood and hesitated, wanting to thank her father for the tasty surprise.

She glanced at him and left the table.

☣ ☣ ☣

Caroline dropped her fork on her plate.

"We can't expect miracles overnight," Roger said. "Let's give it a week or two and see if Adley lightens up."

"I don't know if my patience can hold up," Caroline told him.

Roger patted her hand. "As long as we support each other, we'll do fine." He stared through the arched portal connecting to the foyer.

Caroline laughed. "You look as uncertain as I feel."

"Let's give Dee—" He looked heavenward. "—Adley, the benefit of the doubt. Just a couple of weeks before we try any new tactics."

"There aren't any new tactics left," Caroline said.

Roger smiled at his wife. "I have a feeling that things are going to be different here."

❅ ❅ ❅

Whatever the reason for the uneasy sensations each time she approached her bedroom or went inside it, Adley refused to consider giving into her parent's wishes and changing to the room down the hall. Admitting to them that she was frightened was like admitting she wanted to be treated like a child instead of a teenager. They didn't say a word over breakfast, but Adley felt her parents were holding back on asking her to switch rooms.

She dressed as quickly as possible and then sat in the living room with her headphones securely in place. Adley had borrowed her father's laptop and found it notoriously slow without DSL, as if that mattered. She had no e-mails, except spam and online catalogs. There were zero comments on Facebook. No one responded to her comments, either. Not for over a year. Her rude behavior had earned her the online silent treatment. She wasn't even worth being bullied.

Adley's frustration mounted at not understanding why she felt so hostile. When she tried to do or say something nice, like thanking her dad for the great breakfast, something clicked inside and shut off any of her good feelings. It didn't help that the angry feelings had intensified since arriving at Capilla Manor.

Her school counselor suggested she record her feelings in a journal, telling Adley she needed to vent her feelings in a safe environment without offending anyone. She might have done it if she trusted her parents to respect her privacy, especially her mother, who might do anything to know what Adley was thinking, including reading her journal.

Then she'd probably find ways to try and change Adley and tell her what to do with her life. No thanks.

Adley was miserable enough without letting her mom get into her head. She had to face it. Her days were headed toward utter tedium without a mall, arcade, or movie theater nearby. Her parents didn't care that the desolate vacation made her an unwillingly slave to boredom. And now she see-sawed back and forth between her own imagination and the maddening feeling that something horrible inhabited her room.

It fast became a challenge to fill up the day with anything of interest. Even if the cable had been hooked up, nothing worthwhile showed up on daytime TV except reruns and game shows. To top that off, most all of the movies Adley wasted time watching in Grandma Aggie's DVD collection weren't even in color, and practically none of them ever became a remake. Who wanted to watch an old black and white western called *High Noon* or a love story called *Splendor in the Grass*?

Grateful that bedtime finally arrived, Adley changed into pajamas and crawled under the covers. At least she didn't have to notice how unbearably slow time passed while she slept. She thought to bring only one book, a teen romance that her mother said was inappropriate because of the adult subject matter. It wasn't well written and none of the content was new to Adley, but her mother didn't want her to read it, and that made it worth sneaking off the bookshelf before leaving home.

If they had Wi-Fi access, Adley could have researched free fantasy novels that popped up on Google.

A big yawn filled her lungs. Droopy eyed, Adley set the book on the night stand and clicked off the tiny book light. She muttered, "When is this boredom going to end?"

It took several minutes for Adley to fall into a few solid

hours of heavy sleep, and then her boredom came to an abrupt halt.

☣ ☣ ☣

Suddenly jarred awake, Adley sat up in bed, in the dark stillness of her room. She couldn't remember what woke her up. Disturbing dreams haunted her sleep, but she didn't recall anything specific. She visually scoured the room, assessing every dark space cast by the bright moonlight. Satisfied that all was in order, she lay back down. Shadows lurked just inside of her peripheral vision, tiny noises darted like flies in her mind, and frigid air bit into her feet.

She ignored it all and drifted off toward sleep until a slight scratching underneath her bed brought her back to full wakefulness. Adley's eyes flew open. She waited a moment and heard it again. She'd had enough manicures to know what a nail being filed on an emery board sounded like, but as quickly as it had started, the scratching stopped.

Adley listened for the sound again. Her fingers locked over the edge of the thick comforter and her knees nearly touched her chin. A few heartbeats passed, and then she heard a light drumming, like tapping, directly beneath the bed. The noise reminded her of the shopping trip with her mother last month. While Caroline tried on shoes, Adley, impatient and annoyed, strummed her finger tips on a chair handle. Directly beneath where she lay, the rataplan announced the same waiting, waiting cadence.

From down the hall, she heard a door open then shut. One of her parents was up.

"Mom?" she choked out. "Dad? Is that you?"

The tapping noise moved to the end of the bed, closer to the door.

"Mom? Dad?" she called louder.

Her bedroom door opened, and her mother turned on the overhead light. "What is it, dear?" Caroline's hair was tousled, sleep still reflected in her eyes.

"Something's making a noise under my bed!"

Caroline looked at her daughter, taking in Adley's large round eyes and the comforter drawn just below them.

"Adley, what is it?"

Roger's voice sounded from down the hall. "Everything okay?"

"Adley thinks something's under her bed," Caroline said.

"Something is there!" Adley insisted. "I heard it! And not just once. It's been making noise for a while now."

Roger joined Caroline at the door. She calmly entered while Roger looked back down the hall toward the room closest to the master suite. He looked at Adley and back down the hall again.

Caroline walked to the edge of the mattress where Adley last heard the finger-like thumping. Adley gaped in horror as her mother knelt on the wood floor, stooped forward, and lifted the fabric encircling the bottom mattress.

Caroline peered beneath the bed and screamed at the top of her lungs.

Chapter 5

A mouse! There's a mouse under the bed!"
Adley expelled a huge sigh of relief. The scratching and drumming ended up being nothing more than a small rodent.

Her mother wasn't relieved at all that Adley had a mouse in her room. Caroline wailed like a siren, bouncing on tippy-toe from one foot to the other in an Indian war dance to keep from stepping on any furry vermin. Caroline pounced onto the bed for safety and collided with Adley, who had jumped up to avoid a direct hit.

"Get it, Roger!" Caroline shrieked.

She inadvertently shoved her daughter backward, and Adley grabbed the headboard for balance, feeling the top edge give slightly under the weight of her hold. Adley's foot slipped off the mattress, and Caroline kicked her book light off of the bedside table. It fell to the floor and slid under the dresser.

"Mom! Get off of me!" Adley yelled.

A small, white furball headed for the opposite side of the room.

Caroline, terrified by the small mouse, pointed somewhere at the ceiling and shouted, "There it is!"

She hugged the air out of Adley, fiercely protecting her

baby from the germ-infested brute. Before her parents stormed into her room, Adley had been scared out of her wits, expecting the creature to be far more horrifying and deadly, but now she laughed at the sight of her mother scared out of her wits by the tiny creature.

Roger quickly hunted for a container, keeping one eye on the minuscule prey that scurried under the vanity. He found a discarded shoebox, and after a few clumsy attempts bumping into furniture and upending small frames on the table, he successfully apprehended the critter. The mouse rattled against the sides of its cardboard cage.

"Amazing how such a little varmint can cause such a big scare," he said.

Roger quickened his pace out of the room as the mouse thrashed, trying to escape the box. Caroline collapsed onto the bed, dragging Adley down with her, and slouched into the pillows. She slowed her rapid breath before consoling her daughter.

"Are you all right?"

"Yeah, Mom. I'm fine," Adley answered, just as breathless.

"You should have seen your face!" her mother said.

"You should have seen yours!" Adley giggled, and Caroline playfully shouldered her daughter.

"When Dad and I came in you looked like you'd seen a ghost."

"I thought I heard one, but thankfully it turned out to be a mouse."

"Ready to switch rooms?" her mother teased and was immediately disheartened when the sparkle in Adley's eyes died out.

Adley bounded off the bed. "No! I'm not switching. I'm old enough to live two rooms away from my parents."

"Fine!" her mother said. She scooted off the mattress

and raised her hands up in surrender. "Sorry I said any-thing."

"Why can't you and Dad stop hounding me? I don't want to change my room!" Adley crossed her arms for show.

Caroline bit her lower lip, as if considering her re-sponse. "I won't bring it up again. I'll ask Dad not to men-tion it, too. Okay?"

"Okay," Adley mumbled.

Before jumping off the bed Caroline scanned the floor, and sprinted to the door. Adley's eyes narrowed when her mother touched the handle. She didn't recoil at the freezing surface and held it as if it were any other knob in the house, as if the penetrating iciness didn't exist.

"Good night." Caroline said. Before Adley could ven-ture any protest at being left alone in the dark, her mother switched the light off and closed the door.

Adley was a bit leery about the idea of getting out of bed to switch the light back on or to fish the book light out from under the dresser. What if another mouse scampered across the floor, and it had rabies and bit her? She crawled up to the headboard, scrunched her knees tightly to her chest, and pulled the blanket over herself. She remained tightly balled up for what may have been an eternity.

Time passed. Her head bobbed up and down as her eyelids fell shut but snapped open an instant later. Little by little, her rest-starved body tired of anticipating the arrival of a gang of vengeful mice. Her legs relaxed and Adley's head leaned closer to her shoulder. Her body slowly tilted and gradually reclined to the side.

Before her mind completely surrendered to fatigue, Adley imagined a cloudy image forming on her wall adja-cent to the closet. Plain reason and an ardent desire for sleep convinced her that it was merely a tree from the outside creating the scraggly shadowed drawing on the wall. She drifted into a cavern of dismal chambers and unending tunnels as disturbingly odd shapes hovered overhead, but Adley was too exhausted to be frightened by any nightmares.

She finally descended into unconsciousness, oblivious to the inkblot forming into a hunched, deformed skeleton with fangs. The inky specter danced like a flimsy rag doll, flopping upon the walls, and it grew larger with each awkward thrust of claw-like hands.

Curved shadows shaped themselves into crooked black fingers that peeled, smoke-like, off of the wall while the rest of the macabre body remained, as if drawn with smeared ashes. The filmy mass of acutely pointed bone floated to the edge of the comforter, to the outline of Adley's feet protruding under the blankets. Black pincers opened and lightly clamped onto the thick blanket, moving the girl's foot from side to side. Adley shook her ankle, too tired to awaken. The curvy blades dissolved into a snake-like vapor and drifted underneath the bed.

In her sleep, a troubling memory nagged on the edge of Adley's thoughts. She needed to remember something, but a much needed slumber fully consumed her before she realized that the shadows on her wall couldn't have been created by limb-shaped branches and leaves.

There weren't any trees near her bedroom windows.

☣ ☣ ☣

Sheer white curtains subdued the translucent rays of bright yellow sunlight slipping inside the room. Adley woke up uneasy and tense despite the comforting warmth. The scary apparitions she dreamed of the night before robbed her of a good portion of her peace of mind. It was hard to tell if she had suffered one continuous nightmare or if she actually saw her bizarre dreams come to life. She'd seen shadows lifting off the walls and bits and pieces of ivory swirling overhead.

In the last semester of her biology class, she had to memorize the names of the major bones in the human skeletal system. Her dreams reminded her of a particular homework assignment where she had to label the name of a bone on the line beneath its picture. Femur, tibia, fibula. Was it human bones she envisioned floating above her bed?

She had dreamed the tip of something pointy swiped lightly along the bottom of her foot, and she tried again and again to brush it off. It felt the same as the first time her feet swung over the mattress, but the eerie touch in her dream felt just as real.

Adley leaned over the edge of the mattress. She let her head sink toward the floor and lifted the bed skirt. She peeked upside down under the bed. Nothing was there, yet it felt like she hadn't been alone. Last night she heard the same scratching and tapping as she fell asleep. There was only one explanation.

Another mouse had found its way into her room.

Despite being tired and unsteady, Adley tumbled out of bed and picked out a T-shirt and jeans, socks and underwear from her dresser. Then something tapped and scratched under the bed. She grabbed a pair of socks, her shoes, and juggled all the clothes as she hurried to the door.

Adley hit the handle downward with her shoe and yanked it open. She scrambled into the hall, let her clothes fall to the carpet, then turned around and stared at her bed. She heard nothing and the dust ruffle didn't move. She touched the handle with the tip of her finger. It was bitingly cold. A sock slipped easily over her hand, and she pulled the door shut.

Adley grabbed her clothes as if they were her last possessions on earth and hurried downstairs to change inside the maid's quarters before she joined her parents for breakfast.

☣ ☣ ☣

"Good morning, sleepyhead," her father greeted.

"Wow! You look like you could use more shut-eye," her mother said.

"I was up half the night waiting for a giant mommy mouse to take her revenge out on me," Adley sniveled. She rubbed her bloodshot eyes and waved a palm in front of an imaginary headline. "Girl kidnapped by jumbo furry mammal."

"It would probably want one of those expensive imported cheeses for ransom," her dad said.

"Have some breakfast." Caroline set a plate stacked with hot blueberry pancakes in the middle of the table. "Dad and I are going to sweep and mop downstairs today and dust all the furniture. You can finish organizing your room."

"How about I help you clean instead?" Adley's voice carried an unexpectedly enthusiastic lift.

Roger and Caroline exchanged wide-eyed glances.

"Do you think you'd like to finish straightening your room first?" Caroline asked cautiously.

"No. That's okay. I'm almost finished. Besides, the rooms here are so big. It'll take us all day just to clean the lower level."

"Thanks. We'd really appreciate any chores you could do," Caroline said.

"I'm going to get some more orange juice," Adley said and left the table.

Roger smiled happily after his daughter. He leaned over and said to Caroline, "We may have to call a pet store and order a dozen more mice."

"I'd rather clean the house by myself than see another mouse," she said.

⚠ ⚠ ⚠

After breakfast the Lange family went straight to work. Drapes were gently vacuumed and then flung open. Floors were laboriously swept and mopped. They broke for lunch when the cable company knocked on the door to install the new box and wiring.

Caroline was afraid they'd become lethargic after they had eaten with ravenous appetites, but Adley jumped from the table as soon as she swallowed the last of her sandwich. She washed it down with a gulp of milk and said, "Let's get moving!" Her unexpected lead recharged her parents, and they dived back into a cleaning frenzy.

As Adley had predicted, it took most of the day to make the downstairs presentable. The three Lange's used every ounce of energy stored in their arm and leg muscles. Every swipe of furniture polish or glass cleaner brought the home closer to its original splendor. Furniture glistened, floors shined, and windows were free of streaks. Wood polish and glass cleaner scented the air.

The large grandfather clock in the entryway struck five in the evening and the Lange's were stunned at how long they had diligently worked after their lunch break. Dinner was a simple affair of pasta and salad but surprisingly pleasant because Adley happily participated in the light conversation. Much to her dismay, it was impossible to escape the dreaded arrival of bedtime.

Adley approached her room cautiously, as if she confronted a grizzly in the wild instead of a mouse. She covered her hand with the front of her shirt, then slowly pressed down on the frosty handle and pushed the door open. On a count of three, she rushed to her dresser, ripped clean pajamas and underwear out of the top drawer, and ran back into the hallway, grateful not to hear any wayward noises.

She showered in the bathroom next door to her room and, after putting on her pajamas, she had an idea come to mind. Adley figured if she asked her parents to help in searching for the wayward mouse, they'd have her change bedrooms. But maybe if her mom or dad heard the noises, they'd help her thoroughly investigate her bedroom. She devised a simple plan to get one of them to visit in her bedroom for more than a few minutes.

She poked her head into the master suite and saw her mother first. "Mom, can you tell me what you think of the way I arranged my school pictures in my room?"

Caroline smiled as she gave her husband a raised brow and then accompanied her daughter down the hall.

"Sure, honey. I'm glad that you want to consider my input," she said as they walked side-by-side down the long corridor.

Adley tensed as they neared the door to her room, not knowing what to expect. She tugged once, then twice, on the sleeve of her pajamas and pulled it over her palm, holding it in place with her fingers before pushing down on the handle.

Her mother didn't question why, but she looked at Adley as if her daughter had spun her head in a full circle.

"Handle's dirty," Adley said.

Caroline didn't appear convinced, but she kept quiet and followed Adley into the room. Adley showed her mother a group of family photos atop the vanity and a trio of school pictures set in frames well placed on the wall.

"I think they're perfect where they are, honey," Caroline told her daughter. "I especially like the arrangement above the dresser."

"Thanks, Mom. Um, what do you think I should do with—" She scanned the tops of furniture and the walls, conjuring an excuse to keep her mother in the room long enough to hear the same noises that worried Adley. "What should I do with the vanity? Leave it against this wall or slide it next to the bed?"

Caroline leaned against the door jam and seemed to carefully consider her words. "I think the vanity may not fit next to the bed because the wall isn't wide enough," she replied and held her breath for Adley's reaction.

Adley looked at the wall. "Um, yeah. You're right," she agreed. "That part of the wall isn't as wide as the vanity."

Uncomfortable silence followed and heightened Adley's anxiety. She couldn't repeat her mother's words all night. She wanted to fabricate another excuse to keep her mom with her, but no other ideas came to mind.

Caroline pushed off the door. "You did a good job arranging things, Adley," she said and headed out of the room.

"Uh, wait! What about moving some other pieces of furniture around?"

"I'm afraid the larger pieces of furniture limit the ways you can arrange them," her mother said. "You can't really do much with the layout." Adley pressed her lips together and nodded. Caroline squinted at her daughter. "Well, I'm going to bed now—"

Adley grabbed the sleeve of her mother's robe when she tried to leave the room. "But, Mom! Wait!"

Caroline stared down at the desperate grasp.

"Sorry." Adley withdrew her hand and saw the crease of doubt in her mother's forehead. She wanted to tell her mom that she was bothered by something crazy in her room but that seemed childish. Adley had made such a stink, insisting she have the room and demanding she be treated like an adult, yet here she was acting like a kid, afraid of what was, most likely, another stupid mouse. Although she didn't want her parents to think of her as a cry-baby, Adley didn't know how to communicate her anxiety like an adult.

"Adley, do you want to tell me anything?" Caroline said.

"Yeah. No. What I mean is—I don't want to stay in this house anymore," Adley stammered. "It makes my skin crawl. I want to go home and sleep in my own bed!" It was stated the best way Adley could manage without admitting she was frightened.

Caroline touched her daughter's shoulder. "I know it's hard to think about Grandma dying here, but she went peacefully in her sleep. She really did love her home. Give it a few days and I'm sure you'll change your mind about Capilla Manor."

That was the last thing Adley believed. The freaky events made Capilla Manor far from what a real home should feel like, even if was just mice.

"Try to get some rest," Caroline said. "You'll feel better in the morning."

Adley almost hoped her mother would insist once more on her taking the room closest to the master suite. Instead, Caroline exited the room and shut the door behind her. Unsettled, Adley seriously considered sprinting after her mother. Part pride, part fear, kept her riveted where she stood next to the door.

She whirled around and stared at the furniture, as if the

decorative pieces had been rearranged while she wasn't looking. The only things that had moved were her growing anticipation and jittering nerves. Adley didn't breathe, just listened. Nothing frightening assaulted her ears and, except for the occasional lonely yelp of a distant coyote, all remained quiet. Her eyes shifted to the ruffled fabric running the circumference of the mattress. Nothing moved.

Adley forced in a long breath and let it drain out. She left the overhead light on and climbed into bed, burrowing inside layers of blankets. Again, she listened. The silence was as disturbing as the unease that consumed her the night before, only tonight, after the long day of housecleaning, it was more difficult to stay awake.

Her eyes no longer focused on the incandescent light of the bulbs in the ceiling fixture, and her limbs soon relaxed. Nervous tension eased with the peace found in deep sleep.

All was well and as it should be until hours later when Adley snapped awake. Her mind worked to dissolve the sluggish fog of sleep. The first thing she noticed was the overhead light.

It was off, and the room had been swallowed by pitch black.

Chapter 6

The first warning had been the overhead light. Adley distinctly remembered leaving it on before going to sleep, but now the room was hostage to an unsettling gloom. She blinked several times, and her eyes adjusted to the silver lunar rays that snuck past slits in the curtains.

Something touched the bottom of her feet, a slight tickle running like an electric line from the pad of each foot to the heel. It took a fraction of a second to process the information: if a spider hid inside her bed, it couldn't trace an identical track upon the bottom of both feet, simultaneously. And unlike the rodent that scurried beneath her bed the night before, this one was under the covers.

Adley kicked furiously at the blankets as something jabbed at her feet over and over. She screamed for her parents to help, an outcry that exploded in her room. The agonizing appeal went unheeded by the work-worn couple.

Like an agile gymnast, Adley sailed off the bed while blood pumped through her veins at full speed. Blankets rustled behind her, and the slight noise hammered in her ears. The dim light revealed a triangular lump beneath the comforter, making its way up toward the pillows.

Adley bolted to the door and cried out when the wintry

fixture felt like it burned the palm of her hand and fried her skin like droplets of water in hot grease. Forced to relinquish the handle, she yelled again for her sleeping parents, but they didn't hear the disturbance.

A snake-like hiss drove into her ears. She glanced over her shoulder and clearly saw a bony white object, a skeletal hand, scuttle with an adept spidery stride across the comforter directly toward her. Ignoring the pain searing her skin, Adley grabbed the handle, tore the door open, and vaulted into the hallway.

She stared at the claw-like spider. It dropped over the edge of the mattress and crawled into the obscure depths beneath her bed. An eerie snicker rose up from the onyx expanse before she slammed the door shut. She bolted downstairs, not wanting to stick around and discover the origin of the reptilian cackling.

In the huge family room, Adley burrowed into the overstuffed sofa and curled into a tight ball. Her palm had reddened at the touch of the freezing handle, and she held it to her chest. Adley pulled an afghan over her body and covered every inch of her exposed skin below her eyes. She listened for the slightest unnatural noise from above and heard nothing for the longest time.

Her head bobbed up and down as slumber fought to overtake her, yet Adley was determined to stay alert in case something had followed her downstairs. An occasional thump and hiss from the second story kept any decent sleep away. As long as the clamor originated from her room, Adley felt she'd be safe, separated by the ceiling from the unbelievably hair-raising commotion upstairs.

Gradually, her body slumped against the cushions and her mind melted into the freedom of sleep until the first signs of sunlight brightened the lengthy room. Adley's eyes bolted open and darted nervously about the high ceiling, not in appreciation of the elaborate crown moldings and ornate ceiling tiles. She listened for any of the fretful noises originating from above the kitchen, in the bedroom she had demanded for her own.

Adley kept alert while considering what she might have seen and heard only hours before. She saw something in her room and it was alive. Mice didn't hiss and if she wasn't mistaken, despite the impossibility of it, she could have sworn she counted five legs on whatever scurried under her bed.

It had to be a mouse, with a tail she'd thought was a fifth leg.

Telling her parents that she saw another critter would be the perfect way to end up in the room next to theirs, which might not be so bad anymore. Instead, she'd ask again to take the servant's quarters downstairs. If they thought the room down the hall was too far, then the downstairs unfurnished suite had to be out of the question, but she'd give it another shot.

It seemed to take forever before the sun broke fully over the horizon. Adley straightened out her legs, painful though it was to unwind the tight muscles. After a few stretches she paused to listen for any unusual racket from the vicinity of her bedroom.

Adley tiptoed to the bottom of the stairs and tilted her ear toward the top of the curved staircase. She placed a tentative foot on the first step and worked her way upward, hearing only random creaks of the wooden floorboards supporting the adobe tiles.

At the topmost step, she peeked at her parents' door. Closed. She unnecessarily inched quietly along the carpeted corridor and eased her bedroom door open to see what lay inside. She peered into the room and saw nothing amiss. Except for the rumpled blankets, the room was in perfect order with a glimpse of red and lavender clouds between the curtained panels.

Adley had to get out of her pajamas and into some clean clothes. She'd spend the next day out back or walking up and down the graveled road that led to the main highway. It didn't matter what she did as long as she was not anywhere near the second floor.

She surveyed the bed skirt. It didn't move. The heavy silence pressed in and shook Adley as much as whatever crawled into her bed last night. Her eyes remained fixed on the dust ruffle, and she debated entering the room.

"What is it?"

Adley jumped in the air and twisted as if she was about to return a difficult volley across a net, practically giving herself whiplash.

"Mom!" she shouted. "Why do you keep sneaking up on me like that?"

"Quiet down, Dee—Adley. You'll wake Dad." Caroline looked over her daughter's shoulder. "What's got you so unnerved in your room?"

It was a chance to tell her mother about the thing that crawled under her bed and the freezing handle on her door. Adley looked downed at her hand and absently rubbed the blisters.

"I saw this weird spindly-legged spider thing under the blankets."

"I think your imagination is going wild," Caroline said.

"It crawled under my bed."

"I knew it." Caroline's eyes darted about the room. "We have mice!"

"It didn't look like a mouse," Adley countered.

Caroline started down the hall. "I'm going to get your father."

"Wait!" Adley called out in a panic.

Her state of anxiety surprised Caroline, and she walked back to Adley's room.

"What's the matter, honey?"

"Um, will you like, um, wait while I get my clothes?" Caroline crossed her arms, and Adley explained the need for an impromptu security guard. "I need you to look out for the mouse."

Her mother dropped her arms and nervously rubbed her fingers together. She scanned the floor. "I don't know how much help I can be if a mouse pops out for a visit."

Adley waited.

"Sure," Caroline answered. "Go ahead and get your things."

"Thanks, Mom."

Adley dashed about her bedroom. In record time she grabbed wildly at under garments, socks, shirt, pants, shoes, and purse. Her arms were full, and Caroline pulled the door shut, not flinching in the slightest when she touched the silver handle.

"If I had known you could get your clothes that fast, I would have put a mouse in your room every morning before school," Caroline said, but Adley didn't reply.

Her mother walked to the master suite, and Adley headed for the staircase. She peeked back down the hall toward her bedroom. A dark shadow seemed to enshroud the entire area in front of her bedroom door. The longer she stared, the darker the shadow grew, pulsing like a huge stain of black energy, throbbing to the same pounding beat of her fearful heart.

Adley shook herself out of the daze and ran downstairs.

☣ ☣ ☣

Adley barely ate any meals. She watched black and

white movies without the sound and passed the day in a trance. All because of some stupid mice. Her eyes tired of reading and watching pharmaceutical commercials, reruns, and Grandma Aggie's old movies. Soon it was time for bed all over again, and Adley marveled at the quick passage of time. She trudged upstairs, and her dad called from his desk inside the master suite.

"Adley?"

She stood at the bedroom door. "Yeah, Dad?"

Roger didn't take his eyes off his computer screen. "Your reading light broke when it fell under the dresser. I found a table lamp in the garage and thought you might like it for your room."

Her voice fell flat. "Great." The creepy feelings weren't going away with any amount of light.

Her father looked up. "I also replaced the bulb in the last fixture at the end of the hall. It was getting kind of dark down there." Adley looked over her shoulder to the far end of the wing, still enshrouded in shadow.

"Thanks, Dad," she said with little enthusiasm and started down the hall.

Caroline saw the disappointment on her daughter's face. She set her novel down and stepped out of the room.

"The lamp has an old rawhide cover that needs to be replaced," she called after her daughter. "But the lamp itself is beautiful. We can paint it white. It'll do for now. I'll show you."

Caroline put her arm around Adley and walked with her to her room, showing no alarm at the darkened mist at Adley's door.

Her mother stepped directly into the onyx smoke and the entire black aura floated away to the window at the end of the hall. Caroline didn't notice anything amiss.

The hand carved wooden dowel lamp had three curved

legs, a work of art if not for the hideous animal shade. Caroline noticed Adley's immediate dislike of the rawhide light cover.

"Imagine it with beautiful fabric, maybe a solid, to match the curtains or the vanity settee."

"Yeah. Maybe."

"I don't blame you for not liking it, but your dad was just trying to be helpful." Caroline sat on the bed. "It would be a fabulous room without the ugly headboard."

Adley thought that a new bed wouldn't make a difference with an invisible monster cloud hanging around in the hallway and a funky spider thing crawling around under her bed. She decided to grab her pajamas and sleep downstairs.

"For now, it would be a lot easier to replace the lamp shade than the bed," Adley said.

"Maybe we can shop for a bed online."

"We'll be back home before it arrives," Adley said.

Caroline pressed her lips together, looked down, and then put on a quick smile. "A pastel pink shade might look nice or maybe an off-white accordion style?"

"What about pink and white stripes to match the curtains?" Adley asked.

She knew it was a horrible idea, but she had to keep the dialogue going as a ruse to keep her mother in the room. In record time Adley's pajamas were on, and her clothes were tossed inside the closet hamper. She started in on clothes for the next day.

Caroline flinched at the gaudy idea of a striped shade. "That might be too busy for the rest of the room."

Despite Adley's anxiety, fatigue settled in. She yawned. "Yeah, you're right." It would only take a little longer to grab some jewelry, her make-up, and underclothing from the drawers. "Either one of your ideas would work."

Adley picked up her shoes from the closet floor, slid a fresh pair of jeans off a hanger, and yanked a nice T-shirt from another. Now to make her exit.

"Did I tell you that I wanted to get a degree in interior design?"

It had been a long while since her mother shared anything personal, and the question caught Adley's attention. "What? No, you never told me that."

Caroline repositioned herself against the headboard, a pillow behind her head. She crossed her legs at the ankles and rested comfortably on the bed. She stared upward, as if a movie screen had appeared on the ceiling, one that only she could see as it played film clips from her past.

Adley set the small pile of clothes on the dresser and lay next to her mom. Caroline put her arm around her daughter and proceeded to share stories about her college days that Adley had never heard.

Her mother relayed funny adventures of all night toilet-papering by her sorority of the frat house down the street, using hundreds of rolls of colored paper. A homely boy in her biology class had a crush on Caroline, and her roommate sent a Valentine to him signed with Caroline's name. He followed her around the campus for months.

The story telling lasted for a while, and the last adventure Adley heard was the time her mother went to a party with upperclassmen, not realizing she wore two different colored shoes.

Adley didn't share enough moments like this with her mother. She listened attentively but soon nodded off to the hypnotic lull of Caroline's soothing voice.

Caroline's arm throbbed under Adley's head. She had

fallen asleep. Caroline brushed hair from her daughter's face and her lovely features emerged. She marveled at Adley's natural beauty as she slept.

Sliding out of the bed with as little movement as possible, Caroline pulled the comforter over her daughter. She stepped lightly to the door then switched off the light. As she pulled the door closed, a black form rushed across the room, like a hand with long fingers.

Caroline thought it was the winged shadow of a night owl flitting past the window.

Chapter 7

A dley dreamed of the cold. An arctic current invaded every cell of her body. Her nose, fingers, and feet iced over. Every limb felt chilled from the biting frost. It was like waking up in a polar cave, yet a buoyant cloud floated below her body and her head was nestled on a soft, chilly cushion.

A soft tapping rose from under the bed and startled Adley into sudden awareness. Her mother was gone, and she was alone in the room. She bolted upright. Adrenaline surged, and she scrambled to her feet, holding onto the ugly headboard that provided leverage atop the springy mattress. The four inch wide wooden slat capping the frame shifted under her weight, loosening up more than the last time she used the frame to stay balanced. It was a silly observation to make when she was consumed with fear.

Her heartbeat throbbed in her ears, loud enough to make it hard to hear anything else. Adley forced herself to swallow air, long pulls to slow her heart rate, to keep the blood from pounding out of her veins. She waited in unnerving silence but didn't hear another sound.

She inched her way to the foot of the bed, looked down, and spied her dull reflection on the shiny hardwood floor. An unwelcome tapping crossed the floor beneath the headboard to below where she stood at the edge of the bed. Clumsily, she stumbled back to the headboard, sinking into the comforter and mattress with each step. She listened. The same tapping tailed her underneath the bed, from one end to the other, stopping below the headboard.

"Crap," she whispered and a distinct hiss filled the room.

Adley's heart beat faster and her head spun with indecision. Should she make a run for it? Yell for her parents? To heck with them thinking she was a baby. Her mouth opened wide but her vocal chords refused to budge. A guttural sob was the best she could muster. Adley heard another tap, convincing her all the more to get out of the room.

If she took a flying leap off the bed, she'd be at the door in a few long strides. Although, with socks on, she'd slide and possibly lose her footing. Adley came up with an idea. She took her socks off and wriggled one onto her right hand to pull the door open in one swift motion. She rolled the other sock into a tight ball and planned to hurl it to the far side of the room, away from her escape route. It could buy a couple of seconds to get her out the door.

Ready to shove off, she tossed the make shift ball toward the windows. No predatory varmints chased the sock, but she did feel a tug on the comforter at the foot of the bed. Something was coming to get her, and it occupied the space between her and the only way out of the room.

On impulse, Adley blindly reached for the ugly bedside lamp and wrenched with all her might, ripping the cord out of the socket. She raised it into the air, ready to strike. The ethereal light of the crescent moon revealed a single ivory finger at the edge of the mattress, curled with a tip as sharp as a knife, beckoning her forward, a tiny macabre invitation to join it at the foot of the bed.

A loud metallic snap rang out but rather than coming

from the creature, the loud click sounded when her mother opened the door.

Caroline turned on the light and gasped at the sight of her daughter, who had all the makings of a combat-ready commando, preparing to assail the air with an antique Spanish lamp in one hand, a sock on the other.

"Do you see anything on the floor next to the bed?" Adley whispered.

Her mother took a glimpse at the bed then paled. "The dust ruffle fluttered," she said to Adley. "Oh, no! Roger! Roger!" her mother shouted.

Caroline vaulted on top of the bed and collided with Adley. They hugged and called out.

"Roger!"

"Dad!"

Without delay, their rescuer's footsteps pounded down the hallway.

Mother and daughter tried to stay balanced on the springy mattress and clung madly to one another.

"Mom!" Adley called out. "Did you see it? Did you see it?"

"No! Did you?"

"Then why are you screaming?"

"Because I saw the dust ruffle move!" her mother shouted.

Roger flew into the bedroom, clutching a golf club, gallantly prepared to bogie any intruder, no sillier looking than Adley with a lamp in one hand and a sock on the other. His wife and daughter, eyes wide and white, were a spectacle of arms, legs, and lampshade fused together.

"It's another mouse!" Caroline yelled. "Don't just stand there! Get it! Get it!"

"Let me guess," he said calmly, and stepped forward. "It's under the bed."

"Dad! Watch out!" Adley warned. "It's some kind of spooky hand or something!"

Roger delivered a blank stare to his daughter then knelt on the floor and laid the five iron beside him. He lifted the bed skirt and inspected the dark area. "My gosh!" he yelled.

Adley and her mother screamed. Her father lifted a white article, as if he were holding a soiled diaper, touching as little of it as possible.

"Lucky thing I set the club down. I almost killed your sock." He tossed the cotton garment onto her bed and made an obvious assessment of the matching one on her hand. "They go on your feet, sweetheart."

Caroline blew out the air stored in her lungs. "Thank goodness that's all it was!"

"Mom!" Adley yelled. "You saw it! A sock couldn't make the dust ruffle move!"

"Now, honey," her mother explained. "I was slightly upset at the time."

Roger extended his hand and assisted Caroline to the floor.

"Slightly?" her husband questioned.

"I threw my sock at the window. How could it get under the bed?" Adley said to her father.

"Lousy shot?" Roger took the antique lamp away from his puzzled daughter and offered his hand to help her down, but she ignored it.

"You said you saw the dust ruffle move!" Adley shouted at her mother.

"It was moving because you were jumping on the bed!" Caroline reasoned. "I was horrified at the thought of seeing another mouse, just like you were, honey."

Adley pounced on the floor and jabbed an accusing index finger toward her mother. "You saw it, Mom, and you know that's not what it was!"

"Calm down, Deedee," her father advised.

"I will not calm down, and my name is Adley!" the girl shrieked.

"I think we should have an early breakfast, Caroline," Roger sternly announced.

"I think so, dear."

"I can't believe this!" Adley said. "You saw it!"

"That is quite enough!" Her mother spoke through slightly clenched teeth. "I'm not going to keep arguing. Come down to breakfast and, if you must, we can calmly discuss what happened. After you've settled down."

Caroline followed her husband out of the room, and it didn't take long for Adley to register that she was standing alone on the floor.

"Wait for me!"

Adley ripped the pile of clothing from the dresser and catapulted after her parents. She pulled the door shut with her socked hand. As the handle clicked in place, curiosity got the best of her. She cocked her head and listened.

Something tapped impatiently on the other side of the door. She wisely backed away and ran downstairs to join her parents.

☣ ☣ ☣

"I think it would be nice to have breakfast this morning by the bay windows in the family room," Caroline told her husband in the kitchen. She placed their meals on a two-tiered rolling tray, and Roger pushed it through the swinging doors to the living room.

Adley had sunk onto the sofa, leveling the remote at the television. For twenty-five minutes colorful images had blurred by her eyes. Caroline called Adley to the breakfast table, once, twice, then three times before catching her attention. Adley sat down and yawned. Roger and Caroline exchanged glances.

"Dee—uh, Adley, you look like you need to get out of here for a while. Would you like to take a drive with us this morning?" Caroline asked.

"Sure," the girl grunted.

Pajama-clad and snarly-haired, with puffy eyes and sallow skin, she dragged a piece of Belgium waffle around her plate, etching curvy lines in the syrup.

"Are you feeling well, honey?" her father asked.

"Yeah," came the short reply, and she finished the rest of her meal in silence.

Adley's dirty clothes amounted to a small pile in the laundry room off the maid's quarters. She'd wash and stash the clothes downstairs. After she dressed, the family left for Minero, a small town off Highway 9, a few miles east of Capilla Manor. Adley's mood improved dramatically once they were en route. She almost forgot about the mice and tapping noises. The best and most logical explanation for the outlandish and unreal occurrence was precisely what her mother told her it was. She let her imagination run wild.

The high desert vista filled each window as the car traversed the country highway. They sped past the closest residence to Grandma Aggie's, one mile down the road. It was a large, single-story older ranch house with stables and corrals. The outbuildings required as much repair as the dilapidated barn.

"Gosh," fussed Adley, "who'd want to live in there?"

Her parents grimaced. The scare that nearly silenced Adley at the manor made a rapid disappearance.

"It's not like there are rusted cars or discarded water heaters in the yard. It seems to be in good condition for such an old house," her mother said. "The place just needs some cosmetic work like Capilla Manor, that's all."

"More like an entire face lift," Adley sneered.

Roger and Caroline exchanged disappointed glances. Caroline leaned over the cup holders and whispered to her husband. "Are you thinking what I'm thinking?"

Roger kept his voice low. "You mean do I have any pangs of regret at having included Adley on the drive regardless of how forlorn she appeared this morning?" Caroline nodded. "Fortunately, it won't take much longer to get to the center of town."

Adley huffed in the back seat and her bangs flew up. She didn't bother reminding her parents that she could hear them whispering from the back seat without her headphones. After all, she couldn't blame them for her own lousy disposition that seemed to come and go at will.

She noticed that the stores were located on a two-block road and nearly every business housed multiple businesses within. The grocery store also harbored the post office and utility company. A small diner was a gift store and pawn shop. The library served as the local newspaper and sheriff's office.

Adley fought the urge to complain but soon her inner grump took over. She was disgusted by the rural lack of modern conveniences and entertainment. "They don't even have a Starbucks!" she whined. "This place is so boring!"

Roger's shoulders dropped. "So much for a cheerful tour of the community."

Adley couldn't help raising a fuss when she saw store windows opaque with grime. She complained that the trees lining the center divider were dried out even though she really didn't care about the city landscaping, and she criticized the unpaved parking lots. She also inwardly berated herself for letting the uncontrollable urge to spout negative remarks creep back up to the surface.

Roger pulled into the diner parking lot. Tires crunched on the gravel as he parked in front of the quaint eatery.

"How about a cup of coffee, Caroline?"

"Sure," she said.

"You guys went through an entire pot during breakfast." Adley's tone was filled with accusation.

The Langes exchanged conspiratorial looks and continued sliding out of the car.

The aged diner, older than the ranch they had driven by on the way into town, needed as much repair. Once inside the clean but run-down building Adley said the restaurant was in repulsive condition.

The fake leather booths were too dusty, the curtains too dingy, and the faded linoleum floor had spots so worn they'd probably pool water if any was spilled on them. Though the store was on the opposite end of the building, Adley said the merchandise was most likely overpriced.

When she criticized the waitress for being too skinny, her father suggested, "Why don't you explore the library next door while your mother and I have our coffee?"

Adley rolled her eyes. "Whatever."

"Mornin', folks! The name's Anne Marie," the waitress warmly greeted. "So you're Aggie's family? Movin' into her old haunt, er, uh, house, huh?"

Adley made note of the woman's choice of words.

"Actually," Caroline replied as she glanced at Adley, "We're only vacationing."

"Well, it'd be nice to see more people in town," the waitress said.

"Excuse me. I think I'll explore the fabulous library," Adley dryly announced.

She slid out the booth, stomped out the door, and left the restaurant, wondering if it would have been better to stay home alone at Capilla Manor.

Chapter 8

Adley plodded toward the library. A beat-up motorhome had been parked off to the side of the lot. Weeds protruded from the bottom edges of the tires and tumbleweeds were caught underneath.

Drought resistant shrubs bordered the front of the building, thriving but spaced far apart with patches of thirsty ground in between. An old hitching post stood outside the structure, and a muscular spotted horse had been tethered to it. It snorted, and Adley stuck her tongue out at the animal. She shouldered the single glass door.

A man wearing faded jeans and a plaid shirt, pinned with a sheriff's badge, leaned against a battered counter and sold a copy of the local paper to an elderly resident.

Adley looked back at the horse. "Figures."

The man handed the old woman her change. "See ya later, Hilda."

Hilda returned the farewell. "See you at Bingo, Sheriff."

Then the man gave his attention to Adley before she rounded the first shelf of books. "Good morning, young lady. Anything I can help you with?"

"No. I'm just looking."

"Let me know if you need—say! Aren't you Aggie's granddaughter?"

Adley kept walking, and her eyes focused on the row of bookshelves. "News travels fast," she said, deadpan.

"You sorta favor her. Where are your folks? Sure would like to say hello," he called out.

"My *folks* are at the diner," she called back. Adley didn't know if the man was too dumb to catch the blatant sarcasm or if he chose to ignore it.

"I'll head on over. Holler if you need anything."

He left Adley standing alone in the solitude of the shabby library. She shuffled up and down the few aisles, scoffing at the small selection of books. Although she wasn't familiar with most of the authors, she sulked in disapproval, judging the books as outdated and uninteresting.

When she rounded the last aisle she was startled to see a boy sitting alone, reading at one of three small tables. He wore washed-out jeans, a faded black T-shirt with the sleeves torn off, and overworked riding boots. The boy let his eyes wander from what he was reading and gave Adley a terrific smile, making him that much cuter. No way would a cute guy smile at her. She figured he was making fun of her like the boys did at school. She huffed loudly and turned around to leave.

"I'd be grouchy, too, if I had to stay in that wasted mansion."

Adley peeked back around the corner of a shelf. "How do you know where I'm staying?"

"Are you kidding? You mean you haven't seen the size of this town?"

His skin rivaled the color of caramel and his short hair shined the darkest shade of ebony. He leaned back with a slender but muscular arm slung over the chair next to him.

"Yeah, well, I'm not into small towns. See you later."

Once again Adley started in the other direction. The boy called out. "Hey! A bunch of girls from Animas High are at the mall today, trying to earn money for new cheerleading uniforms. They think they're better than everyone else. Maybe you could meet up with them. You'll feel right at home."

Adley's hot temper boiled to the surface. She stormed back to the table. The teasing light in the boy's eyes and the tiny lift at the corner of his mouth made her all the more furious.

She scowled. "What makes you think you know what I'm like or who I hang out with? You don't know a thing about me, and I'd like it to stay that way!" Adley straightened her spine and pulled her shoulders back.

"You're Adley Lange," he said. "Grandma Aggie's granddaughter. And you think you're staying for the summer at Capilla Manor even though your parents have already decided they're going to live here permanently."

"You're a liar! We're only here on vacation," Adley pointed out to the boy, even though he was right about everything else. She was rattled by the thought of spending six weeks at Grandma Aggie's mansion, but the idea of living there was a nightmare she couldn't endure. "For your information, we're only staying for the summer and are not planning on living there at all!" She did an about face and pounded her feet into the linoleum floor.

"I guess it's true. You didn't know."

Adley didn't want to give him the satisfaction of the last word. "I'm not going to stay here and listen to your lies!"

The boy shouted as she stomped down the aisle. "Sorry about what happened to your grandma. I bet she'd still be alive if she hadn't been pushed down those stairs!"

Adley marched back and slammed her palms on the wooden table. "What do you mean? I don't know where you got your story from, but it's wrong. My grandma fell down those stairs by accident!"

"It was no accident."

He was a bit too certain of what he said and had an all-too-familiar cocky attitude. "Who are you? What makes you think you're so smart?" she demanded.

"My name is Victor Trumillo, and if I didn't know anything, I'd still be smarter than you."

Adley ignored the ridicule. "Why did you say my grandma was pushed down the stairs?"

"My mom, Maria Trumillo, worked at Aggie's for nearly ten years. You probably never met her because Aggie sent the staff home when your family came to visit, not like you visited your grandma more than a handful of times." Adley crossed her arms over her chest and glared. "My mom started work in the early morning and left in the evening with the cook. Once a week the gardener came, and he left when they did. No one in their right mind ever stayed overnight, especially after the 'accident.'"

"Grandma liked coming out to see us. My dad flew her out for every visit."

"Yeah, I know. My great-uncle always drove her to the airport. Aggie was afraid one of her employees might spread rumors, or secrets, and scare your family away."

"What rumors and secrets?"

"Everyone knows that place is haunted."

"Hah!" Adley chucked her chin a bit. "It's not haunted. I've spent three nights in my grandmother's house, and I haven't seen any ghosts."

"I didn't say it was haunted by ghosts," Victor smugly replied.

"What else can it be haunted with?"

Victor tilted his head, as if about to gauge Adley's reaction. "It's haunted by a creature that takes on the form of a skeleton."

Less than a second later, Victor kicked the chair out from under the table and slid it next to her. He sat up straighter as Adley dropped into the seat. "Now I'm seeing ghosts," he said. "Your face turned all white."

Adley didn't argue with Victor. Slumped and defeated by the revelation, she looked at him across the table. Victor relaxed back into his chair and kept silent a few moments as Adley regrouped. She wet her lips, gulped, and whispered, "What makes you think that's what's running around inside my grandma's house?"

"It's only in one room," he explained. "The room with the bed made of bones."

"There isn't a bed made out of bones anywhere in that house!" Adley meant to sound more convincing but, even to her own ears, her words sounded like she was pleading against hearing the truth, denying that her summer home had given way to a wicked invasion.

"I've only been in Aggie's a few times but I wasn't allowed upstairs on account of what's hiding on the second story. My mom told me about it, though. She says it's in the west wing. It's in the room with a different handle on the door."

"How is the handle different?"

"It's made out of hematite," Victor said.

"Well, you're wrong, Mr. Know-it-all!" Adley was relieved that the haunting was nothing more than a tall tale. Local folklore. "For your information, the only door without a crystal knob in the entire mansion has a silver one on it. I ought to know. It's my bedroom."

Victor's raven-colored eyes widened, and his jaw dropped. "Now I really feel sorry for you," he whispered.

"Why do I possibly need or want your pity?"

"Hematite is a stone that has been used for thousands of years by those who believe in its magical properties," Victor explained in a kinder, softer tone. "It's said to absorb negative energy, like the evil inside of your bedroom. And hematite resembles dark silver."

Adley's heart raced, and she made a poor effort to hide her fear. She shook off the chill that crawled up her spine and pressed further. "So why use it on a door handle?"

"Gypsies believe that installing a hematite handle on a door will keep evil confined to a room."

"Where was this monster before it supposedly, you know, before Grandma Aggie had her accident? And how did it get stuck in my room?"

"I don't know where it was before but Great-Uncle Pablo might know. He drove to Aggie's with a few other locals who suspected things weren't exactly right. They went in the house with sacred objects, including the hematite handle, and they backed something upstairs, into the farthest corner they could find. Aggie couldn't walk unassisted by then, but she refused to leave. No one wanted her alone upstairs, so they brought her bed down to the first floor."

"You left my grandmother all alone with whatever it was?" Adley scolded him.

"After the accident, we couldn't find a live-in nurse or housekeeper anywhere who was willing to stay overnight, and like I said, Aggie refused to leave. She said it was the home where her son grew up. Anyway, after it happened, those who drove the creature upstairs volunteered to stay the night to protect her. She insisted that no one stay inside, at least not past the evening."

"Even so, why would she want to stay there alone?" Adley asked.

"That's the kind of lady she was." Victor spoke with admiration for her grandmother. "Sheriff Flatley thought it was a robber that caused her fall, even though nothing was taken from the house. He didn't believe the manor was haunted but he let us use his old motorhome in case the intruder came back. We took turns staying the night outside until the day she died."

Adley was stunned into silence. People served guard duty to protect her grandmother, a very bad sign of what could be hidden in her summer home. She felt as if she was a girl in a scary movie who'd had the sudden realization that her parents were aliens.

Victor leaned forward and whispered, "You've seen it, haven't you?"

"I don't know what I've seen," she confided, "but it's crazy to think that it's what you say it is. It has to be…mice."

"It's a curse." Adley raised her eyebrows. "Maybe I should tell you the facts," he continued. "Then you can decide for yourself whether or not you believe that your grandma's place is haunted."

Adley and Victor heard the sound of the library door opening and were startled by the sheriff's robust baritone.

"Hey there, Adley Lange! Your parents are fixin' ta leave in a bit and want you back at the restaurant."

Adley gazed upward. "I'm fixin' to leave in a few minutes!" she hollered back with a Texan drawl, and Victor suppressed a laugh.

Before the door shut itself, they heard Sheriff Flatley's footsteps bite into the gravel as he headed back to the restaurant.

Adley spoke to Victor without the fake accent. "Listen, can I call you later, this afternoon?"

A huge smile lit his face. "Sure!"

"It's not like that," Adley explained.

Victor grinned. "Of course not."

"Ugh! I need more information. That's all!"

A smug smile plastered his face as he took a piece of paper and a pen from the backpack slung behind his chair and scribbled down his phone number.

Adley crammed the note into the pocket of her jeans, and then wrote down the number to Capilla Manor for Victor.

"We live in the ranch house almost a mile from you," he told her. It was his home that Adley had belittled earlier. Lucky thing she didn't mention it to Victor. "If you want we can meet at the trail behind your grandma's instead of talking on the phone. I can ride my horse over."

"That's your horse out front?" she asked. "I figured it was the sheriff's."

"Naw," he chuckled. "They use trucks out here."

"Did you just say there's a trail behind my grandma's?"

"You haven't seen it?"

"I haven't gone out back. This is only my fourth day here, and I've been too busy freaking out about a mice-infested room," she snapped, but Victor didn't respond to the bite in her remark.

"Something scared you pretty bad, and I know it wasn't a mouse." When Adley didn't reply, Victor said, "When you go out back, you'll see a small dirt path off the left side at the back of the property. It leads behind the backyard into the woods. I can meet you near the big pine tree at the start of the trail from Aggie's thirty minutes after you call."

"My parents won't let me go hiking alone."

"Tell them you'll stay within calling distance. That always works."

"I don't know if I can pull it off. My parents didn't even want me taking a room down the hall from them. Wished I had listened. Still, they'd freak if I asked to go hiking alone."

His friendly face became etched with urgency. "You need to know a lot more about what's happening at your grandma's house."

He was deadly serious. Adley mentally recapped the intimidating experiences that had taken place in the past four days: the tapping sounds, weird hissing, and possibly a five legged creature. Regardless of how unbelievable it was, her security had been threatened, and Adley didn't know anyone else who could help her. It felt as if she was drowning and her parents refused to throw her a life preserver. She had to speak more at length with Victor. The sooner, the better.

"I'll call you when I get home, and we'll set a time to meet." She stood to leave.

"I'll see you then," he said, "and tell you more about Capilla Manor."

"Why do you pronounce it that way? You're supposed to say 'Ca-pill-a.' You know, like swallowing a pill?"

Victor leaned forward and shared yet another secret. "It's you who are mispronouncing the name, *señorita*." He pronounced the title with a perfectly rolled 'r.' "The word is Spanish. 'Ca-pea-ya,'" he enunciated. "It rhymes with 'See-ya.' You know, as in 'so long, good-bye, see ya'?"

"All right. I get it, but what does it mean?"

His eyes narrowed, and his words cut like a knife through her peace of mind.

"It means 'Death House.'"

Chapter 9

Adley left the library, not knowing if she should have thanked Victor for scaring her even more out of her wits. She returned to the diner and found the waitress and sheriff-librarian-reporter with her parents.

"And then the parrot points at the frozen chicken and says, 'What did he do?'" Anne Marie said.

The sheriff and her parents burst into a fit of laughter, a four-person party. The waitress smiled at the success of her bird joke and walked away from the table.

Roger spotted Adley standing near the door.

"Hey, there! I was just about to have the sheriff send a posse out for you!"

"Hah-hah," she said dryly and folded her arms across her chest.

"I'd best be going now," the sheriff announced. "It was a pleasure meeting you." He shook Roger's hand and tipped his hat to Caroline. To Adley he said, "Well, little lady, did you happen to meet Vic Trumillo in the library?"

Caroline clamped a cupped palm over her mouth, and Adley caught it before her mother dropped her hand back into her lap.

"Yeah, I met him," Adley said, keeping an eye on her mother.

"His family lives closer to you than anyone else around here," the sheriff said.

"Did you say Trumillo?" Caroline asked, not bothering to hide her curiosity.

"Sure enough, ma'am, but don't concern yourself with them. Why, they're good people and all, but pretty much keep to themselves. See y'all later."

The sheriff sauntered back to the library. Roger and Caroline exchanged uneasy looks.

"Do you think they're the same ones who sent you those letters?" Caroline whispered to her husband.

"Most likely," Roger said.

"Why would they write to you?" Adley asked her father, and then questioned her mother. "What was in the letters?"

"Nothing for you—"

"—to worry about. I know." Adley looked off to the side when she cut her father off.

"Adley," her father lectured, "it's impolite to interrupt people mid-sentence, whether you know what they're going to say or not."

Adley frowned but didn't apologize. Roger dropped a few bills next to the check, and Anne Marie strolled back to the table.

"You folks leavin' now?" she asked.

"Yes. We have to get going," Caroline said. "It was so nice to meet you, Anne Marie."

The Langes said goodbye to the woman at the door and piled into the car.

The ride back to the mansion was quiet until Adley asked, "Mom, why did you freak out when the sheriff said Victor's name?"

"Oh, well, um…" She glanced nervously at her husband. "We've heard the Trumillos are a strange lot, into the occult. But like the sheriff said, it's probably nothing to worry about. He thinks they're nice people, but all the same, Dad and I would prefer it if you didn't hang around that boy."

"He's a nice kid," Adley said, defending Victor.

"Oh, I'm sure he is," Caroline sounded cheerful yet unconvinced. "But they have different views than we do, and I'm not sure they're healthy ones."

"Victor's mother was a maid for Grandma Aggie, and Grandma loved Mrs. Trumillo."

"That may be so, but we'd prefer you to stay away from them, Deedee," her father said. "They're way too superstitious."

"The name's Adley, Dad. And what do you mean they're too superstitious?"

Her father opened his mouth to speak, but Caroline explained, "They think that your grandmother's house is haunted." She laughed. "Can you imagine? When Grandma was alive, some of the Trumillos performed some sort of a séance in her home." Both of her parents shook their heads.

"Why did they do that?" Adley asked. Her muscles tensed all at once.

"Some people believe a dreadful thing lives in the mansion and takes revenge on people," her mother said. "Some ancient curse or something. Of course, your grandmother said it was a bunch of nonsense. Supposedly, the Trumillo's believed the curse was real and wanted to get rid of it."

"They probably made a bundle charging for their services," Roger muttered.

"We don't want you exposed to people who believe in that uncultivated kind of thinking," Caroline said.

"What if it *is* haunted?" Adley said. "What if Grandma didn't tell Dad just so she could get us to move out here?"

Caroline swung her head toward the back seat. "Don't tell me that Victor boy has gotten to you already!"

"Of course not, Mom," Adley reassured her. "I meant that—"

Roger used his firm and serious father voice. "You keep away from that Trumillo boy. Is that understood, young lady?"

"Yes, Dad." No sense arguing with stubborn adults. Adley had enough on her mind and wasn't in the mood to finish the debate.

She decided to phone Victor the moment they arrived at the house and tell him not to call her. Despite all the peculiar things going on inside the walls of her temporary summer home, it wasn't a smart move to tell her parents about her meeting with "that Trumillo boy."

She had no way to prove all that had happened since moving in. If her parents didn't believe in ancient curses, they'd have a hard time believing a freaky spider creature lived in her bedroom. Although Adley felt as if her heart had leapt out of her chest and into her stomach when it crawled under her comforter, she wasn't ready to rule out mice. Maybe she only imagined something with five legs. Still, she wanted to find out about any long ago curses. To do that, she needed to talk to Victor.

The afternoon sun blazed directly overhead when Roger pulled the truck onto the native sandstone circular driveway. He drove to the other side of the house and parked underneath the carport, draped with twisted limbs of dried out vines in dire need of trimming.

"Which of those windows belongs to my room?" Adley asked.

"Why, the first three on the left, the second floor up. Can't you tell by the striped drapes?" her mother said.

"But there aren't any trees by my windows!"

Two nights ago, straight and curved lines of tree branches outside her window created the shadow of a skeleton.

Examining her windows from the outside, the group of tall and shady Texas umbrella trees stood in front of the east wing, not near her bedroom on the west side of the structure. There wasn't a single tree in front of her windows to make any kind of a shadow against her wall.

"The sun doesn't really shine too long in that direction because of those hills," her father commented, pointing west as he escorted Caroline and Adley to the massive front doors.

"You really don't need a lot of shade on that side of Capilla Manor," Caroline said.

Shade was nowhere near what Adley needed. She spoke in a monotone. "It's Ca-pea-ya, Mom. As in 'so long, good-bye, see ya.'"

"That's what my mother used to say," Roger said.

He inserted the key into the lock, and a loud crash of shattering glass erupted within the mansion. The clamor died down an instant later, and Roger hesitated before opening the front door.

"You stay here with Adley," he whispered to Caroline.

"But Dad," his daughter protested, "we don't know who, or what, is inside!"

His glanced at Adley. "One visit with that Trumillo kid and your imagination goes wild."

Caroline gripped her husband's arm. "Why don't we call Sheriff Flatley?" she said in a hush.

"Don't worry, darling," he assured her. "I'll be fine."

"Be careful, Roger!"

He nodded and then proceeded into the silent foyer while his wife and daughter huddled together as if they had to keep each other warm.

A black dot soared on an up-current in the distance, and they both jumped when the hawk screeched as it dived toward the ground for its prey.

Caroline and Adley tensed, unimpressed with the majestic high desert environment, and listened for any further hint of disturbance.

"Maybe we should call the sheriff, Mom," Adley whispered.

"I would," Caroline spoke as softly, "but I left my phone charging on the dresser."

Adley peeled her mother's hands off of her arms. "Mom, you're going to bruise me."

"I'm sorry, honey." She gasped. "Did you hear that?"

They hugged each other again.

"What did you hear?" Adley whispered.

"Footsteps," Caroline said.

They cast wary glances around the yard for any sign of danger, and a voice jolted them out of their shoes.

"It's the strangest thing." Roger kept his eyes on the foyer and didn't see them jump. "I've checked every conceivable area where I'd find something broken. Upstairs and down, in every room and closet, in the attic and the basement. I can't find a single speck of broken glass, china, or mirrors anywhere. There's no sign of a break-in. Nothing has been taken or vandalized. I don't know what to make of it."

Adley couldn't resist an off-handed remark. "Maybe it was a ghost, Dad."

At first he was offended by her clever wit, but then he glanced at his wife, and the two of them chuckled nervously.

"I wonder if someone is out back in the woods," Caroline said as she closed the front door.

"It came from inside the house," Adley said. "It sounded like it was upstairs—inside of my room."

"Don't start," Caroline warned her daughter. To Roger she said, "I remember you saying once that sound carries through the canyons up here."

"That's true. Sound always carried from behind the house," Roger said. "I'll check out back."

His wife nodded and followed Adley upstairs.

More out of anger than bravery, Adley stomped up the stairs and marched right to her room, determined to settle the matter of skeleton curses.

Tired of being afraid and from not sleeping, she swept through the black shadow at her door and tugged on the handle.

It remained icy to the touch. A freezing gust of air licked her face as she pushed the door opened.

Suddenly feeling safer in the hallway, Adley scanned the room from side to side and from ceiling to floor to see if any broken glass was littered in her room. She looked on the floor beneath each window for any sign that indicated the presence of an intruder, and then she studied the perimeter of the bed for any clue that might signal something otherworldly.

Caroline spoke from down the hall. "Are you all right, dear?"

"Yeah, Mom. I'm fine." Adley closed her door and joined her mother in the master bedroom. She sat on the bed just as Roger entered the room.

"Not a darn thing outside, either." Adley didn't think he'd find anything. The crashing noise had to have something to do with whatever lurked in her room.

"Are you guys going any place else for a while?"

"I'm going to take a nap," her mother said. She sat on the bed and took off her shoes.

Her father sat at the desk with his laptop. "And I'm going to check e-mails from the office. Did you need something?"

"I wanted to check out that trail behind the house."

"Maybe now's not a good time," Caroline said. "Someone who broke that glass could be out back."

"I didn't see one shard of glass anywhere. I think it's safe," Roger said.

Adley found it interesting that her father didn't make a bigger deal about the noise. She might have mentioned the thought if she weren't planning on meeting Victor.

"When I was a kid, we used to hike through those back trails from sun up to sun down. Three miles west, you'll hit the Continental Divide. A small meandering creek runs along the tree line, which is why we have a forest of scraggly saplings running behind the house. With the piñon pines and low lying mesquite they provide good coverage during a heavy wind and a little shade in the summer. A few coyote dens lie a half mile east of us, and a natural spring that feeds the stream lies shortly past that near the Trumillo ranch."

"Did you grow up with them?" Adley asked, only perking her ears up at the mention of Victor's last name.

"No. They moved in shortly after I left for college." Roger stood up, "It'll take me a few minutes to get my hiking boots on."

"Uh, gee, Dad. I kinda wanted to go alone."

Both parents opened their eyes wider. Her father said, "If you're afraid to be in your room, how are you going to feel safe outside in the woods?"

"We can't explain the noise we heard when we got home," her mother said. "It may not be safe."

Adley tried to put a lid on the familiar but distressing anger welling within.

"Please don't make me a prisoner inside this house."

Roger and Caroline looked to each other for a response, but none came forward.

I'll be fine," Adley said. Then she hastily added, "I'll stay within calling distance."

Chapter 10

Adley jogged downstairs to the kitchen and pulled the paper scribbled with Victor's number out of her jacket pocket. She wished she hadn't forgotten her cell phone in California. Finally she had someone to call, she needed to call, and had to depend on a landline.

There were so many weird things to consider inside Capilla Manor. In the library Victor said the hematite handle kept a bad spirit contained inside her room. She wondered why her parents couldn't feel the icy cold of the stone fixture. And there was no simple explanation of the broken glass, the sound her father wrote-off way too easily.

Across from the oak butcher block, a phone sat on a small built-in desk with a reading lamp positioned over the top of a blotter embossed with flowers. Adley stroked the floral pattern and imagined Grandma Aggie writing letters and addressing Christmas cards. She picked up the phone and punched in the combination of numbers to get Victor on the line.

She cradled the receiver in her neck as she took a couple of water bottles from the refrigerator and set them on the counter along with some fruit snacks from a drawer. In the pantry she fished for granola bars and a plastic shopping bag to carry the food.

After a few rings she heard a warm greeting on the other end of the line.

A woman with a Spanish accent asked, "Hello?"

"May I speak to Victor?"

"Yes, you may." The woman cupped her hand on the receiver, and Adley heard the muffled voice say, "Hurry up! It's a girl! She wants to talk to you!"

"*Ay Diós*, Mama!" Victor said to his mother. "Hello?" he asked.

"Hi. It's me. Adley. Can you come over now?"

"Sure. I'll see you in fifteen minutes."

"You said it took thirty minutes to get here," she reminded him.

"It does, if you've got a slow horse," Victor said. "See you in fifteen."

☣ ☣ ☣

In the downstairs restroom, Adley stared at her reflection and carefully brushed out her hair. She applied lip gloss and blush. Turning from side to side, she studied her appearance. She decided that the make-up had nothing to do with Victor. She left her purse on a robe hook in the bathroom, not about to take it back upstairs.

Adley didn't want to appear anxious, not that she cared what Victor thought. She surfed channels in the family room for another five minutes before she shut off the TV and unlatched the French doors leading out to the patio.

After a brief coursing through tall dried weeds toward the rear of the yard, she found the trail Victor told her about. The bag of snacks and bottled water swung at her side as she made her way past the dirt path lined with saplings and shrubs. It led to a wooded area, landing her right at the base of a big pine tree.

Adley looked behind her and could barely see Grandma Aggie's sizeable home beyond the brush. A thick wooded line of trees—mesquite, piñon pines, and juniper ran for miles either side of her, along a shallow creek, and purple mountains filled the vista beyond.

A huge spotted horse, different from the one at the library, nibbled at the scrub underneath the surrounding trees.

"Wow, what a cool horse!" Adley said.

Victor patted its neck. "Her name is Sweet Pea."

"I guess you must go riding through here a lot."

"Used to. Not since…well, what happened to Aggie."

"You mean because of that dumb curse?"

"Yeah. Now I ride to the north and east of here."

"Tell me what you know about this thing in my room."

Victor sat on a large fallen tree trunk and patted the spot next to him. Adley sat a few feet away and offered him a snack and bottle of water.

"Thanks," he said, and Adley stared as he took a long swig from the bottle and finished off a granola bar in three bites. After another drink, he related the tale of the manor.

"Okay. The whole thing started in the seventeen hundreds when Spain was ruled by King Ferdinand."

Adley stood up. "What in the world does the king of Spain have to do with the problem in my grandmother's house?"

"Just calm down and listen!" He tugged on her arm and drew her down closer to him than she was before. "I'm trying to tell you how this whole mess started. Do you want to know or not?" Adley glared and crossed her arms but didn't speak.

Victor glared back at Adley, mimicking her facial expression and stiff back. "Like I was saying."

Adley laughed. "Okay. Go ahead. Tell me."

"Got another one of those crunchy things?" He tried to peek inside the bag, but Adley tugged it out of his grasp.

"Not until I know the story."

Victor shook his head when he laughed. "So the king hired this large gang of really mean guards to defend his city because looters were always trying to steal the gold that Spain had stolen from Mexico during its expeditions. One of the king's guards, the meanest one, went up to some gypsy guy, called him a grave robber, and slashed his arm. The gypsy got pretty ticked off because the guard thought he was stealing."

"How in the heck did the gypsy know what the guard was thinking?"

"Who's telling the story?" He glared at Adley. She huffed and crossed her arms. "To a gypsy, being accused of stealing from a grave was unforgivable slander."

"Isn't that what gypsies did? Rip people off?"

"Yeah, but not dead ones already buried." Victor became more animated as Adley's interest peaked. He narrated like a professional speaker, and his arms flailed to and fro as he told the tale.

"Anyway, they fought like crazy. Finally, after fighting for a long time, the guard hit the ground, fell onto his own blade, and was mortally wounded." He touched Adley's arm, his dark brown eyes commanding her attention. "This is when the gypsy started to curse him, but the guard died before hearing the final words. Here's the thing. If a man is cursed but dies before the invocation is completed, the curse falls back onto the one who made it in the first place."

"You mean, what the gypsy said was used as a curse against himself, instead of the guard?"

"Right." Victor nodded. "My great-uncle knows the exact words, but basically the gypsy said that the oldest child in the guard's family, and in every generation from then on, would die."

"Hold on!" Adley said. "Even if this was true, what does it have to do with me and my family?"

"You're a descendant of the gypsy who started the curse," Victor said.

"We're not even Spanish! 'Lange' is a German name. Duh! And my mother is Irish and Russian," Adley happily reported, relieved of the tension that built during the telling of Victor's tale.

Victor shrugged. "Guess it doesn't matter then. Like you said, it's a crazy story." Victor appraised the way Adley crossed her arms, as if this time warding off a chill. "I don't have all the answers, Adley."

She liked hearing Victor say her name. He pushed a wayward strand of hair behind her ear.

"So all the gypsy's kids and their kids and their kids died at the hands of…a curse?"

"No. Remember, not all the kids are involved," he said. "It kills only the oldest of each family. The demon can also make horrible accidents occur, like with your grandma."

Adley set her fists on her hips. "That's the stupidest thing I've ever heard of!"

"Only this morning it seemed like you knew what I was talking about, and now you deny it?"

"I'm not denying a thing! I just don't believe in your kooky curse."

"It seems like the few nasty episodes of whatever happened in your bedroom make the gypsy story hard to ignore," Victor said.

Adley took in the sunlight streaming through the canopy overhead. "Okay, suppose I buy your crazy curse story. Why did it go after my grandma and stay under her roof?"

"Obviously one of you is a gypsy descendant."

"That's stupid. I've already told you we're not gypsies."

Victor remained silent. His confidence disturbed her.

"So maybe it's better to take precautions, like if this was a real curse. So how does one go about—" She felt silly for asking it. "What I mean—if you want—that is—" she stammered.

Victor completed her choppy sentence. "You mean, how does one stop the curse?"

"Yeah." Adley acted as if it wasn't important but she was all ears.

"I don't know," he said.

"What?" Adley roared. She jumped to her feet yet again and landed in front of Victor. She vigorously shook him by the shoulders. "You don't know?" She glanced at the path leading back to Capilla Manor and lowered her voice. "What do you mean you don't know?"

Victor smiled up at her and made a deliberate act of looking at her hands on his shoulders and where she stood between his knees. Adley gulped.

She took a step back. "Sorry."

"For someone who thinks it's such a stupid fairy tale, you sure are bent out of shape," Victor said in a gentler voice

Adley sat back down and regained her composure. She absently watched a tiny beetle crawl underfoot and spoke in a near hush. "I'm simply wondering how to end a curse, that's all."

"I know you saw something that scared you, Adley. And I know you aren't telling me all that's gone on in your room."

She weighed his comment. "I don't know what I saw or heard. But you're right," she admitted, "I'm very scared." She paused, confused by wanting to be honest but afraid to trust him. "If a gypsy can curse a man, can't he just do a counter-curse?"

"Yeah. The good news is that all curses can be lifted." Her thoughts brightened with hope, but any optimism died out when she saw his brows crease together. "But the bad news?"

Victor didn't want to alarm her further. A lump formed in his throat as he prepared to tell her more.

"A weird ghoul lives in my bedroom," she reminded him. "I mean, how bad can it get, right?"

Victor toyed with a rough piece of decaying bark clinging to the tree trunk by a fibrous vein.

"Tell me, Victor. Please," Adley said.

"It's just that we don't know what the counter-curse is," he apologized.

Her voice rose in pitch again. "You can't just say 'I remove the curse' and click your heels three times?"

He scowled. "Get serious, Adley"

"That's great," she moaned. "I may have been cursed by a gypsy-psycho-thing, and you don't even know how to stop it!"

"Your ancestors have been trying for decades to find a counter-curse and so has Great-Uncle Pablo. He uncovered documents from the ship that carried the gypsy's family here when they fled from Spain. A list in the manifest records recorded everything belonging to a Rodrigues family, including a little furniture and some household goods. A book was listed in the records that my great-uncle believes explains the powerful rituals. It was described as large with an embossed, leather cover."

"Where is it?"

"The book had been crossed off the manifest list," Victor said.

"More good news," Adley scoffed.

"Great-Uncle Pablo thinks it was crossed out because the custom agents didn't find it. He thinks Rodrigues hid the book because it was so sacred, filled with powerful ancient gypsy lore handed down by word of mouth for hundreds and hundreds of years until someone decided to write it down a couple of centuries ago."

"So without the book no one knows the exact wording needed to end this type of curse?"

Victor shook his head. "No, but we're pretty sure we know where the sacred manuscript is hidden."

She hopped off the tree trunk. Her enthusiasm was an odd mix of excitement and desperation. "Where?" she pleaded.

He reached out for her arm and had her sit back down, only now much closer than before. Adley felt the sides of their thighs touch, and Victor kept his hand on her arm.

"We think it's somewhere inside Capilla Manor," Victor said.

"Well, that's not a big deal. I'll find it and—"

He interrupted her. "We tried, Adley. After Aggie's accident, my mother made it her personal mission to find the gypsy book. She and my great-aunt, Gloria, scoured everywhere, from top to bottom. They went through every door, drawer, and cupboard. They searched from the cellar to the attic. My mama tried to find hidden compartments and fake walls but didn't find a single one."

"Which means that it's not inside or it's too well hidden." After a beat Adley asked, "This isn't something we can pick up at the local bookstore, is it?"

"No. It was written by hand."

"Your great-uncle knew how to make the handle for the door. Why can't he come up with some kind of wording to end the curse?"

Victor sighed. "Some things are common knowledge to

those in the metaphysical field. Spiritualists know that hematite absorbs negative energy. But ending a curse? That's different. It has to be worded exactly as it was originally stated."

Adley slumped. "What am I going to do?"

Victor acted as if he instinctively knew she felt alone with such a huge problem and placed his arm around her shoulder. "Great-Uncle Pablo might be able to tell us if there's anything else we can do. He's on his way up to a friend's ranch a few hours away. I'll call him when I get home. Until you can talk to him, I really think you should sleep downstairs in the family room."

"Why?" Adley defiantly crossed her arms. "Do you think I'm that scared?"

"No," Victor said, capturing her with sure, dark eyes. "It will be safer if you do."

Chapter 11

Adley realized a muscled arm had draped across her shoulders. It thrilled her. It frightened her, too. She slapped her palms on her thighs and stood up.

"Guess I'll see you later."

Victor escorted her to the top of the dirt trail. Adley stole glimpses of him as they walked side by side. He was a head taller than her and more than cute. Dimples creased each time he smiled. He caught her tiny smile at the corner of her mouth, and she feigned interest in a low branch.

"Aren't you going to thank me?"

She tore a leaf off the tree. "You want me to thank you for nearly scaring me out of my wits?"

"For offering you an explanation and a way out."

"I only have a way out when I find the *Curses for Dummies* manual," she snapped.

Victor crossed his arms. "However mad you come across to others, I know that your anger is nothing more than a show to disguise your fear."

Adley didn't deny his accurate observation. It unnerved her that he knew her defenses almost as much as the thing in her room.

"You sound like a shrink."

He shrugged. "I learn things from my great-uncle. Listen, Adley, don't worry," he said as she trudged away from him down the dirt path leading to the backyard.

"Why shouldn't I be worried?"

"Legend says that it doesn't get really bad until you see it take the shape of a skeleton's hand," Victor said.

Adley froze in place. She couldn't reply. Victor stepped over to her and placed his hands lightly on her shoulders. "Look at me, Adley." She looked up into his earthy brown eyes filled with concern. "I know something strange is going on at Capilla Manor, and it's best to tell me all of what you saw."

"I saw something, but I don't know what it was."

Tension fringed his words. "Think carefully, Adley. What did it look like?"

"I'm really not s—s—sure," she stuttered. "It could have been a—a hand. Made of bones," she added.

"Oh, man." Victor exhaled loudly and ran his fingers through his thick, black hair, as if her heavy burden was now his. "Keep me up to date on whatever happens, no matter how foolish you think it is, all right?"

She paused, pursing her lips, weighing the importance of what she had to say. "We heard glass breaking when we came back from town this afternoon, but my dad searched inside the entire mansion and out back, but he didn't see one single broken piece anywhere."

Victor shook his head. "Oh, man, Adley. I'm not sure what that means, but I'll call you as soon as I hear from my great-uncle. Anything else?"

"No." Adley hesitated a moment. "Except there's this black shadow cloud thing that hangs outside my bedroom door. No one sees it except for me." Victor started to say something but Adley added, "Oh yeah. And the handle is as cold as ice to the point that it stings my hand and leaves blisters practically every time I touch it, but my mom and dad can't feel it."

Victor shook his head. "Oh man, Adley. I don't know what that means either, but it can't be good. I'll call you as soon as I find out anything."

"Hang up if one of my parents answers. Okay?"

"Why?" The tone in his voice changed, slightly tinged with anger.

"Because my parents talked to the sheriff when we were in the library."

"Oh, I see." Victor looked about at the trees. "Sheriff Flatley is a good man, but he doesn't agree with some of my family's beliefs."

"I know, Victor. I'm sorry."

"No need for you to apologize," he replied. "I'm used to people who are afraid of what they don't understand. A lot of people are like that."

"I know exactly what you mean. Before all this weird stuff started happening, no way I'd believe in wacko curses. I can't remember a time when I've been so scared," she admitted.

Victor rubbed his hands up and down her arms, and she instinctively held onto his strong shoulders. He lifted her chin with the tip of his finger and stared into her eyes. "My family will do everything we can to help."

An incredible blanket of warmth wrapped itself around Adley. She'd never felt so safe, so secure, so scared, and it had nothing to do with an ancient curse. This was different from being frightened of a foreign creature. It was like being happy and afraid at the same time. She cleared her throat and stepped back.

"Call me later," he told her.

"I will." Adley smiled. At the top of the dirt trail, she waved as Victor easily mounted the mare.

He blew her a kiss, and left Adley dazed as he galloped away.

She ambled down the path to the back yard. A coyote or a dog howled not too far away, a mournful cry like a desperate warning of things to come. She looked up at the second story windows of Capilla Manor, darkened, hiding something behind the planes of glass. The animal howled again, more insistent and in closer proximity to the house. Odd that she found it safer to run inside.

☣ ☣ ☣

Victor was sorry for the callous remarks he made at the library. Seeing her outside in full sunlight lit up Adley's face. Her beautiful features remained unaffected by her ashen complexion each time they spoke of the gypsy's curse and the wretched monster that lurked in her bedroom.

Her fear touched his soul. When he looked beyond that fear, he noticed her latte-brown eyes, the spattering of freckles dusting her nose, and her cheeks tinged with a natural pink. Her slender body promised more womanly curves.

What he thought of her up until that moment in the library had instantly vanished as his primal need arose to protect her. However, on his own, he wasn't certain what form of protection he could offer against anything paranormal.

Still, something reached down inside of him, out from the past, from a time far away, as if they had already met, as if he had already fallen in love with her.

He found that a very weird feeling, maybe even scarier than the creature in her room.

☣ ☣ ☣

Adley sat in the den and found it not wise to watch the clock. Time oozed slowly when she was looking forward to something pleasant, like having to wait for the next time she'd hear from Victor. She contemplated what Victor had told her, and time managed to zip by like a rocket, as she thought about the idea of a curse, knowing that eventually nightfall had to come to Capilla Manor.

Adley decided to take Victor's advice and sleep downstairs, as far away from her room as possible. The thought of going into it alone scared the wits out of her. Fortunately she'd laundered her clothes. They were tumbling in the drier which meant she'd have clean pajamas for the night and clean clothes for the following day.

☣ ☣ ☣

Adley succeeded in avoiding her room for another twenty-four hours. She had yet to convince herself that it was mice creating the strange noises and sights in her bedroom. She also wondered if she actually saw a five legged creature crawl off of her bed. It terrified her to know that she could be under the same roof with anything so threatening, and it saddened her to think that her parents would think she was crazy if they knew she was starting to believe the history surrounding the curse. It would be far worse if she were hurt—or killed—by a supernatural being.

Even if her parents did believe her, they'd want to return home. Adley didn't want to stay another moment in her grandmother's house, yet she didn't want to go home just to be shut in her room, fight with her mom, rarely see her father, and most likely, never see Victor Trumillo again.

She liked boys, and before all her unexplained anger set in, they liked her. Yet something about Victor placed him far apart from the other guys she knew at school. It was like she'd been friends with him forever. Adley found it comforting to know that Victor believed her nightmarish stories. He made her smile, and expressed genuine concern about her lack of safety in the old mansion.

Victor gave Adley something to look forward to. She wondered if the curse didn't exist and if her parents decided to stay in the area, would she and Victor stand a chance of being friends, especially if he knew what she was really like. Adley didn't know if it were possible for her to change. She didn't even know what made her so angry, let alone how to fix it.

Since she had no choice but to remain at Capilla Manor, every spare moment would be spent searching for the ancient volume Victor's great-uncle said the gypsy family had brought from Spain. She wondered if that was enough to prove to her parents that her imagination wasn't the cause for all the improbable events taking place in her room. And then again, that might be a mute issue if she didn't survive it.

☣ ☣ ☣

Adley thought of using the excuse of resurrecting the garden simply to be outside and away from her room, but it also gave her the opportunity to search the spacious garage for the gypsy manuscript under the guise of looking for gardening equipment.

She found her parents enjoying their coffee in the family room. "Mom? Dad? Do you think you can get me some seeds?"

Caroline didn't think she heard correctly. "You mean like plant-in-the-ground seeds?

"Sure, hon," Roger answered. He whispered to his wife, "My prayers have been answered."

They never thought she could hear their loud whispering.

To Adley, Roger said in a more cheerful tone, "I'm surprised you've taken an interest in gardening. When Grandma was alive the yards were beautiful and now..." Roger gazed at the dead plants and brown grass that dominated the backyard.

"Most all of your grandma's tools are in the garage," Caroline said. "First, you'll have to soak the ground to make it easier to pull weeds out from the area you want to plant in. We can work together, if you'd like."

"That'd be cool, Mom," Adley said. "I'll check out the garage right now."

She left the room, but not before hearing her mother's comment to her father: "No, *my* prayers were answered."

Leaving her parents open mouthed in the family room, Adley rolled her eyes at the ceiling, yet again.

☣ ☣ ☣

Grandma Aggie's garage had been thoroughly organized. All the gardening equipment had been stored away in nooks, shelves, and drawers clearly labeled in a corner of the huge area. Other than typical home maintenance tools, a lawn mower, a back-up generator, and her father's SUV, the huge four-car garage—formerly a carriage house—was empty.

Adley searched through every bare cupboard and drawer. No secret compartments or books were found. She placed trowels and gloves in a basket, lifted a metal rake from a hook, and took the implements out to the back patio. It was too late in the evening to begin her outdoor project, but she'd start promptly the next morning.

After dinner the Langes enjoyed an old movie in the

family room, the original black and white version of King Kong. When it was over, their daughter graciously cleared away the popcorn bowls. Roger held his hand out to his wife to help her off the sofa. As Adley had predicted, bedtime arrived too soon.

She snuck into the maid's quarter to retrieve her pajamas but all of her clothes were gone. Adley ran toward the study to ask her parents about the missing laundry, but they had already retired for the night. She was certain her mother found the stash of clothes and took them upstairs. Adley ran up the circular staircase to the top floor but avoided looking down the hall toward her room.

"Mom?"

Caroline was already in bed and glanced up from her book. "Yes, honey?"

Roger looked up from his desk.

"Did you happen to get my stuff from the downstairs room?"

Caroline set the book on her lap and peeked at Roger for a fraction of a second. "I did, sweetheart. All of your clothes and things are in your room. Dad and I were willing to negotiate on you having the room down the hall, which I'm thinking you're regretting these days, but even so, a bedroom on the first story is out of the question."

Both her parents steeled themselves at the expected verbal onslaught.

Adley had already expected that response and didn't care that her mother put her laundry away. However, now she had to concoct a new excuse to avoid being alone while she retrieved pajamas and clothing from her room. For the rest of the night while her parents slept, she planned to search for the gypsy book downstairs. But even before all that, she had to know something.

"Mom, where were your parents from?"

Adley heard her father's audible sigh of relief. The abrupt change of subject seemed to please her mother, too, as if she was glad Adley had an interest in the family history. Both of her parents were most likely expecting a temper tantrum because she wasn't permitted to have the room downstairs.

"Your Grandmother Mary, my mother, was born in the states but her family came from Ireland and my father, Grandfather Orvic, was from Russia," Caroline said. "They met in Scotland where they were both students, but I've told you all this before."

Adley plopped onto the loveseat in the sitting area. "Yeah, but that was a long time ago. I forgot." Adley enjoyed the romantic how-they-met story, but her real interest wasn't in hearing the genealogy. Stalling for time was the real culprit, next to learning the roots of her family tree.

"Well, they met when they were students at the Edinburgh University." Caroline reminisced while her daughter and husband gave her their attention. "Grandmother Mary was a real knock out and Grandpa didn't know how to get her attention, especially because the upperclassmen were constantly surrounding her.

"Every Thursday afternoon she'd walk by the fountain near the cafeteria after her music class. One day Grandpa asked his friend to play a traditional Russian folk song on his accordion. Grandpa danced in front of the entire student body. At the end of the performance, everyone applauded. Grandmother Mary was tickled and let him walk her to her next class. They were never apart after that. They moved here not long after they graduated from college."

"That's so cool. What about Grandpa Orvic's parents?"

"His mother, Ivanka, came from Russia and my great-grandfather, I can't pronounce his name, was Czechoslovakian."

"Thanks, Mom." Adley was relieved to have some of her worries alleviated. German and Scottish and Russian ancestry. No gypsy blood, no homeless nomad ancestors, wandered in her family. There had to be another reason why her family had been affected by the gypsy curse.

She lumbered out of the cushy sofa to begin the mad routine of grabbing clothes out of her room.

"And if anyone cares, not that I feel slighted, of course, my father, Augustus Lange, was from Germany," her father said.

Adley paused before leaving the room, "Great, Dad!" She really meant it. A burden lifted off her shoulders. If only there was another explanation other than a dumb curse as to why she was being victimized by some unknown inhabitant stalking her bedroom.

She was out the door and in the hallway when he called out, "And Grandma Aggie was Spanish!"

Chapter 12

Adley whirled around and reentered her parents' room. "Say again, Dad?" She leaned on the door-jamb to keep her balance. "You said Grandma Aggie was born in London. Grandma Aggie was English!"

Caroline spoke up. "Just because she was born in London, doesn't make her English."

"Technically, she is English," Roger said. "Half, anyway. My father, Augustus Lange, was born here in the states but both of his parents came from a little village that used to sit outside of Dusseldorf on the west side of Germany. I took your mother there for our honeymoon."

"It's so beautiful, Adley. You'd love it. Maybe we can plan a family vacation there," she suggested to Roger.

Adley didn't know why she was impatient for more bad news. "Dad, what do you mean Grandma was only half English?"

"My mother's name was Agatha Elizabeth Wilkes, the daughter of an English woman, Sondra Wilkes, and my grandfather was Armando Rodrigues, a Spaniard," he said. "The Wilkes family frowned on him because he was considered to be a peasant. A gypsy, actually."

"But you n—never t—told me!" Adley choked.

Caroline shifted her eyes to Roger then back to Adley.

"It's not a terrible thing, Adley. I think it's actually nice to have such a colorful family tree."

"No one really knew much about my grandfather," Roger reported. "He died before I was born."

"But you're an only child!" Adley pointed out uselessly.

Roger glanced at Caroline who was just as confused about the obvious, yet unexpected observation. "True, I am an only child but that makes me all the more special," her father quipped. "You look disappointed. Don't tell me you have a hard time with gypsy ancestry?"

"No, uh, thanks for telling me, Dad."

The history lesson ended on a sad note. Adley eased out of the room. She staggered into the hallway and grasped the handrail at the top of the stairs. Sapped of energy, her body dragged her down, and she slumped onto the top step, looking hopefully down the length of the well-lit hall. Maybe she simply exaggerated the darkened mist in front of her bedroom door. But even with ornate electric wall sconces neatly spaced apart illuminating the entire hallway, and a new bulb in the farthest fixture, the area fronting her bedroom still looked gloomy and forbidding.

So she was a real Spanish descendant after all, without any brothers or sisters which qualified her as the oldest child. But her father didn't have any siblings. How had he survived? She wondered why he hadn't gone through any of the dismaying episodes that she endured.

For whatever reason the curse affected her, it had, and if Victor was right, then that inexplicable apparition was out to get her, and she had to find out how to stop it.

Adley went through the ritual of stealing clothes from

her own room and rushed back into the hallway just as the tapping and hissing started. She slept downstairs in the family room and woke intermittently to a variety of noises. How could her parents think it was mice? Twice she woke abruptly to a loud thump, too loud to be a mouse, unless a group of a hundred jumped off her bed at the same time.

After a light breakfast Roger and Caroline relaxed in their suite, but Adley remained downstairs. The moment her parents were out of hearing range, she scoured the lower level for the manuscript. In the living room, she pulled apart the sofas and opened every cabinet. She moved furniture and lifted carpets in hopes of finding a hidden trap door. She held her breath and stuck her hand into every dark closet corner hoping to find a hidden cupboard.

In the kitchen, Adley pushed dishware aside in the cabinets and reluctantly swept her hand over the highest shelves. Her search for a sliding wall panel or secret drawer proved futile. The search continued in the formal dining and living rooms, but she found nothing. After hours of futile searching and nearly losing all hope of defeating the sinister entity that haunted her bedroom, she dialed Victor's number.

"Hello?" the boy asked.

"Hi. It's me," Adley said. "What are you doing?"

"Chores. They never end, especially during summer vacation."

"I guess I better let you go then."

"No! It's okay. Is everything all right?"

Adley started to cry. Maybe it was his concern for her that made her feel safer. Perhaps what touched her so deeply was a near-total stranger offering her comfort when her own parents didn't.

"What's wrong, Adley? Are you okay?"

"I'm okay. Really. I just didn't sleep well. All night

long there were tapping noises and scratching. And then there's that dark gloom floating in front of my room. And there's something else, Victor."

"What is it?"

"You were right. Last night I asked my parents about my ancestors, and my father said he has Spanish blood on his side of the family. His grandfather was a gypsy."

"I'm sorry, Adley."

"Did you reach your great-uncle?"

"Yes. He said we can't do much without the gypsy's manuscript. All our answers are in that book. He tried a lot of rituals to keep the curse from hurting Aggie, and the only thing that worked was putting the handle on the door."

"I've been looking for the book all morning. I've gone through the entire first floor and the garage. I guess I'll have to search upstairs, too."

"I would help you," he offered, "but considering how your parents feel about my family…" His voice trailed off.

"I know. I'm sorry. They're such hypocrites."

"They're not that bad, Adley."

"Yes, they are. They're always telling me how no one is better than anyone else and how it's our behavior that sets us apart from others. And look how they're behaving toward you because of your last name. It's not right, and it's not fair."

"You know the angrier you are at your parents, the less afraid you sound," Victor said.

"Great. My anger makes one problem go away but it makes an awful lot of tension in our family. But that's the least of my worries. I have no idea what this curse is about or how bad it's going to get."

"Great-Uncle Pablo didn't have time to tell me much. He said to call if it gets worse."

"That's one call I hope I don't have to make," Adley said.

"Let's put our heads together and see if we can come up with a plan."

"But you said we needed the book," she reminded.

"Yeah, I know." He hesitated. "Do you think you'd like to meet me again? At the trail?"

"I'd really like that."

"You would?"

"Yeah," she answered. Her heart swelled, not with relief at getting away from the freaky curse, but finally with something good to look forward to.

"Okay. I've got some chores to do. I can meet you in an hour at the big pine. I'll see you then."

"Thanks, Victor."

His voice softened. "It's nothing."

"That's not true. You believe me, and you're willing to help me. I'm really glad that we met. I'm sorry I was so rude to you at the library."

"It's okay," he replied. "I know you were scared."

"I still am," she said.

"I like this other part of you, Adley. Not the scared, apologetic girl but the one who appreciates me."

"Thanks," she said, glad he couldn't see her face turn red.

"It won't be long before I see you. I'll feed the horses and muck the stalls as fast as I can. See you soon."

"Bye."

Adley hung up the phone after his farewell but wanted desperately to keep him on the line until he was ready to visit. It was only an hour, she assured herself. She had to get dressed to meet him, and that meant another trip to her room for something to wear.

She'd get more than one change, her pajamas, jewelry,

and her make-up, too. She'd stash her things in the bottom drawer of the maid's dresser where her mother was least likely to find them. Adley would take them out when her parents weren't around. She'd also keep doing her own laundry but only when she knew her mother wasn't washing anything.

Fortified by the thought of seeing Victor, she climbed the stairs and forced herself to walk toward the dark shadow occupying the space at the end of the hall. She pressed her ear to the door and didn't hear a sound.

Luckily, her mother came out of her room.

"Hey, Mom." Adley brightened her voice. "Um, could you, like, um, please help me to pick out an outfit?"

"Sure," Caroline strode down the hall and met her daughter at the bedroom door. She kept her arms crossed tight against her chest, seemingly suspicious of Adley's sudden dependence. "But since when did you need my help picking out clothes? You haven't done that since you were in kindergarten."

"When I was at the library, Victor Trumillo—"She thought her mother grimaced. "—well, he told me about some girls who hang out around here. Sometimes they go riding on the trail outback. I wanted to, um, see if they came by."

Her mother smiled approvingly. "Well then, that calls for a pair of your best jeans and that pretty blue V-neck blouse." Her mother started to leave.

"Mom!"

"Yes, dear?" Caroline stepped back to the door and watched Adley rush to the closet.

Adley knew it wasn't possible to grab more than one change of clothes without raising suspicion. "Let me grab my shirt and see if it's the same one you're talking about."

"I'm sure you know which one. I bought it for you during spring vacation. Remember?"

"Uh, I think so." Adley grabbed her boots, the blouse,
and jeans from the closet. "This shirt?" She held it up as she
headed to the dresser for her purse and more jewelry.

"That's the one," Caroline said and, again, started out
of the room.

"What about this necklace?"

She heard her mother sigh, but Caroline came back into
the room. Adley plucked socks and a bra from her dresser
drawer.

"Your silver heart locket is a good choice. And the
matching earrings." Caroline tossed her chin at the dresser
to a set of silver heart shaped studs.

Adley made small talk as she scurried out the room.
"Mom? Uh, could you shut the door behind me?"

Caroline squinted her eyes suspiciously at her daughter. "Sure."

"So is it all right if I take a walk around the trail
again?"

"Yes, but don't stay out late. And if those girls happen
to come around, you should invite them in."

"Sure," Adley said, knowing an introduction to Victor
was highly unlikely.

Adley felt her mother's eyes staring after her as she
scampered down the hall with her clothing bundled in her
arms.

☢ ☢ ☢

Adley changed into her clothes in the upstairs bathroom. Only once did a pipe rattle and hiss, but she didn't
necessarily chalk that up to the strange creature in her
room. She dressed as quickly as possible, hoping the noises

were caused by bad plumbing. She raced downstairs into the servant's room, wondering how such an unbelievable thing could be happening to her as she stashed her pajamas in a dresser drawer.

Before they came to Capilla Manor, Adley's out of control verbal attacks were her biggest problem. Sometimes something snapped inside that made her want to lash out at anyone who showed her kindness or understanding. Her bad temper wore at her, and Adley had no idea how to keep the onrush of hostile feelings from exploding. Her inexplicable behavior was almost as baffling as the stupid gypsy curse, a curse she still hoped didn't apply to her. But then she met Victor, and her anger was manageable. She felt more in control of her feelings.

Adley stared at her reflection in the bathroom mirror and brushed her hair. She heard a noise above her in the east wing of the house. Victor said the "thing," whatever it was, couldn't leave the confines of the room. Adley fumbled with the silver jewelry and clasped it into place, then heard a noise again. A hissing, like pressure releasing from a water pipe. She scanned the area, but there was no apparition in sight. She quickly applied concealer onto the puffy dark circles beneath her eyes.

"Aaaa," she heard, not able to pinpoint the direction of the sound. She stood still. "Aaad—leeey," it whispered, drawing out each syllable of her name.

She shoved her make-up and brush into her make-up bag. Maybe the thing couldn't leave the room with the silver handle, but it somehow had the power to create noise in other parts of the house. In any case, the maid's suite no longer felt safe. Adley grabbed her things off the counter, ran out of the bathroom, grabbed her pajamas from the dresser, and dashed to the far corner of the family room.

After stashing her pajamas in a neat pile behind the so-fa, she sprinted around the furniture to the French doors.

"Aaad-leeey!" someone whispered behind her, but no one was there.

Adley rushed out through the doors leading to the pa-tio. She ran off to meet Victor at the big pine tree and hoped nothing followed her up the trail.

Chapter 13

Adley hiked across the dead brush and dried weeds, recalling how she first thought Capilla Manor a stupid name until Victor told her at the library what "capilla" meant. Then it made perfect sense, but who named it that, and did they know that someone was going to die in the house? Did they know about the curse?

Adley felt helpless. She'd barely learned about her family history and had no idea where she'd go to learn about gypsy lore. Maybe her dad would let her use his computer tonight. Maybe the library in Minero had a computer. Maybe it even had a book on gypsy curses. She was desperate for answers and held onto the hope that she could find the key to end the waking nightmare.

A gust of fresh desert air swirled about her, wafting through the trail, slightly cooling the shelter under the surrounding evergreens. She sat on the felled tree trunk, closed her eyes, and inhaled the lovely sage and mesquite aromas that drifted in abundance down the hillsides. Rays of sunlight found their way through overhead branches and felt as comforting as Victor's voice on the phone.

At the thought of him, she opened her eyes and locked onto his dark irises. He was a distance away on Sweet Pea, but he had reigned in his mount and stopped completely. He smiled and nudged the horse. It followed his silent command and cantered forward. Victor pulled on the reins only a few feet from where Adley sat and slid effortlessly off the mare.

He let the leather reins fall to the ground. Sweet pea nibbled on grasses at the base of a tree stump. "You look relaxed," Victor observed. "Finally."

"Sometimes it's nice to just sit and be quiet."

He sat next to her and their shoulders touched. "I guess things are pretty crazy in your world right now."

"You can say that again," she agreed.

"I guess things are—"

She playfully jabbed him in the ribs. Victor laughed and grabbed her hand. He looked at her pale fingers and stroked the back of her hand.

"Victor, why is it that my dad is still alive? I mean, if this curse thing is supposed to get the first child shouldn't my dad be—" She gulped. "—dead or something?"

"I don't know. Are you sure he's an only child?"

"I'm positive. Grandma Aggie told me once that she wanted lots of kids, but she couldn't have any more."

"I can't figure out why it skipped a generation. A curse doesn't exactly list conditions, like the number of children parents have to have in order to qualify for death."

"I wish there was something we could do without the manuscript."

Victor put his arm around the frightened girl. "My uncle told me he'd call if anything came to mind. All he said was not to go into your room."

"What if we left? What if we went back to California?"

She felt Victor's arm tense slightly at her suggestion. "Actually, I asked him that myself. My great-uncle said it will seek you out until the end of your days."

"Well, now I feel better," came her dry and bitter response.

"My great-uncle is at a ranch a few hours north of here. He said I was to call him if anything bad happened, and he'd rush back down. Until then, there's not much he can do."

"But what if something happens—worse than me hearing creepy noises and seeing dark shadows?"

"I'd hate to hear and see things like that. I don't want to imagine anything worse."

"I'm glad you don't have to." Adley smiled. "Let's take a walk."

"Sure." He made a clicking noise to his horse. Sweet Pea responded by following at a slow pace behind the couple, content to nibble sparse patches of grass.

"How long did my grandma put up with that thing before the handle was installed?"

"My great-uncle put it on after she fell down the stairs."

Adley remembered what her mother said on the drive to the timeworn property. Grandma Aggie said she was pushed by sticks when she fell. What else felt like sticks? The mechanical claw of a vending machine at an arcade? A skeleton's fingertip? The hair rose up on the back of her neck. A hole just had to exist in her interpretation of the psychotic events.

"Aggie had Great-Uncle Pablo nail the windows shut," Victor said. "He even buried tiny hematite beads around the outside of the window frames and all around the door to help keep the creature inside the room when someone left the door open."

"But how did it get into Capilla Manor in the first place? How did it know where to look for the gypsy's descendants?"

"I'm not sure. I'll ask my uncle. I do know that a curse has a life force all its own. It hangs around, waiting for the right time to strike. My great-uncle said that more insane stuff kept happening after Aggie's accident but nothing else physically hurt her. Remember that you told me how you heard glass breaking?" She nodded. "I told my mama about that and she said that everyone who worked at your grandma's house heard glass breaking at one time or another, but they never found a single broken piece. The gardener said he heard snakes hissing but never found anything more than a lizard outside."

"I've heard all of that," she reminded him.

Victor felt her shiver. "I wish there was more I could do to protect you." He pulled her closer to him. "You've got to find that book, Adley."

"I know, but like your mom, I've searched everywhere downstairs. In every room, in the garage, the maid's quarters. I've pulled the cushions off the couches, stuck my hand inside every corner of every closet but found nothing. I can't think of another place to look. Except upstairs."

"Maybe if your parents go someplace, I can come over and help you look," he offered.

"I wish. Other than going into town for coffee the day I met you, they seem to love hanging around the death house."

"Maybe you might try convincing them to let you sleep in the maid's quarters downstairs."

"They vetoed the idea when I first got here. But it's just as well. Today I was in the maid's bathroom and it sounded like—" She shuddered. "—like something said my name."

"What?" He responded loud enough to make Sweet Pea snort in response. "But that's impossible! It shouldn't be able to get past the handle!"

"I didn't see anything, any lumps or spider hands. I just heard it."

"All the same, I'm going to call my great-uncle and ask him about that," Victor told her. "He pulled out a cell phone. "I forgot. You can't get signal in this part of the woods."

"Even if I wanted to sleep in the maid's room, you can't imagine the roadblock my parents can put up when they really want something their way. I had to pitch a fit to get the room of doom, and that was me just being down the hall, let alone downstairs."

"I hate to say it, but they were right not to want you to have that room. Only they gave you the wrong reasons for not wanting you in it. What about taking one of the other rooms, across the hall and closer to your parents?"

"At first I was thinking of taking a room next to theirs, but now that's way too close for me to be near that thing." Adley stopped walking and leaned her head back to look directly up at Victor. "Thank you."

He smiled and embraced her with his eyes. "For what."

"You're the only one who believes me, Victor. I don't know what I'd do if we hadn't met."

Their eyes remained locked and both relished the surge of energy between them. One lifted up the other, and Adley swore they'd start rising above the trees at any moment. Victor's lips came closer to hers and, in that second, nothing else in the world existed. Nothing else had meaning except the wisp of breath she felt on her nose, his arms so tenderly wrapped around her.

"Deedee! I mean, Adley!" They heard her father calling from the distance.

Victor pulled back, brought back to reality. "I'll be right there!" Adley bellowed toward the general direction of the manor.

Victor grabbed his ears and shook his head from side to side. Adley grinned.

"I'll stay here until you're closer to your house," he told her.

"Adley!" her father called again.

"Coming!" Victor burst out laughing, and she asked in a normal tone, "What's so funny?"

"You're so delicate and little, but your voice can sound like a bulldozer!"

Adley shook her head. "No wonder my mom and dad cringe just before I throw a fit."

Victor took her hand, and they started moving quickly toward the big pine tree. "Are you still throwing fits?"

"Only when I don't get my way."

"Uh oh!" Victor stepped away, but Adley reached out and pulled him back to her.

"I don't know why. I told you it's uncontrollable sometimes. I don't mean to get so angry, but I do."

"I've only seen you get mad when you don't want to admit the truth."

She cocked her head to the side. "Huh." That gave her something to think about.

"Adley!" Caroline called from over the tree line.

"Coming!" Adley shouted back. "I've really got to go!" she said and pulled away, but Victor kept holding her hand. "They're coming!"

"Call me tonight, before you go to bed," Victor said. "I can stay on the phone with you until you're ready to fall asleep."

She smiled. "That would be really nice."

They were nearly at the bend when Victor leaned down and kissed her soft, freckled cheek. "I'll see you later."

He mounted his horse and cantered away just as Caroline and Roger came up the trail.

Her mother stretched her neck, trying to glimpse the person who just rode off.

"Looks like you caught up with those kids from the school," she commented.

"Just one," Adley replied and quickly changed the subject. "What's for lunch?"

Caroline was about to say something, but Roger took her hand and shook his head, no more than a flicker of movement on his part. Still, Adley caught the tiny motion.

"What do you feel like eating?" Caroline followed his lead, and trailed her husband and daughter along the path which led back through the yard of the old manor.

Caroline squinted back at the dirt course leading into the woods. Adley knew she wondered who the visitor was. Caroline kept her lips pressed together, and Adley was grateful not to have to lie about the mysterious friend.

Thanks to Victor, Adley's cheerful smile had to be more than either of her parents had witnessed in months. She willed herself to lose the ridiculous grin she saw reflected in the glass of the French doors.

She opened one for her father and waited for her mother to pass before entering the house.

"Why thank you, good sir," her mother joked.

"Need help in the kitchen, sweetheart?" Roger offered his wife.

"Why don't you guys chill, and I'll fix us some sandwiches?" Adley said.

Her parents stopped in their tracks, but Adley continued into the kitchen.

☣ ☣ ☣

"Am I dreaming?" Roger asked quietly.

"Not unless I am, too. Please! Let it last!" Caroline pleaded heavenward.

They sat in the corner group of sofas in the living room, holding hands, relishing Adley's change of attitude.

"Let's try not to say anything about her social life that might set her off," Roger said.

"Fine by me," Caroline said. "Believe me. The last thing I want to do is spoil her good mood. But I think I have an idea why Adley is unusually good-natured."

"What's that?"

Caroline smiled. "The obvious. A boy has to be involved, and I hope it isn't that Trumillo kid. The last thing our daughter needs is someone telling her spooky stories of family curses and horrible monsters."

Roger looked up at nothing in particular for a moment before he spoke. "Well, something Adley in a happy state, and even if it were the Trumillo boy, it would be worth it."

"I'm sure that she met one of those girls from the local high school. If it was that Trumillo kid, he'd be scaring her with all that family curse nonsense. No, it has to be a different person she met on the trail for Adley to be this happy."

"She was definitely happily distracted by the company she kept during her time out back. She's more cheerful than she has been in months," Roger said. "Look. It seems harmless enough, and although we don't want to interfere, we can still make it a point to carefully find out if Adley is hanging out with a good crowd of kids or someone she's safe around."

"I have to admit that I'd feel better knowing it was another teenage girl who visited our daughter on the trail," Caroline said.

"We have to trust that we've taught Adley how to make good choices," Roger said more to himself than his wife.

"When should we tell her about the house?"

"If it wasn't for all the problems she's having getting to sleep, we should have told her already. Why don't we tell her after we take care of the rodent problem in her room?"

"That's a good idea," Caroline agreed. "If she hates living here so much, the least we can do is make sure she likes the room she's in."

"I can't imagine how she'll react when we tell her we decided to move here," Roger said.

"We'd be crazy to turn down any of the offers on the California house, Roger. They're so much more than even the realtor expected."

"Let's not tell Adley just yet," her husband suggested. "She'll find out soon enough anyway."

"Did you check under her bed?"

"Yes, but I didn't see any mice, and I can't tell how they're getting into her room," he said.

"Maybe a hole in a window screen?"

"No. I checked. They were painted shut, but I'll wait until I solve the mouse problem before starting another project like prying the windows open. Besides, Adley doesn't seem to mind. I'll just concentrate on getting the mouse out for now."

"That's a good idea. The last thing Adley would want to know is that her room is infested with mice."

"It only sounded like one or two," Roger said.

"But you have to admit," Caroline pointed out, "that was an awful lot of noise for one mouse to make."

Chapter 14

Despite what Victor told her about the curse, the day had been wonderful. Adley couldn't stop thinking about him and their walk together. The stupid curse took a backseat during most of the conversation. They laughed a lot and not once did Victor look at her with disgust or anger like the boys at her school did.

Adley wondered if it was her imagination, or if Victor had been going to kiss her before her parents called out for her. It had to be the curse that interested Victor. It was their only common link, and once they were able to get rid of it there would be no reason for Victor to visit her. He might stop being nice to her or stop talking to her altogether.

He could have been just teasing her, relishing her fear when he told her about the scary gypsy family history like her parents said. Yet, if it was all an act on his part, there was no reason to be nice to her when no one was around to see how he treated her. If he really didn't like her, there was no point in asking her to call him before she went to bed.

Adley had to admit she didn't have much experience with boys and interacting with them. Her feelings told her that Victor seemed genuine and honest. Maybe he really was a sweet guy. Whether it was a farce or not on Victor's part, Adley enjoyed their earlier interaction and decided it made her feel better to believe that he really was a good person. Regardless of what happened between them, at least she had fond memories of that morning to enjoy.

With her thoughts focused on Victor, Adley was happy throughout dinner, and her mood probably gave her parents a pleasant surprise. She was so lighthearted she barely noticed when night fell upon the decaying residence, and for the first time since staying at Capilla Manor, Adley couldn't wait for bedtime.

From the moment she left him in the woods, she started looking forward to calling Victor later that night. Of course, she didn't want to seem desperate. Her last issue of teen Cosmo cited desperation as one of the top ten reasons why guys broke up with girls.

Adley decided to wait until eleven to call him, otherwise, she might wake up someone else in the family. Better make it ten when she called. Even so, all the adults would be in bed. She shouldn't call later than nine. Who was she kidding? She was ready to call him right then, and her parents hadn't even gone to bed. Time passed quickly while Adley hung out with Victor but it took forever for the time to arrive when she decided to call him.

If Adley remained friends with Victor, and dared to hope for more, she'd want to have her cell phone. Talking to Victor all night on the phone was a good alternative compared to thinking about him, and it served as a good way to keep her thoughts distracted from what lurked in her bedroom. Maybe her dad would get her a pay-as-you-go phone for her birthday when they got Wi-Fi, and at least pay for service to last until the end of summer, that is if her parents wanted to stay in the twenty-first century. For now, she'd have to use the phone in the kitchen.

Grandma Aggie had old fashioned plug-in phones throughout the house. Her dad had mentioned buying a new system with cordless phones if they ever planned to live at the mansion. Like that would happen. He never stayed home at their own house and rarely visited his own mother. Knowing she wasn't destined to live in Capilla Manor was mostly a blessing, but when Adley thought of Victor, she didn't want to leave the area.

After her parents retired for the evening, Adley changed into her pajamas and called Victor. He answered the call.

"Hi. It's me," she said.

"Hey. I was just thinking of you. How are you doing?"

"Fine," Adley told him.

"I don't know how you can say that. I'd be scared stiff staying there."

"Look, Victor—" She loved saying his name. "—I want to be honest with you. I'm freaked out and all by the story of the curse, but having a mouse in my room explains a lot. The noises, the tugging on the comforter. It makes sense."

"What about the shadows and those weird feelings you get?"

"That's just my own crazy imagination."

"Did your parents tell you that?" he asked somewhat defensively.

Great. She'd made him mad. Maybe she should have kept her mouth shut. "Just when I decide to be honest with you and tell you how I feel—"

"What?" he asked.

"Never mind."

"No, say it," Victor prodded. "I don't mean to upset you, Adley, and I'm not trying to scare you. Heck, I don't have to with that nasty thing living in your grandma's house. But you can't explain away all the creepy things that have been going on. You're doubting your own senses and what you've been experiencing in order to talk yourself out of the truth of what's really happening inside that house."

Adley listened, not reacting to his honest opinion. "If I see or hear anything else that can't be explained, I'll tell you, and then we can figure out what to do. Okay?"

"Okay, but promise to tell me anything, regardless of how stupid it sounds. Is that a deal?"

"Deal," she said, relieved that she didn't blow it. She didn't want to risk losing Victor's friendship now that he'd just entered her life.

Adley felt better knowing that telling him the truth didn't affect their budding relationship.

"Did your parents tell you they decided to live there yet?"

"I told you, they never said anything to me about it but—" She considered the idea. "I guess if they were thinking of moving here, they wouldn't have told me. They probably thought I'd have a fit if they didn't bother asking me about it."

Victor asked her straight out, "Would you have? Had a fit, I mean?"

Adley huffed. "Probably. Yeah. I told you before, sometimes I get so angry, and I can't seem to control it."

"I wonder if that has anything to do with the curse."

"Victor, please. Don't bring that up again. Something freaky is happening, I admit it, but I'm not fully convinced some kind of evil spirit lives in this house because of a curse. I don't even want to talk about it anymore."

"All right, all right. I don't blame you for not wanting to talk about it." An awkward pause stifled their conversation until they spoke at the same time.

"Do you, like, read much?" he asked.

Her question was, "What's your favorite movie?"

They laughed and another momentary pause lapsed,

this time without any discomfort as they waited for the other to speak.

"Ladies first," Victor said.

Adley laughed. "Yes, I like to read, but I haven't done much lately. I can't seem to concentrate. Besides, I haven't had much free time with my busy social life in Hachita," she joked.

"I hope I can fill up your calendar a little."

Her heart swelled. "Me, too, Victor." Adley heard thumping from somewhere upstairs. "Someone's up. At least, I hope it's my mom or dad compared to what it could be. I've got to go. If I'm not in my room, they'll come downstairs to look for me."

"What if it's not them, Adley? Making that noise, I mean."

"It's one of them. I just heard a toilet flush. I have to wait until they're asleep before I can come downstairs."

"Gosh. Are they like the police or what?"

"No. They only started being overprotective in the last few months. Since the evil Adley personality started taking over."

He didn't laugh at her dark sense of humor. "You're not evil. If you were, I wouldn't want to be with you."

Adley didn't hear a hint of sarcasm in his voice. It didn't sound like he was joking at all.

"You say that now, but just you wait 'til I get mad at you."

"You've been a little grumpy every now and then, especially when we first met at the library," Victor admitted, "but that was just because I freaked you out about the history of Capilla Manor. I think you're great, Adley."

She didn't know how to reply to that. She was speechless, a rarity for the opinionated girl. Another loud thump resounded over the kitchen.

"Great. They're in my room now. I've got to go."

"In your room? Are you sure it's them?"

Adley crooked her head to listen. "It doesn't sound like the usual noises. I don't hear any hissing or wicked laughing."

"I don't think you should go into your room."

"I'll just check and see if it's them, then come back downstairs," she assured him.

"Okay. But if it really is something freaky, I want you to call me right away, okay?"

Her heart fluttered. "Okay. I will."

"Promise?"

"I promise," she said, smiling.

"I hope you have a good night's sleep. Downstairs."

Adley laughed. "Thanks. You sleep well, too. I've got to go!"

"Talk to you tomorrow?" he asked.

She wondered if he could feel her big smile across the phone lines. "You'd better."

"Bye, Adley."

"Good night, Victor."

She hung up the phone and, in high spirits, ran across the room, and sprinted up the stairs. At the top of the stairwell, no one was in sight.

"Huh." They probably went back to bed, but she wanted to make certain her mom wasn't waiting for Adley in her room.

Adley walked down the long hallway, toward the shadowed area. A light touch on the freezing handle let her know that all things hadn't changed since meeting Victor. She switched on the light and took a few tentative steps inside the room, leaving the door wide-open behind her. A quick check of the floor revealed no mice or any other furry animals that could scare the living daylights out of her.

The floor was a bit cool to the touch. Lucky thing she'd worn a thick pair of socks. Confident that her parents were in bed for the night, she turned toward the door, but it was completely closed. The overhead light flickered off and on. She glimpsed a hulking shadow lurking in the corner of her room between the closet and bedroom door. As dark as night itself, the black figure started to take shape right in front of her eyes. Then the lights went out completely.

Adley stepped backward to the door and the handle was colder than ever. The tips of her fingers felt as if they sizzled, so she stuck the singed fingertips into her mouth, her eyes focused on the corner.

She reached back for the light switch. If the bulb still worked, the obscure image would disappear the moment the light when on. The bright flash relieved her sense of unease when she looked back at the corner but only for the briefest moment. As predicted, the shadow was no longer there.

Now it stood right in front of her.

A long string of bones whipped out the top of the obsidian mass, tethered on the end to a spidery hand. It whipped itself straight at her. Adley jerked to the side and the clawed limb smashed into the door and locked it. Adley couldn't scream but she ran to the other corner of the room, farthest from the door. She grabbed a frame off the dresser and threw it at the dark mass. The shadow dissolved. She willed every ounce of strength in a sprint for the door. From out of nowhere, the hand shot out in front of her and spread its fingers like a catcher's mitt ready to grab whatever came its way.

Adley slid beneath the bones and into the door as if she was sliding into home base. The spindly object grabbed her foot as she hit the door. Adley kicked at it and her foot crushed the bony hand. It broke into pieces that scattered across the floor, clattering like a bowl of marbles.

The creature cackled and whispered clearly into her ear, "Aaad—"

"Shut up," she shouted. "Don't say it! You have no right to say my name!"

She grabbed hold of the handle, ignoring the freezing burn on her skin. She yanked the door open and looked back.

Five skeletal fingers with deadly sharp tips flew directly at her face.

Chapter 15

With lightning speed, Adley slammed the door behind her. She heard the creature pummel against the closed door.

It must have shattered again.

She hunched over in the hall, gasping for breath.

"Deedee!"

Adley jerked out of her frightened stupor. Her father's voice was reassuring, and she didn't care that he called her by her baby nick-name.

He ran down the hall and looked at her door. "What's the matter?"

Her pale skin and frantic eyes told him she saw something, but he doubted it was anything more than another rodent.

Caroline called from their bedroom. "Roger? What is it?"

"It's a monster!" Adley shouted back and ran toward her mother.

Caroline heard the absurd remark but enveloped her daughter in a comforting embrace. "It's okay, honey. You were just having a nightmare."

"No! I saw it!"

"For goodness sakes, this has got to stop!" Her father's

remark was tinged with disgust. "It's only a mouse or two." He reached for the door.

"Cover your hand or else it will burn your skin!" Adley said.

Roger shook his head and pulled on the handle. He held up his palm, to show her nothing had happened, and pushed the door open. From her mother's protective hold, Adley gauged his reaction.

Roger looked back toward Caroline and Adley. "Well, aside from the bedding being torn apart, everything looks okay."

"I wasn't even lying down on my bed!" Roger gave his daughter a warning look and entered her room. Adley yelled, "No, Dad, don't go in there!"

"Dad's going to be fine." Caroline held Adley in a tight embrace and the girl rubbernecked over her shoulder. Her father didn't tear out of the room. He calmly closed the door behind him as he walked back out.

Caroline escorted her daughter to the love seat in the sitting area of the master suite and Roger followed. "Are you okay?" he asked.

Adley simply nodded and shook in her mother's arms.

"You can sleep in our room if you'd like," Caroline said. What Adley really wanted to do was to call Victor and apologize for not believing him. She wanted to be as far away from her bedroom as possible. She wanted to be completely outside of Capilla Manor.

"Can I sleep downstairs?" At least she'd be closer to the kitchen phone.

☣ ☣ ☣

Both Roger and Caroline walked downstairs with their daughter.

"Adley, I'm sorry for shouting at you when you had such a terrible fright, but your ludicrous behavior is wearing on my patience," her father said. She returned a blank stare. "I'll make up the couch with some blankets and a pillow." To Caroline he said, "Maybe you can make us some of your creme de la creme."

Caroline agreed to make Adley's favorite hot drink, mentioned in a cartoon with talking cats and mice, no less. Her mother invented the drink of warmed milk, sweetened with sugar, and sprinkled with cinnamon. It always had a calming influence. Maybe it was only a psychological reaction, but her nerves were frayed, and Caroline couldn't think of another way to stop Adley's shuddering.

As soon as the hot drink was ready, all three cuddled on the cushy sofas in the corner of the family room and drank their hot beverages. Adley finally dozed off, and her parents tucked warm blankets around her.

"Should one of us stay down here with her?" Caroline asked.

"We should see if we can hear anything making noise upstairs. Maybe one of us can sleep in Adley's room to see if we can find out where the mice are coming from."

"I think one of us needs to stay with Adley." Caroline tightened her protective arm around Adley's shoulders.

"What we need to do is make Adley take the room next to ours. You have to admit, Caroline, this is really getting out of hand."

She kept her voice low. "Don't you see, Roger? It has to be Adley's idea to make the switch. She's trying to force us into making that decision for her with her silly behavior. Later, she'll completely resent us for making her change rooms. What we really need is an exterminator."

"Why do we need all that poison for just a couple of wayward rats?"

"It stands to reason that more than one mouse frightened Adley in her room tonight," Caroline said.

"Yeah, but she acts like there's a bogeyman hiding underneath her bed." Roger said.

☣ ☣ ☣

Apparently, while Adley slept, Caroline brought down a fresh change of clothes. Adley found them on the coffee table the next morning, and she changed as the fog of deep sleep cleared.

Although phones were located throughout the lower level of the house, she felt the most privacy in the kitchen, even if it sat directly beneath her bedroom.

"That's the last time I'm sleeping in that room," she told Victor.

"I don't blame you. I wouldn't even sleep in that house," Victor told Adley. "I've been trying to reach Great Uncle Pablo, but reception is lousy where he's at. He's not getting his calls."

"Keep trying. Please keep trying." She exhaled and tried to blow out her frustration. "I wish you didn't have so many chores to do."

"Me, too. You know, you can call me anytime you need to."

Adley smiled. "I know. Thanks."

"I mean it, Adley. I'll drop everything to make sure you're all right. I'd come right now if you really wanted me to."

"Of course, I want you to, Victor, but then your chores will pile up, you'll get into trouble, and your mother won't let you visit me because I'm such a bad influence."

He laughed. "I think she'd understand. Maybe I should tell her everything that's happening. I haven't been giving her all the details, but she's actually pretty cool. Next time we're on the trail, we can go to my place, and you can meet her."

Adley, mildly surprised, had to double-check. "You want me to meet your mom?"

"Sure. Why not? I know you'll really like her."

"I'd like that. I'll call you if anything terrible happens." If Victor liked her enough to introduce her to his mother he must really like her, and not because of the creature haunting her room.

"I'd like to think that you'd want to see me even if there wasn't a curse on your family," Victor said, confirming what she'd just thought.

"I do want to see you, but I can't help thinking about this all the time, and I need to find a way to make it stop. I don't want you to think that you're just a distraction from my daily horror of living in Capilla Manor, but you make me feel better, Victor."

"I'm glad for that. Do you want me to come over? I mean, I'll just get out of here right now."

"Won't you get into trouble for not doing your chores?"

"Maybe. Honestly, I think my mom will understand. She knows the curse is real. Even if she didn't, you're worth any trouble I'd get into."

Adley hoped he didn't hear her tiny gasp, surprised to hear him tell her she meant that much, and it felt really good.

"No, Victor. I'll just stay out of my room, and if it gets really bad, then I'll call you."

"Promise?"

Only Victor could coax a smile out of her in such a traumatic time. "Yes," she said. "I promise."

"Good. I'll call you when I get my chores done."

"Thanks, Victor. For everything."

His whispered voice soothed her. "I'm glad to help, Adley."

"Bye," she said.

Adley didn't want to end the conversation, but how silly to say "You hang up first," "No, you——" It was hard not to ask him to come over, but what could he really do to solve the problem until he spoke with his uncle?

Over breakfast, Roger and Caroline made several attempts to speak with Adley about the incident in her room, but she refused to discuss it. There was no use. If they didn't believe her last night, she didn't think she had a chance of them believing her at any other time.

Adley tossed her pajamas into the washer before going out back. Then she coaxed on a pair of small work gloves. A patch of ground behind the main patio marked the first part of the yard that she would reclaim. The dirt, hard as rock, made the task in the warm sun more of a challenge than she expected.

At least it was a problem she could do something about.

☣ ☣ ☣

"It'll help to water first," her dad said as he stepped outside. "Once the ground is soaked, it'll be a lot easier to pull the weeds out." Adley stood up and watched him drag a long irrigation hose off a spinning reel. "Start at that corner and snake this hose back and forth until you get back here," he said. "We might as well soak it all at once."

Adley took the hose without objection, glad for her father's company. After laying down the irrigation hose as her father directed, he turned on the water. The two picked up several dark green plant containers and ceramic remnants of broken pottery. After tossing the debris in the trashcan, Roger and Adley ripped out dead vines embedded in the stuccoed walls of the house.

Caroline served them lemonade and sandwiches for lunch. Father and daughter worked up a healthy sweat, and Roger finally called it a day. After lunch, her parents were surprised to see Adley cleaning up the backyard again, yanking on weeds closest to the hose.

"If she physically exerts herself, she may get exhausted and finally have a good night's sleep," Roger said.

Caroline nodded. "And most likely in the family room."

☣ ☣ ☣

Caroline brought out a tray of food. "I know how much you enjoy eating outdoors." A small section of the ground had been cleared of weeds, and Caroline praised Adley. "Wow, I can really see progress. You'll have this garden looking beautiful in no time."

The compliment gave Adley a sense of accomplishment. Eventually, it was too dark to continue her work, and she showered in the maid's quarters.

It wasn't until she stepped out of the shower stall and onto the plush carpet that she realized she had no clean clothes to wear. Wearing her bath towel to the laundry room, Adley found that with her mind set on working outside, she forgot all about putting her pajamas into the dryer. Even in the summer, the house was too chilly at night to wait while her pajamas dried. The clothes she'd worn outside were soiled and smelly, and that meant a trip to her room.

Rather than get fresh pajamas or a robe from her room, she would ask her mom to get them for her. She sprinted up the stairs and glanced down the hall. The light in her room was on. A shower of light stretched across the hall through the dark mist to the opposite wall. Someone, or something, was in her room.

She peeked into the master suite and saw her father typing at his desk. She knew better than to interrupt him while he worked.

With caution in every step, Adley ventured ever so slowly toward the room. She tilted her head and peeked inside. Caroline sat on her bed with her nose inside a home decorating article. It startled her to see Adley.

"For goodness sakes, Adley. Why are you walking around in a towel?" Caroline pushed the door shut after Adley took her time entering the room.

"I forgot to grab pajamas before my shower," she said.

"I wanted to show you some decorating ideas, but I'll leave you alone to give you some—"

"—no! No!" Adley interrupted. "You can talk to me about it while I get on my jams."

"Okay, dear. Wait 'til you see the curtains that I found. They'll look great." Caroline took her place back on the bed, her feet on the floor, touching the dust ruffle. Adley put her night clothes on in record time.

This was an opportune moment for Adley to also get the clothing she needed for the next morning. "What did you have in mind?" she asked her mother, going through the all too familiar routine of opening the closet and pulling out pants and shoes at record speed.

Caroline patted the mattress next to her, the last place Adley wanted to sit. "Come take a look."

Adley stared at the dark shadow under the foot of the bed. "Why don't you tell me what you have in mind, Mom? I'm not much of a decorator, and I really want to hear your ideas."

She gushed with appreciation because she didn't have to be alone in the room. She piled her clothes on top of one another until an array of garments draped across her arm while Caroline suggested that they begin with Adley's favorite color.

Her mother actually had great ideas. Soon Adley was caught up in the excitement of the interior design lesson, coupled with the feeling of safety while her mother stayed in her room. She folded the clothes and set the stack on her dresser, then joined her mom on the bed, sitting cross legged on top of the mattress beside her. They spoke for quite a long stretch, brainstorming a variety of approaches to create a room that Adley could call her own, not that she planned to sleep in the room again. She scooted to the middle of the bed, lay back, and relaxed. Her mother read short articles she clipped from other magazines.

"Let me read you some great tips I found on choosing the window dressings most appropriate for your room."

"Just do it, Mom, and surprise me. I trust your style and taste," Adley said.

The woman pressed her palm to her chest, obviously taken aback by the unexpected praise. "It's a rare occasion these days when I receive a compliment from my daughter."

"I know. I'm sorry, Mom. I guess I haven't been myself for a while."

"Thank you, sweetheart. I really appreciate hearing you say that. Let me tell you the changes I'm considering so you'll at least have a chance to veto anything you might not like."

"Sure, Mom. But why go through all the expense of redecorating. We're not going move in here, are we?"

Caroline smiled at Adley and paused before speaking. "This is the only room that doesn't look good enough to show anyone who might want to buy the house. We might as well make it something you like while we're here."

Adley was glad her mother wanted to include her in the process, although she could care less about decorating the room. What she really wanted was to get out of Capilla Manor altogether without sacrificing her new friendship with Victor.

Caroline read aloud, and even though the conversation was simply a ruse not to be stuck in the room alone, Adley basked in the comfort of her mother's presence. Her breathing steadied, and she stretched out, staring at the ceiling. She smiled contentedly as her mother's voice, a soft and reassuring drone, lulled her into a peaceful and secure slumber.

☣ ☣ ☣

Caroline smiled. She had lost her audience. She was inwardly bursting with anticipation at Adley's reaction once her daughter saw her new room. Maybe in the next day or so, Caroline could take Adley out to the mall, an hour's drive away, and have Roger paint the room while they were gone. She also wanted Adley to pick out new linens and a new bed.

The unattractive headboard caught her attention. What was Aggie thinking? The awful design and dreary color were counter-intuitive to the rest of the room. The slat capping the top of the primitive headboard had started to separate from the rest of the frame. That cemented her decision, and when Caroline ordered the new bed, she hoped to find another knob to replace the gaudy silver handle on the door.

Caroline set the magazine on the bedside table, casting an eye on her dozing child. She smoothed the strands of hair around Adley's face and gently kissed her on the forehead. Perhaps Adley could find happiness within their little family again. Her night terrors had to be outgrowths of Adley's guilt due to her terrible behavior. In the last two days, she'd shown promising signs of wanting to be a family again—gardening, doing laundry, fixing meals. A new bedroom might solidify her positive changes.

Caroline lovingly wrapped the comforter around her daughter and rose carefully from the bed so as not to disturb her. She turned off the light and closed the door as quietly as she could. She heard a muffled noise as she walked away from the room. Adley was more than likely snuggling under the blankets.

Caroline smiled to herself, remembering Adley's comment regarding a giant mommy mouse. The last thing a mother had to worry about in the quiet high desert of the Hachita Mountains was any kind of a monster going after her daughter.

Chapter 16

*W*ake up! *Wake up! Get out!*

Adley flinched at the command inside her head. But get out of what? What happened to the light? And what poked at her feet? Adley groped around for something familiar, and reality crashed into her nightmare. She sprang up like a jack-in-the-box and frantically studied her whereabouts. Why on earth was she in her room? Her mother had been reading to her.

Oh no! I fell asleep in my room!

The moon cast a bluish glow on top of her furniture, the floor, and onto her bed. Movement beneath the covers told her she should have woken up earlier. Adley's eyes locked on the lump moving toward her foot. She frantically scooted back to the headboard and the comforter ripped open. A long, thorny fingernail shoved its way out of a little hole, jabbing the air, as if trying to find her foot.

Adley held her breath and gaped at the fabric, paralyzed at the sight of the comforter as a large gash widened with each slash of the knife-point nail. She steeled herself to take a flying leap and jump off the bed, but her footing wasn't secure on the cushy mattress, and her feet tangled in the clump of blankets. She fell back against the headboard.

The thing under the blankets stopped moving, as if finally aware of her location.

Adley clutched the headboard as she kicked at the folds of fabric to free her legs. She held hard onto the wooden frame, and accidentally detached the wood strip that topped the length of the headboard. Slightly askew and with just enough moonlight, the broken board revealed a compartment containing a leather rectangle with gold corners. It was a thick manuscript lodged between the wooden sides. The gypsy's text that the Trumillo's had been looking for had been hidden in her headboard all along!

For a fraction of a second it was quiet, too quiet, and Adley whipped her head around to face the evil intruder. Gone. The silence only lasted a second longer. In the next instant, a claw-like hand attached to a rope of bone shot out from under the bed, and lunged for her foot.

The pointed talons burned her skin and searing pain engulfed her ankle. Adley cried out and acted on her first instinct. She kicked on the hard bone pressed into the bottom of her bare foot, and stomped again and again on the sharp talons clutching her ankle until she felt the slightest relief. She kicked again with all her strength and shoved the thick string of bone off the bed and across the floor. The clacking rope recoiled and sailed backward under the bed.

Adley took a herculean leap to the door and immediately slid on her fuzzy acrylic socks. Her arms flung out like a surfer to keep her balance. As she skidded toward the door, the appendage exploded from under the bed like cannon fire and slammed its long fingers against the door, a skeletal hand preventing her escape. Adley skated into a U-turn and skittered back onto the bed.

She stumbled across the mattress back to the headboard and held on for dear life to retain her footing. Before she could scream for her parents, the snake-like arm flew straight at her, and Adley jerked to the side. The bones smashed into the ivory-colored headboard and broke apart. All the pieces rolled to the floor and under the bed as if the room was at an angle. Deadly silence engulfed the room, except for Adley's uneven breathing. She snapped out of the trance and knew she didn't have long to escape.

Something clicked and Adley's gaze darted to the foot of the mattress. The skeletal hand crawled spider-like up the edge of the bed. It stopped, and its bony fingers tapped against each other. Adley's instincts kicked in and she jumped off the side of the bed, but the plan to run toward the door failed. Her legs were knotted in blankets and sheets, and she hit the hardwood floor with a thump. Only the merest primal grunts came forth from her clogged vocal chords as she flailed her legs against the tangled covers.

Her heart pounded like an impatient fist on an unanswered door and the life-giving organ nearly ruptured when the mutated collection of bones jumped off the bed and onto her foot, clawing at her ankle again. She kicked hard and sent the thing sailing back under the bed. The bony hand skidded out of control on the slick floor. Adley finally jerked herself free of the blankets. She clumsily barreled for the door with a single sheet wrapped around her ankle.

She recovered the use of her voice, but her scream was overpowered by an inhuman howl that filled the room. She didn't dare look back. Terrified, she was inches from the door when a menacing growl sounded behind her. Adley shrieked an indecipherable call for help as she wrestled with the stinging handle. The door gave way. She scrambled to her feet, but fear put her off balance. Adley tripped on the last fold of linen and pitched forward, her weight sending her into a touchdown across the threshold, half in, half out of the room.

The cadaverous hand clamped down on her foot and

she writhed helplessly, tears streaming down her face, a prisoner in a powerful grasp.

"Nooo!" she screamed.

With a surprising show of strength, it slowly pulled her back into the room, dragging her toward the bottom of the bed. Adley clawed at the carpet fibers in the hall and mustered every single ounce of energy in her body. She directed her energy into a single adrenaline-powered kick that collided with the hellish entity. It careened across the polished surface of the floor to the darkened depths beneath the bed.

Adley's survival instinct gave her an adrenaline surge, and she clambered to her feet, reconnecting with the door, not caring if the icy handle singed her hand. The skeletal appendage charged at top speed as she flung herself into the hallway, seized the handle, and wrenched the door shut.

The wooden barrier shuddered as the bloodless hand slammed against it and clattered into another noisy collection of rolling fragments. Adley's knees buckled, and her body collapsed onto the floor. She shivered in a bundle on the carpet.

☣ ☣ ☣

Her parents clamored down the hall. "Adley!" her father shouted.

"What's going on?" Caroline called behind him.

They knelt beside their daughter and her onset of tears amplified into a salty overflow down her cheeks.

"It's in my room!" Adley pointed to the door. "It tried to pull me under the bed!"

"What did?" Roger asked.

"That thing!" she cried back.

Roger and Caroline exchanged distressed looks.

Her father cradled her in his arms and tried to soothe her. "It's okay, honey."

"No! It's not okay!" She struggled wildly as her mother smoothed the damp hair away from her forehead and felt Adley's burning skin beneath her fingers. "I saw it! It's under my bed!"

"You have a fever, sweetheart. You must have been hallucinating," her mother calmly stated.

"I wasn't hallucinating!" Adley screeched.

Her father stood up, and Caroline took her daughter into the crook of her arms. Roger wanted to see what was in the room, once and for all, that scared her so badly, and he started for the door.

"No! Don't go in there, Dad!" Adley warned.

"Sshhh!" her mother cooed and rocked her ranting daughter in her arms. "It's okay, Adley. Honestly, you're acting like an alien lives under your bed."

"It's not an alien!" she shouted hysterically. "It's a skeleton hand! It grabbed my foot and tried to pull me under the bed!"

Roger's expression remained blank during her tirade. He shared another doubtful look with his wife. Their daughter had gone off the deep end. Maybe it was time to call the family therapist again. He pushed the door farther open as Adley tried to wrestle free of her mother's hold.

She violently lurched away from Caroline and lunged for her father's foot. "No, Dad! Stop!" she pleaded.

"It's okay, sweetheart," he reassured her.

He tilted his head at his wife, and she picked up the cue. Caroline pulled Adley back into her arms, and this time she kept a firmer hold. After he peeled away from his daughter, Roger stuck his hand inside the bedroom and switched on the light. The room remained cast in onyx.

"The bulbs must have burned out."

"No, they didn't!" Adley countered. "It must have broken the lights!" she said, despite her hoarse voice. "It only likes to come out in the dark!"

Her parents didn't reply, and Caroline felt Adley's body slump into exhaustion. Her adrenaline supply must have hit empty.

Caroline laid her palm flat against Adley's forehead, grateful to have good reason for her temporary madness. "Roger, she's burning up. Why don't you change the bulbs while I settle Adley in our room?"

He nodded, closed the bedroom door to prevent the escape of any mice, helped Caroline lift Adley to her feet, and then jogged downstairs.

Caroline escorted the shaken girl to the master bedroom. "Sit down, honey. Everything is going to be all right," she said in a hypnotically soothing voice.

Several minutes later, Roger returned to the master suite. "Well, I fetched replacement bulbs and a small stepladder from the garage then put the new bulbs in."

Caroline had an arm around Adley and looked at her daughter as she tenderly smoothed her hair down. "I just love that Victorian fixture. With the lights on in the evening, it makes the room look like it's glowing in a sea of soft light. Don't you think so, honey?"

Adley didn't respond.

"The vanity chair was upended, there was a tangle of blankets on the bed, and the comforter was all balled up," Roger said.

"Did you check underneath the bed and the other furniture to see if another mouse got into the room?"

"Yes, but no mouse. Everything else was in proper order." Roger shifted his gaze to Adley and spoke as softly as Caroline. "You managed to kick a hole in the comforter."

"The claw tore the covers," she whispered, her voice raw from all of her screaming.

Roger frowned, and Caroline wondered if he felt as disappointed as she did that Adley refused to give up her fantastic story.

She quickly offered an explanation. "Adley hallucinated, dear. It's the fever." Adley incoherently mumbled a contrary opinion. "Will you get the ibuprofen from the medicine chest and a glass of water?" Caroline said. She changed to a delicate tone of voice as Roger had when she next spoke to Adley. "Why don't you sleep in here with us tonight?"

"Okay," Adley muttered.

Caroline decided to press her luck. "If you want, Dad can move your belongings to the room right next to ours tomorrow." She held her breath and waited for an earth-shattering tantrum.

"No," Adley said, and that was the end of her argument.

☣ ☣ ☣

Frustration settled in with Adley's fatigue because even as she said it, she realized that the truth really did sound like a crazy hallucination.

Too shaken to say more and too emotionally depleted to clearly express her thoughts, Adley remained immobile on the comfortable loveseat in her mother's protective embrace. After tonight, no way she was going to go back upstairs, into her old room or any other room on the second floor.

Her right hand stung when she wiped her tears, bringing her back to full awareness of the newly formed blisters spattering her palm where her skin had been burnt. The tiny bit of evidence fueled another round of proving that she had been telling the truth.

"Look." She sniffed and showed the swelling white boils to her mother. "The handle was so cold it froze my fingers."

Caroline inspected her palm. "Your temperature is so hot, sweetheart. They're just fever blisters. Your skin always turns red and blotchy when you have a fever. You're flush all over."

It was true. Adley's face felt warm and was probably as red, if not redder, than the palm of her hand. "I'm not making this up, Mom," she said, trying to make her mother see the truth. "What about my ankle where it hurt me?"

Caroline examined the red marks. "We heard you stumble in the hallway. You have a carpet burn, honey. That's all."

"Why won't you believe me?"

Caroline seemed to melt at her daughter's desperate plea, just as Roger entered the room with a glass of water and the fever reducer. "Here, honey, take this," he said.

Adley obediently swallowed two blue pills, exhausted by the ordeal and too weary to argue any further. The dizzying effects of the traumatic incident combined with the medication rapidly overcame her will to convince her parents of what really happened.

Roger lifted her up from Caroline's protective embrace and let her mother tuck the warm blankets around her. Adley snuggled into a comfortable position, feeling secure and out of danger. The master suite held no unease nor did she sense a bizarre or harmful presence. There was no tapping of a violent claw scrambling for her limbs.

Adley fell asleep, reassured by her parents' presence, knowing that she was safe.

For now, at least.

☣ ☣ ☣

Not much time passed before the morning light invaded the master bedroom and penetrated Adley's eyelids. She glimpsed herself in her mother's full length mirror and had all the makings of a shipwreck victim. Her tangled and matted hair partially hid bloodshot eyes, and her pajamas were wrinkled and dowdy.

It wasn't her imagination after all, but a deadly menace that lived in her room. Victor had been right all along. The curse was alive and well. Too bad she couldn't convince her parents that it was real. Worn and haggard, she didn't think she was up to spending one more night at Capilla Manor. Six days in a scary place far exceeded her quota.

Both her parents were wide awake and dressed. Caroline read a novel, nestled on the loveseat next to Roger, who skimmed the paper.

"Well, good morning, young lady," he greeted kindly.

Adley smiled half-heartedly at him. "Morning, Dad. Morning, Mom."

Both smiled tenderly and returned the sentiment to their peace-deprived daughter. Adley thought they were like two soldiers, guarding her from horrors they didn't believe in.

Roger hesitated. "Your mom and I want to know if you'd like me to bring your things into the room next to ours."

"Can't I sleep in the downstairs room?"

"Maybe in a few days but for now, we're not sure that's a good idea, honey," Caroline said. "We'd really prefer it if we could keep a closer eye on you."

"Just until these horrible nightmares end," Roger added.

"Yeah. Okay," she said, appreciating the offer.

Her parents looked stunned.

"Aren't you going to put on some fresh clothes, honey?" her mother asked.

"I guess so," Adley answered.

"I can go to your room with you, if you'd like," Caroline offered.

"Yeah." Adley's tone was as enthusiastic as a person who was asked to test for land mines. "Let's go now. While it's still morning."

Roger and Caroline exchanged glances as their daughter crawled out of the security of their bed.

With her mother at her side, Adley shuffled to her room like a zombie, completely undone by the previous night's events and very aware of where they were headed.

Chapter 17

Adley no longer saw the point in stubbornly insisting that her room lodged a sinister ghoul. She realized it never appeared in front of her parents. They never took notice of the dark cloud hovering at her bedroom door nor could they feel the true temperature of the hematite handle. Both of them reasoned that her high fever caused the hallucinations, easily explaining her claims of a skeletal spider. They said the fever also produced the redness on her hand, and the carpet caused the severe burns around her ankles.

Her mother escorted Adley to the door at the end of the west wing. Once there Adley's legs wilted like cooked pasta, and she ferociously held onto her mother's arm.

"That was some nightmare you had," Caroline commented.

Adley glared. Obviously, her mother thought it impossible for her to be frightened by what she claimed existed in the room, yet even Adley agreed that the story sounded bizarre and hard to believe.

Caroline stood guard at the door and watched Adley dart nervously across the floor. Adley glanced at Caroline's sorrow-fill eyes and knew her mother felt helpless, unable to alleviate her daughter's fear.

Adley zoomed to and fro, tossing clean clothes and shoes into a pile in the hallway. The clothes she prepared the night before lay in a heap next to the dresser. She might as well get all she needed out of her room while she had the liberty to do so. Her mental list included Victor's phone number scrawled on a scrap of paper inside her dresser drawer, make-up, and her backpack.

She planned on phoning Victor and meeting him out back, wanting to tell him the latest horrible details she suffered in the dark morning hours. She needed to tell someone who believed her. Maybe he'd be able to calm her frazzled nerves where her parents had failed.

Then she remembered the book, almost having forgotten the most important article on her list, a much-needed tool if she wanted to save her own life and end this maddening but formidable curse. Hopefully the mystical recordings were going to be of use to Victor's great-uncle. They had to find the right counter-curse to bring an end to all the craziness.

Now that she remembered the gypsy writings in the headboard, Adley realized the problem of removing it from the bed without arousing her mother's suspicions. If she told her parents about it, they might try to take the manuscript away, and that would mean the end of her chances at finding a way to end the curse.

The predicament of getting the book out unseen was easily solved when Caroline said, "I have to use the restroom, honey. Will you be all right for a minute by yourself?"

The truth was, Adley didn't know if she'd be all right, but she had to get the hand-written text and, to do that, she had to be alone in her room.

"I'll be okay for a minute or so," Adley told her.

Caroline smiled. "I'll be right back."

Caroline made a beeline to the bathroom next to Adley's room—and, much to Adley's relief, left the bedroom door wide open.

Adley walked slowly to the side of the headboard. Each encounter with the gruesome creature grew more terrifying than the one before, and she didn't know what to expect. She needed reassurance that any cries for help were going to be heard by one of her parents.

"I'll be done soon!" she called out.

"Fine!" her mom yelled back from behind the closed bathroom door.

Adley yanked on the buckled wood. The panel didn't give so she shoved the slat upward with the heel of her palm. The wood lifted but snapped hard back into place. She shouted to her mom as she tugged, "I'm getting my clothes, okay?"

"For Pete's sakes, Adley!" her mother called. "You don't have to tell me every detail of what you're doing! I won't be but another minute!"

In a swift and gallant motion, Adley hopped onto the bed and heard the distinct tapping beneath her. She stood still but didn't feel any jerking on the bed covers. This might be her only chance to get the gypsy manuscript. All things considered, it was definitely worth the risk. Or at least it seemed so until she heard something whisper her name.

Adley heard the toilet flush and knew her mother would wash her hands and return shortly. With that knowledge, using all her strength, she caught her finger tips under the wooden slat and lifted up. The wood splintered but it didn't matter. She didn't plan on sleeping in that bed ever again. Adley peered inside the headboard.

The leather cover was in partial view and the rest was buried in the same darkness that haunted the floor below.

Swallowing hard, she slowly lowered her hand into the dark space. Adley felt the rough edges of the unevenly bound parchment sheets and spread her fingers wide to cinch the book in hand. It was heavier than it appeared, and she grunted as she tugged upward.

She managed to lift the book half-way up but bony pinchers firmly latched onto the lower half, gripping the spine. She yelped but the sound was muffled in the tug of war, a game of life and death. Adley refused to release her claim on the gypsy's recorded history.

"Let go!" she ordered through clenched teeth and heard a hissing sound, like the spitting a cat makes as it arches its back in a defensive posture. Or when a snake is about to strike.

She pulled harder and almost had the book completely out of the headboard. Calcified fingers released their fierce hold on the manuscript. The hand launched itself from the elaborate cover and landed on Adley's arm, pinching her skin with its sallow nails. She pressed her lips together and grunted instead of crying out. Her arm throbbed painfully, and her heart pounded with a primal drumming in her ears. The pain and fear didn't deter Adley from concentrating on her task, determined as she was to end the curse with the precious information that could only be found in this book.

Positioning the bound pages just so, Adley used the wood slat like a hammer, smashing the bones between the leather cover and the board. The fingers crumbled instantly, falling into the dark space inside the headboard, and she ripped the book free. She bounced across the mattress and jumped off her bed, sprinting for the door with the sound of clacking bone right behind her.

Adley heard the bathroom door open and dove onto the personal belongings heaped in the hallway. She shoved the life-saving book into the middle of the pile. Spinning around, she looked back into her room. A pair of red, beady eyes retreated into the mysterious veil under her bed just as Caroline stepped next to the rumpled pile of clothing.

She took in Adley's ashen face and heavy breathing. Apparently, her daughter had another fright. Adley picked up her belongings in a hurry.

"Can I help you with that, honey?"

"No. I'm okay." Adley said in a barely audible voice. "I have to do it myself."

Her mother delivered a pity-filled smile at her daughter, not knowing Adley kept a historical relic out of sight. Caroline latched onto the door and snapped it shut. Adley watched her mother examine the handle then her fingers. Nothing. Caroline walked ahead of her daughter, and Adley heard hissing and snickering as they marched through the hall toward the stairs.

"I know you're upset because you weren't able to make your dad and me believe that your room is host to some kind of monster, but you need to stop that immature muttering under your breath, Adley."

Adley clutched her bundle of possessions and whispered behind her mother, "I didn't say a thing."

☣ ☣ ☣

The well-preserved manuscript now in Adley's possession was the key to finding a way to rid herself of the horrifying curse. The cover was written in Spanish and Adley definitely needed Victor's help in translating the book. Besides, she admitted to herself, she didn't want to look at it alone.

Adley called Victor from the kitchen. He picked up the phone just as she heard footsteps heading toward the room.

"Hello?" he said.

"My parents," she whispered. "I'll call you after break-fast!"

She hung up on Victor as her parents entered the kitch-en, but she was frustrated, because she'd wanted to tell him about the manuscript, and disappointed because she didn't get to speak with him.

Her parents headed directly for the coffee pot and the cups Adley had set out for them.

"Hey! You made coffee." Roger said, inhaling the in-viting aroma.

"Thank you, sweetheart," Caroline said. "Who was that you were on the phone with?"

Adley stiffened. "Some kid I met in town."

"What's her name?" Caroline asked, excited that her daughter made a friend. "Maybe Dad knows her family."

Adley caught her dad nudging her mom lightly with his hip as he set his coffee on the counter. Maybe her parents had agreed not to question Adley about her hiking buddy. Even so, the anger that she had practiced holding in check successfully since meeting Victor seeped out.

"Do I have to report every little thing I do, who I meet, or what I'm thinking? You might as well lock me in a cell right now!"

Caroline pursed her lips.

"There's no need to be rude," her father lectured. "Your mother and I are simply concerned about your safety. It's our job as parents to know what kind of people you're hanging out with."

"Why can't you give me a break? Have I ever hung out with gangs or drug dealers? Have I ever been stupid enough to get into a stranger's car or help a grown man look for his little lost puppy?" Adley looked from her father to her mother with her fists planted firmly on her hips. "I wish you'd both stop treating me like some stupid kid!"

Her mother crossed her arms and sulked. Roger draped his arm around Caroline's shoulders and whispered something gentle and soothing in her ear.

Adley felt bad, not about telling her parents how she felt, but how she said it. Caroline kept quiet after that, and Adley felt her mother's silence as bothersome as her own outburst. If they asked her again about her new found friend, Adley would have to choose between telling her parents the truth or a lie.

If she told the truth, that she was hanging out with Victor whom they had expressly forbidden her to socialize with, she'd never know how to rid herself of the curse, and she'd miss him terribly. On the other hand, she could lie and say Victor was someone else. A nagging conscience insisted that she tell the truth, but Adley ignored it. She had another option. Change the subject.

She considered the tension in the room and did her best to speak in a kinder voice. It helped to imagine Victor standing next to her. Although the disturbing incidents were limited to the inside of her room, and usually at night, Adley prepared a few ideas while staring out the bay windows, any reason to keep from spending time inside the mansion.

"Can we eat breakfast on the back patio?" she asked. "It's so nice out. And it just seems more relaxing to breathe clean air while we're eating outside." Especially since something intimidating on the inside of the house wanted to kill her.

"Sure. It's a beautiful day," her father agreed.

Caroline nodded.

"I'll set the patio table," Adley volunteered. She pulled the rolling tray out from under a cabinet. She gathered dishes and linen. "Uhm, so can I like, go for another walk on the trail after breakfast?"

Her parents looked at one another and shrugged.

"Sure," her father said.

"You said you'd stay within calling distance," Caroline reminded her.

"I will." Adley pushed the cart toward the silverware drawer and bit back any hostile remarks.

"Your mom is planning to do some shopping in Deming," Roger said and glanced at his wife. "Would you like me to join you on your hike this morning?"

"Uh, no, thanks, Dad. I'd like to go alone."

"You be careful," he cautioned. Adley inwardly groaned at the forthcoming lecture but remained silent. "When I was a youngster, most all the kids roamed these hills," he continued. "The sheriff said it's still very safe here, but I don't want you to take any chances. If you see any wild animals or strangers, I want you to turn around and come right back here where it's safe. Is that understood?"

He waited for her reply. He and Caroline looked like they were both holding their breath.

"Yes, Dad."

Her parents both exhaled at the same time.

☣ ☣ ☣

Roger and Caroline watched Adley add utensils to the rolling tray and then push the cart out of the kitchen to the patio. Caroline toasted bagels, and Roger brought fresh fruit and cheese out of the refrigerator.

"That's strange how Adley didn't protest your hiking guidelines," Caroline said.

"So is her irrational insistence on a monster living in her room, but you were right, Caroline," Roger said. "All she needed was a good scare to come out of that nasty shell."

"It's not like she's all the way out of it, but it is an improvement," Caroline added with a smile, "My guess is she met a boy and didn't want to tell us."

Roger stopped slicing an orange. "A boy? The only chance she had to meet someone is when she was away from us during our visit with Anne Marie at the diner. You don't think she was with Victor Trumillo on the back trail, do you?"

"Maybe. But he did tell her about a group of girls who go riding up here on occasion. Regardless, Roger, I've been blaming him all this time for feeding Adley's fear, but we really don't know the Trumillo boy very well. We shouldn't make judgments about people without knowing them. Isn't that what we always taught Adley?"

He sighed. "Yes, but you saw the letters."

"He didn't write them," she reminded. "His mother and uncle did."

"The apple doesn't fall far from the tree," he quoted.

"We caught her hanging up the phone in the kitchen just a while ago. She doesn't want to lie to us. Instead of lying and telling us she met a girl rather than a boy, or instead of making up someone else's name, she avoided the subject. I'm sure Adley will eventually tell us about her new friends when she's ready. That's probably the reason for her nightmares. She must be feeling really guilty about not telling us the truth."

"But what makes you think she met a boy?" Roger asked.

His wife smiled at him. "A girl doesn't get a look on her face like that from meeting another girl."

"What look on her face?"

Caroline giggled. "You almost told Adley why I was shopping in Deming today, didn't you?"

Roger smiled. "Yeah. I'd hate to spoil the surprise. I'm sure Adley has forgotten all about her birthday."

"Cake and presents will get her mind off mice. Maybe if she made some new friends she can bring them over. I hope she likes the stuff I'm going to get for her room." Caroline handed her husband a platter of sliced, buttered bagels. "Why don't you take these out to the patio, and I'll grab some preserves?"

He took the plate and headed out of the kitchen.

"And Roger," Caroline added, "remember, we agreed to not ask her again about her companion."

He rolled his eyes at how often Caroline forgot her own reminders. "I've got to admit that now I'm more curious than ever, but I will comply."

Roger bowed to his wife and Caroline laughed. He took the platter out to the patio.

Chapter 18

Butterflies and bees flitted from stalk to stalk on sparse wildflowers in the backyard. The plants that thrived did so because they were determined to live even through crisp desert nights and hot dry days. At least the spattering of wildflowers broke the surface and blossomed into an exquisite array of yellow, pink, white, and purple. Some grew around the deteriorating gazebo, yet any wonder at the beautiful surroundings escaped Adley, who was too distracted by the unearthly being that inhabited her bedroom.

She was glad for having suggested breakfast outside in the fresh morning air, although the yard had been host to an invasion of weeds and thick stalks that drilled up through the hard-packed earth. Adley picked several of the wildflowers and arranged the skimpy bouquet in a small crystal vase. Maybe her parents could enjoy them. The family took their seats at the table, next to the patch of ground Adley and her father had cleared the day before. She realized that they had done enough gardening to make it easier to reach the path at the back of the yard leading to the trail.

"Did you sleep well?" Roger asked his daughter as he added cream to his coffee.

"Probably as well as you did." Adley knew her facial

features were a testimony that she hadn't gotten a good sleep at all. Her father had the same dark circles below his eyes, but he wasn't frowning like she was. "By the way, thanks for letting me sleep in your room with Mom."

"Not a problem. It was like being at a one-person slumber party on the couch, but I hadn't been lying down for more than a few minutes before I heard something scratching," he said.

"Must be the mice," Caroline added.

"Huh," was all Adley had to say.

Roger and Caroline busied themselves in their room after the meal, and Adley offered to do dishes so she could have a good reason to be in the kitchen—downstairs and near the phone. She couldn't stop thinking of Victor and cleaned up after breakfast in record time so she could call him all the sooner.

The dishwasher whirred as she shoved the eggs and milk back into the refrigerator. She tossed the soiled linens into the clothes hamper in the laundry room off the maid's quarters. Adley hurried through her tasks, knowing she was going to talk to Victor and eventually see him.

"Are you all right? I've been freaking out since you hung up on me," he told her as soon as he answered the phone.

"I'm sorry. My parents came into the room, and I hung up because they always ask me questions, which they did anyway."

"Are you all right?"

"Not at all. I slept in my parents' room last night," Adley said and barely kept her voice from cracking. "Victor, it was awful."

"I wouldn't want to sleep in my parents' room either," he admitted.

"Not that. They won't believe me!" Adley whimpered,

not ashamed of letting the boy hear her anxiety. "My parents still think we have mice."

"I'm sure they'd rather have mice than what's really in your room. I know you said to meet at eleven but can you get away a little earlier?"

"Of course! I can leave the right house now if you want."

"I'll be there in twenty minutes." Victor said.

"See you then."

Adley prepared a lunch of sandwiches, chips, cookies, and bottled water and placed it all in her backpack, constantly looking toward the kitchen door in fear that her parents would enter the kitchen.

She slung the pack on her shoulder, just as they entered, and saw their festive smiles. They refilled their cups with fresh coffee and followed Adley into the family room.

☣ ☣ ☣

Caroline clicked on the stereo remote, and easy rock music played quietly in the background. "You must be really anxious to see this friend."

Roger lightly tapped her foot under the coffee table. Caroline immediately berated herself for mentioning the mysterious friend again. Her curiosity was on autopilot.

"I told you. I don't like being here," Adley snarled at her mother. "This place gives me the creeps, something bizarre is hanging around under my bed, and you don't even believe me!"

"Honey, your stories are pretty dramatic," her mother said.

"I knew it! I knew you didn't believe me!" Adley hollered and ran outside, upset with herself for having lost her patience. Again.

"Geez, Caroline," Roger admonished.

"I know, I know," Caroline moaned. "I keep forgetting not to ask about her mysterious friend."

"Maybe she's bi-polar?" Roger asked, half serious.

"I don't think so. It's just this last year she's had a problem. And everything was going so well before I opened my big mouth."

Roger patted her arm. "Redecorating her room for her birthday is going to make a big difference. It'll liven her spirits."

"I can't blame her for not wanting to be in that room," Caroline said. "What, with all those mice. But as soon as we have an exterminator go through it I think Adley will feel differently.

"I finally got hold of the only firm that will come out here, but they can't make it until next week."

"I don't understand why Adley refuses one of the other two rooms," Caroline said. "What if redecorating her room doesn't work?"

Roger sighed. "We may have to arrange a few more family therapy sessions."

His wife nodded. "And I prefer decorating over therapy any day. I'm getting new curtains, pillows, and maybe an unbreakable lamp."

"How about some nightlights?" Roger suggested. "So Adley will stop tripping in the middle of the night and stop waking us up. With all her loud nightmares and the mice, I haven't been getting any decent sleep."

"Nightlights are a great idea," Caroline said. "And I'm getting something else for her birthday."

"What's that?" Roger asked.

Caroline proudly shared her idea. "I'm getting her a new crystal knob for the door. You can take off that old sil-ver one, can't you?"

"Sure. But let's wait until the last minute to surprise her," Roger said.

His wife nodded. "Good idea. I can't wait to see her face when she finds out we replaced it."

☣ ☣ ☣

Adley quickly took the dirt path that led to the felled tree under the big pine. The small area was encircled by heavy woods. Dry grasses and leaves rustled in a breeze, sounding more like rushing water than foliage.

She sat on the rough bark of the felled tree, waiting for Victor. It wasn't a long wait. In minutes she heard Victor's horse canter around the bend. When he came into view at the end of the curved path, the sight of him erased any anxiety she felt up to that moment. She had no control over the stupid grin plastered on her face. Her facial muscles refused to budge when she tried not to smile so brightly.

He easily swung down from the side of the well-trained animal and draped the reins over a sapling. Without hesitation, Adley ran to Victor and gave him a big hug. She closed her eyes and sighed into his neck, grateful to know someone believed her room was host to a monster and glad to feel his warm body in her embrace.

Victor smiled. "Hi."

Adley pulled back and reached out to pat the horse's silky neck. "Who's this?"

"This is Greystoke," Victor replied. "I'm glad you could make it."

"Are you kidding? Even if I were surrounded by cannibals, I think I'd feel safer out here."

Victor put his arm around Adley's shoulders, and his eyes narrowed on her. "I'll protect you."

Adley's breath caught in her throat and she gulped it

down. "I have something to show you." She took his hand and led him to the old tree trunk. "I didn't have time to tell you on the phone this morning. Victor, I found the gypsy manuscript!" She pulled the leather bound package from her backpack.

"This is it? Where was it? My mom looked forever!" He took the leather-bound book into his hands and ran his fingers over the cover. They sat down, side by side, and gazed at the artifact. Adley's life depended on the information written within. Neither of them had any idea what to expect within its pages.

"It was stuffed in the headboard in my room," Adley told him.

"So much for reading in bed." Victor joked at the most unlikely of times, but his sense of humor took the edge off.

"Maybe we can find a simple cure, like a potion or do some type of ceremony to end the curse," Adley said.

Victor frowned. "You know it isn't going to be that simple."

Adley remained optimistic. "So, is this it?" she asked, hope brimming on her words.

"I'm pretty sure. It looks really old. Have you read it?"

"No. The title's written in Spanish, and I'm afraid to look at it alone," she admitted. "Let's look at it now."

"Okay, but first I have to ask you something."

"What?"

"When's your birthday?"

"My life is at the mercy of a supernatural creature and you want to know my birthday?"

"When is it, Adley?" he asked a bit more firmly.

"Actually, with everything that's happened, I forgot that it's coming up." He grimaced and, for a moment, Adley thought he was in great pain. "Victor? What's wrong now?"

"When exactly is your birthday, Adley?" It seemed as

if he fought to maintain his composure. "Don't worry. Please, tell me."

She jumped off the log and stood directly in front of him. "You don't want me to worry? If something paranormal tried to attack you in your own home would you be worried? You told me things don't get really bad until I saw a hand, remember?"

"Like you said, you've only been here less than a week so there's nothing to—"

"Don't say it!" she interrupted him, failing to keep her borderline panic hidden. "I saw a shadow of a hunched figure on my wall the first night I was in my room! And then I saw something like a white spider crawling under my bed. Then it said my name! And last night a rope made out of bones with a hand on the end of it tried to drag me under the bed. So don't tell me not to worry!" she shouted hysterically. "And today it grabbed my hand when I pulled the book out of the headboard!"

She showed him the scrapes on the back of her hand where the skeletal fingers scratched her skin. Adley relayed the events of the entire early-morning ordeal in a fit of tears.

Victor acted on instinct. He set the book aside, stood up, pulled Adley up into his arms, and held her in a protective embrace. He remained quiet while she cried and let out the fear and frustration plaguing her since her first day at Capilla Manor.

"It'll be all right," he soothed, not knowing what else to say. He sensed her upset and anxiety and rubbed his hands up and down her shoulders, then across her back. "I'll be with you, babe, every step of the way."

It was all she needed to hear. His gentle voice and endearment washed away some of the stress, and she relaxed in his arms.

Once she composed herself, she wiped away the last of her tears.

"Now, what's this about my birthday?"

"I wanted to know when it was."

"With all that's happened, I nearly forgot. Can you imagine?" She looked upward and shook her head.

Victor continued to soothe her. "You're okay now. Stay as calm as you can." Adley sniffed. He continued. "Do you remember that I told you the oldest of the Rodrigues descendants is taken by the skeleton?"

"Yes, and we have already determined that I hold that lucky position in my family, thank you very much!" she sniveled.

"Listen to me. I talked to my Great-Uncle Pablo this morning. He told me it comes for its victims at the hour of their birth, and no earlier, so we're okay for now." Adley stepped back, her eyes filled with a haunting emptiness. "Didn't you hear me, Adley?" he asked. "We have time until your next birthday," Victor assured her again. He waited for Adley to speak but dead silence hung in the air around them. "Adley?"

It took great effort but she croaked out, "Yes," but her one-word response dripped with panic.

"What's wrong?" he asked.

Her unfocused gaze and slightly opened mouth told Victor her troubling silence hid some horrible information. His curiosity grew like a balloon filled with too much water, ready to burst.

"Darn it, Adley! Tell me what's wrong!" he demanded.

She finally spoke, her voice hoarse and reluctant. "I'll be sixteen in two days."

Chapter 19

Victor had thought there was more time. Great-Uncle Pablo wanted him to find out the exact time of Adley's birth. Pablo said it was critical that they knew.

Pablo had finally gotten through on his cell phone early that morning and told his niece, Maria Trumillo, about his radiator. One of the steers had reacted to a vitamin shot, crashed into his truck, and poked a hole in the radiator with its horn. The truck had been in the shop.

"When is your great-uncle coming home?" Adley asked.

"He said he'd leave the moment his truck was fixed this afternoon," Victor said. "If it can't be repaired today, he won't be able to come home until tomorrow morning. I tried calling him. They don't have a phone at the ranch where he's staying and he accidentally left his cell phone charger at home. I'll let you know when he gets into town."

"Didn't your mom tell him this was an emergency? We need him, Victor!"

"I didn't tell my mom all that's been happening at Capilla Manor and so she didn't have anything to tell my great-uncle."

"It doesn't matter, anyway. She'd think I was nuts," Adley said.

"That's not it, Adley. I told you that my family knows about the curse. I didn't tell her all the details because I didn't know how she would react, especially after what happened to—" He paused a moment. "—to your grandma."

Tears welled up in Adley's eyes. "Last night was awful, Victor! I don't think I can go through anything like that again."

Victor didn't tell her it was going to get much worse on her birthday.

Adley swiped at the tears on her face, and Victor guided her back to sitting on the old tree trunk. "You know what I don't get?" she whimpered. "My grandma wasn't the oldest! Why did it kill her?"

"It didn't have the power to kill her because it wasn't strong enough. Remember, Grandma Aggie didn't die from the fall but of heart failure almost a year later," he explained. "Her accident is what brought you here. It had to find a way to lure you to the mansion, and it succeeded because you're staying there now."

Adley shifted as if a heavy weight grew in her chest. "How awful that my grandmother had to suffer because of some devastating curse that she wasn't even responsible for creating. Grandma Aggie made a sacrifice for her family, and I just now realized how much my grandmother loved us." She gazed up at Victor. "The fact that my dad wasn't close to her made it somehow sadder."

"That's why Aggie discouraged you from coming out to visit. She had to have known about the curse, believed it was real, and had been trying to protect you from any fatal consequences."

Silent tears streamed down her face. "I'm so sorry she

was injured and unknowingly served as live bait to get us to Capilla Manor. That thing in my room knew what to do to get my parents to her house. Victor, you were right. It was determined to find a way to get to me."

He brought Adley close to him again. "I won't let that thing touch you, I swear." She nodded into his shoulder. "I'm sure my great-uncle will be home soon to help us." He thought a moment. "Two days until your birthday?" he asked again, on the off chance they had more time. Adley head's bobbed slightly up and down. "Great," he muttered. "Adley, listen, this is important. What time were you born?"

"Eight o'clock in the evening. Exactly," she said.

"Are you sure?" he asked.

"Positive. My mom likes to joke that she gave up her favorite TV program to have me." She spoke without the usual joy when she repeated the story. "This year my birthday isn't cause for celebration."

"Then we have up until eight o'clock the day after tomorrow to prepare," he informed her. "Lucky thing the hematite handle is on your door."

"Lucky? You call this nightmare lucky?"

Victor squeezed her shoulder. "As long as the creature is contained within hematite, it won't be able to kill you until the precise hour of your birth. The handle will keep the demon inside your room until then. Once we get you exactly twenty-four hours past your birth hour, that thing can't touch you," he explained.

"I don't know if I can stand one more night in that house, let alone two." The day was warm yet she shivered as if in mild shock. "Victor! What are we going to do?" She paused and looked at him, her eyes pooling with tears. "What am *I* going to do?"

"I'll tell my mother all that's happened in case she

hears from Great-Uncle Pablo tonight," Victor said. "If she does, I know he'll find a way to come home."

"Let's look through the gypsy writings and see what we can find. If the manuscript doesn't yield any information, your uncle is my only hope of survival. And so far, we don't know for certain how much danger I'm in."

"Did you pack us a lunch?" he asked light-heartedly, changing the subject.

"You're thinking of food right now? I just ate and I'm surprised I was able to."

"You have to keep your strength up, Adley."

"You don't have to tell me why," she said.

"This is such an insane nightmare. Maybe you can stay at my house tonight."

Adley dropped her mouth open. "Like run away from home?"

"Just for the next two nights or so."

"That might be a good idea but my parents barely let me go out here on the trail alone. They'd go nuts and call the police if they didn't know where I was. And what would I say? That the Trumillos weren't trying to kidnap me but protect me from an ancient curse?"

Victor laughed. "I guess that was a pretty stupid idea."

Adley snuggled closer to Victor, and he was glad she felt safe in his arms. "Thanks for getting in touch with your great-uncle."

"Did I tell you that he is a shaman?"

"A what?" she asked.

"A wise man." Victor sat on the felled trunk and pulled Adley gently down beside him. "His eyes are very black, and people think they're midnight blue because he's so powerful. He says God didn't know if he should have had black eyes like his mother or light blue ones like his great-grandfather."

"How did his great-grandfather get blue eyes?"

"European descendant."

"I'm glad he's willing to help me. You know, more than once in the last few days I've been extremely grateful for your great-uncle, almost as much as I am for meeting you."

Victor watched her cheeks redden. "My great-uncle says gratitude is a humbling quality, and it gives us a tiny bit of peace." Victor didn't want to take his arm off Adley's shoulders but he needed both hands to lift the heavy and elaborately bound manuscript. He set it on his lap. "Since you're not hungry…" He ran his finger over the gold embossed letters. "Las Palabras," he read with a perfect Spanish accent.

"What does it mean?"

"It means 'The Words.' Very important words that we need to know," Victor said. He opened the handmade work filled with beautiful calligraphy and grand illuminations.

"Wow!" Adley exclaimed, obviously impressed by the artistic hand-drawn letters and pictures. "Go to the table of contents and see if they have a chapter on curses."

Victor gave her a half-smile. "They don't have a table of contents in here." He gently paged through the delicate parchment sheets. "It looks like there are separate sections written by different generations adding their own knowledge and discoveries about the curse."

"Did your great-uncle tell you that was how it was written?"

"No," he answered. "I read it here on the first page."

Adley and Victor saw the obvious changes in the chapters as they continued to peruse the sheaves of old paper. The earlier parts were rich in detail and more artistic, like the hand-lettered Latin bibles displayed under glass at the museum. The middle sections were written in a flowing script, as if they were scribed with a quill pen. The latter drawings toward the back were fewer, less detailed, yet the obvious messages in the rough sketches were more intense.

The drawing that caught and held their attention was of a small, bony hand scurrying toward a crude rendering of a person's foot. It was exactly the image she had described to Victor and he felt a newfound respect for her.

"This thing chased you?"

"Yes. I barely believe it myself."

He gave her a fierce hug. "You're a very brave girl."

They resumed browsing, easily understanding why the Roman numeral XVI, sixteen, appeared so frequently in addition to several drawings of the very bed she had slept in. Quite a few drawings of humans tilting their heads at a perceived sound, their eyes opened wide, wary and scared, also dominated the pages.

"At least we know we found the right book," Victor said,

"Bet it never made the best seller's list." Adley said, copying his macabre sense of humor.

The morbid depictions alarmed Victor more than ever. Until then, he hadn't appreciated her horrific encounters with the curse and the great danger she had been experiencing. She clasped Victor's arm as they skimmed through the book and gaped at pictures every so often depicting various forms of a skeleton. Most of them were canine-like with a large, abnormally proportioned head.

"Did you find any counter-curses?"

"This book is written in formal Spanish. Castilian," he explained. "Not the same dialect as we speak here. Great-Uncle Pablo will definitely have to interpret it." With the tip of his finger, Victor touched Adley's cheek and turner her to face him. "You need to be extra careful tonight," he cautioned. "I don't want you going into that room no matter what. Sleep in dirty clothes if you have to, just don't go into your room."

"That's not an issue, believe me," she replied.

Victor was pleased that she wasn't put off by his fierce protectiveness.

"I put all the clothes and things I need for the next few days in a cupboard under an end table in the family room."

"Can't you have the maid's quarters for your room?" She shook her head. "Why not? It's got a kitchen and its own bathroom."

"Don't you remember I heard it talking to me in there?"

"But it was just noise. Not like in your room where it physically touched you."

"I know it makes sense to want a room that feels like my own apartment, but I think I'd feel trapped in any room."

"I understand." Victor set his hand on Adley's arm and she met his troubled gaze. "Don't go into your room for anything, Adley. I mean it."

By now he knew that she wouldn't take his demanding voice as a condescending insult. He cared for her and she seemed to understand that.

"Relax, Victor. You don't have to keep telling me. I don't plan on setting one foot, one toe, inside that room."

He softened his hold on her arm. "C'mon. Let's take a walk and try not talking any more about it for the rest of the day."

"I'll try," Adley said, "but I'm not sure if I can stop myself from bringing it up. That's the only thing that has been on my mind since my first night here."

Fear clearly etched itself on her face. Victor helped her place the manuscript into her backpack and then hung it on Greystoke's saddle, glad he suggested that they not pursue the subject. They could discuss all the details of the haunting once they met with Great-Uncle Pablo. Victor untied the horse, and Greystoke traipsed behind him. He draped his arm over Adley's shoulders, guiding her along the wooded path, the same trail that led toward the Trumillo ranch.

"We'll beat this. I promise," he confidently assured her. She smiled up at him and he felt his heart lurch at the vulnerability reflected in her beautiful brown eyes.

☣ ☣ ☣

Adley knew Victor was doing his best to make the walk interesting and enjoyable. He managed to take her mind off the gypsy's curse, which had engulfed her like a somber cloud, pointing out various plants and small critters as they strolled along the shaded path, enjoying the leisurely pace.

"I've been wanting to spend a few quiet moments alone with you since we first met. Only, not under these circumstances," he said.

"That's nice to hear," Adley said. "Where do you go to school?"

"Animas High. It's almost thirty miles east of the ranch. That means I have to take a bus to school because it's too far for my mom or uncle to drive every day. I have my driver's license, but we only have my great-uncle's truck so I can't take it to school."

"But who needs a car when you can ride a horse?" Adley said.

Victor smiled. "One day you'll have to ride with me. Once you're in a saddle, it's hard not to get hooked."

"That's cool. What else is there to do out here?"

"That depends on what you like to do. The nearest mall

is at least sixty miles away," he teased.

Adley pretended to scowl at him, but Victor caught sight of her pretty smile. She defended herself. "I haven't missed malls, theaters, or much else. I haven't thought about missing anything since that thing—" Without intending to, Adley broached the painful subject and allowed her dilemma to intrude into their easy conversation after agreeing not to discuss it. She left her sentence unfinished, and Victor felt her shoulders droop under his arm.

"You're going into the tenth grade, right?" he asked, in another attempt to redirect the conversation.

"Yeah," Adley replied. "I'm going to be a sophomore."

"I'll be a junior. Tell me about your school and your friends," he said, unwittingly changing the subject to another sore area in Adley's life, yet instead of clamming up or berating him for opening up the delicate topic, she answered candidly. "I don't really have any friends at school. I guess I'm not very nice. It's like I get mad for no reason and I don't know why."

By admitting the truth to Victor, she felt like a wound had been ripped opened, but it immediately started to heal in the same instant. She needed someone to talk to, to be open with, even if it hurt to speak the truth about her own short comings.

Also, since she might be dead soon, she had nothing to lose by being honest, especially with Victor.

Chapter 20

What makes you so angry?"

Adley didn't get bent out of shape by Victor's direct question. "I'm not sure," she replied. "I guess it's my whole life that makes me mad. I know I've been pretty unhappy with my parents, but even so, they don't deserve what I've put them through, especially this past year."

"Why are you mad at them?"

"I'm not sure," she repeated. It felt like her heart weighed a thousand pounds. "It seems uncontrollable. Even though things weren't perfect at home, it wasn't like my parents beat me or made me live in a closet."

"What are they like?" he asked.

"My dad travels a lot for his work, and it's like he doesn't know me because he hasn't been home when I needed him. My mom does nice stuff for me but doesn't do much *with* me. I feel like she's nice because I'm her daughter, like she's supposed to treat me that way and not because she really wants to." He listened attentively and his silence encouraged her to continue sharing. "But really, Victor, I didn't think all that really bothered me so much. I mean, they give me everything I want."

"Everything but their time?" She nodded, a slow and deliberate movement. "Have you talked to them?" he asked.

"Yeah. Maybe."

Victor frowned. "Maybe?"

"Well, I guess not. I've been too mad to even talk to them. They took me to a counselor once but I told him what I figured he wanted to hear. I didn't want to talk to a stranger. I wanted to talk to my parents but I'm not sure how to do that so—"

"—so that they'll listen and take you seriously?" Victor finished her thought.

She smiled, not offended by his interruption. "It's so cool that you know how I feel."

"Don't try to talk with them when you're angry. You need to wait until after you've calmed down to talk about it."

"You sound like my counselor only he didn't give me any good ideas to make things better."

Victor smiled at her. "Remember, I've been brought up in a house with a shaman. My great-uncle is all about love and peace, like an old hippie." She giggled. "I'm lucky to have him teach me his ways," he said. "And I'm lucky to have found you."

Victor's arm slipped from her shoulder, and he took both of her hands into his. They stood face to face. Static electricity poured over her body, and a tangible humming swarmed about them.

"Do you feel that?" he asked.

"I feel something," she said.

"It's like something electric—"

"Yeah! I hear buzzing, like bees—"

"Wow! That's crazy. I hear it, and feel it, too," Victor said.

"What do you think it means?"

Victor slid one arm around her and pulled her close. His other hand stroked her cheek and he lifted her chin. Adley's eyes saw into his, a midnight sky—the cosmos—and found the other side of the universe. He pressed his lips against hers, and Adley felt her soul come to life. It stirred and rose outside of herself, entwined with Victor's. His lips left hers, and she opened her eyes, preferring the remarkable floating sensation instead of being in her own physical body.

"Wow!" Victor said, and Adley couldn't speak.

They embraced, and Adley knew that everything Victor had told her up until that moment about wanting to protect her, wanting to be with her, had all been true.

"Let's try that again," he said.

Adley didn't think it was possible to duplicate the sensational feelings, but it happened and, to her surprise, his next kiss seemed better than the first and lasted a bit longer. Victor pulled back and inhaled deeply. He leaned his forehead against hers.

"Amazing," he whispered, and Adley sighed. He took her by the hand again. "Come on," he said. They arrived at a dirt passage leading to an immense backyard. Victor pointed. "That's where I live."

From this location atop a small rise, she saw his home standing close to the border of the woods and farther on stood the outbuildings. The structures from the road gave the impression of disrepair but now she noted they were merely in need of paint.

A lovely herb garden grew below what looked like the kitchen window. The multi-level patio exploded with color. Decorative pots filled with well-tended flowers edged the slate tiles covering the patio. Latticework sheltered the chairs and tables from the worst of the sun.

The green lawn starkly contrasted with Grandma Aggie's dried grasses and weeds.

"I saw your ranch when we passed by on the way to town. It's a big piece of land."

"There's a small stream this way." Victor gestured at a hill behind the Trumillo ranch. "I'll show you."

He held her hand during the short hike to the hidden stream and tied his horse to a thick branch, giving enough slack to the rope for Greystoke to drink from the stream and graze on the surrounding grasses. They sat on a flat rock heated by the sun overlooking the water. Victor took off his shoes and Adley followed suit. Right before they slipped their feet into the cool water, he was shocked by the sight of the abrasions on her ankles. He hoped she didn't see his reaction.

"What happened?" he asked with a nonchalant lift of his chin in the direction of her foot.

"I told you that creepy hand attacked me. It grabbed my ankle and cut me. And look," she flipped her palm face up. "The handle on the door is polar cold. It blistered my skin." He was clearly bothered by the sight of her abrasions but before he had a chance to comment, Adley reminded him, "We agreed not to discuss this again, remember?"

He smiled, and a welcome breeze swirled about them, easing the effects of the warm temperature. The cool water soothed her ankles, and she slipped her blistered hand into the water, too, releasing a long sigh of relief. Adley kept up the subject of her difficult relationship with her parents.

"I wish I didn't lose my temper so quickly. It's so easy to get mad, especially when my dad calls me this stupid nick-name, Deedee. It makes me feel like a baby."

"You make it sound like he calls you 'sweety cakes' or 'baby-boopie,'" he said. Adley elbowed him. "I don't think it's a bad name," he told her. She glared at him and he chuckled. "No, really. It's cute. Like you, Deedee."

Involuntarily, her lashes fluttered. Deedee sounded pleasant coming from Victor. It must have made a difference that he was cute, too, and tall and kind. The fact that he liked her also had an effect. Adley would probably let him call her 'sweety cakes' or 'baby-boopie,' too.

She liked him but felt too uncomfortable admitting how she felt. It was too soon to share such personal feelings. Besides, liking a boy this much was new to her, and she wasn't able to define what was reeling inside her heart. It was easier to change the subject. In doing so, however, she had no idea that she was bringing the conversation full circle, back to the subject of the curse.

"Do you argue with your dad like I do with mine?"

"Not since he died."

"He's dead? What happened?" Adley asked and immediately discerned the sag in Victor's shoulders. "I'm sorry. I shouldn't have asked."

"No. It's okay. It's just that I really try—"

"—not to think about it?" It was Adley's turn to finish his sentence.

"Yeah. It happened, you know, and now it's done."

"Well, whatever happened, I'm sorry it did."

"Thanks." The weight of buried memories surfaced and pulled down the corners of his mouth as Victor recalled the details of the tragedy. "My dad died about four years ago. He was riding the trail when Greystoke was most likely spooked and reared. When my dad fell, he hit his head on a small boulder which left a big gash on the back of his skull. He was probably knocked unconscious. I miss him, but I try to focus on the good memories of him."

"I'm so sorry." Emotional intensity charged the air and it told her there was more bad news to the story.

Victor drew in a heavy breath and continued. "This is something you should know, Adley. He left for Capilla Manor shortly before he died." She was stunned as Victor told her more. "Your grandmother called him that morning. She said she had a terrible situation but couldn't tell him about it on the phone. She said she didn't think he'd believe her if she didn't tell him in person."

Adley's protest came out a whisper. "No!"

"She also said that she had something very important to show him."

"What was it?"

"We never found out. We think it might have been the gypsy's manuscript. Great-Uncle Pablo says Greystoke came back by himself, and he rode the horse back up to Aggie's. My great-uncle is the one who found my dad." She gaped at Victor. "He died from exsanguination."

"What's that?" she asked.

His voice dropped in pitch. "My father bled to death," he said.

She held his hand. "Oh, Victor!"

"The thing is, he had a dog bite on his leg, but that's not the only weird thing the coroner wrote in the autopsy." Victor inhaled, filling his lungs with the clean desert air. It was obviously harrowing for him to endure the retelling of his father's tragedy.

Adley laid her hand on his arm. "What did they find, Victor?" Whenever she asked him a question related to Grandma Aggie's it was always bad news.

"His system was full of snake venom. The coroner said my father lost too much blood, but if that hadn't killed him, he might have died from the poison." Adley's hand flew up to her mouth as she silenced herself. Victor bravely finished telling her about the terrible event. "But they didn't find any snake bites anywhere on his body."

"What about the marks left by the dog?" she questioned. "Wasn't it possible that the coroner made a mistake?"

"Teeth are kind of like footprints. You can tell the difference between human tracks and an animal's. And you can tell the difference between a snake bite and a dog's."

"Do you think this has anything to do with..." Adley couldn't finish saying it but he knew what she was asking.

"I have no doubt at all that the thing that pushed Grandma Aggie down the stairs is what spooked Greystoke, but I'm not sure how. My whole family thinks the same thing. We also think Grandma Aggie was going to give my dad the gypsy manuscript, but after he died, she refused to admit she had it."

"Didn't you tell her how important it was?"

"We did, but she was too afraid that someone else would get hurt trying to get it."

Adley hung her head, her posture mimicking Victor's when he spoke of his father. "She died thinking she was protecting us. Protecting me."

"My dad, too," he said with his lips pressed together, as if he were debating on sharing more. "There's something else, Adley."

He was so deadly serious, that she held onto his arm again. She didn't think she could stand one more scrap of information to gnaw at either of their peace of mind. An inner yearning bubbled inside her, and she wanted to relieve Victor's misery. She might be able to do that by helping him talk about what happened to his father.

"What is it, Victor?"

"My dad had the same kind of wounds on his ankle as you do on yours."

That was enough to render them mute for a very long while. Any doubt had been erased for both of them. Adley and Victor's father, Frank Trumillo, had been assaulted by the same creature.

"Wait a minute," Adley exclaimed. "You said it didn't have the power to kill anyone."

"Even with all that poison in his system and the gash on his head, if we found my dad in time, he could have lived. But he bled to death, Adley, because he was alone."

"We've got to stop this!" she said in words fueled with anger.

"It'll be hard to convince your parents that an evil presence lives in Aggie's house."

"I know. I tried to tell them over and over, but they still won't believe me."

Victor seemed apologetic. "I don't mean to defend your parents, Adley, but you've got to admit that it does sound pretty crazy."

She nodded in agreement. "And because I sounded so crazy this morning my parents treated me as if I were made of glass. They have to watch what they say to me. I don't know why or even when I started becoming so hard to live with. Sometimes I don't even recognize myself. I don't like who I've become."

"You're a good person, Adley. It's not you who needs to change, just some of the things you do."

"Yeah, well, the worst part is that I might not have time to make any changes, good or bad. My parents might never have the chance to love me again." She sniffled and wiped her teary eyes on her shoulder sleeve.

Victor took her hand into his and smiled. "Didn't we agree not to talk about the curse?"

"It's hard not to."

"For the record, I got past your angry defenses, and I see a girl that I really want to know better. You're beautiful, Adley, inside and out." She pressed her lips together, embarrassed by his wonderful compliment. "Let's try again," he said. "Even if for a short time, let's just think of this as a grave—I mean big, inconvenience."

Adley smiled at his unintentional play on words. Being in a grave would be a terrible inconvenience. Despite the oral blunder, she saw that he was a kindhearted boy and truly cared for her.

Victor leaned over and kissed Adley again. They both felt a surreal lifting out of their skin and opened their eyes at the same time.

"What's the matter," Adley asked. "Why did you pop your eyes open like that?"

Victor laughed. "I needed to make sure I wasn't floating in the air. Why did you open yours?"

"Me, too," Adley giggled.

He kissed her again, a quick peck on her lips. They leaned shoulder to shoulder and, for a bit longer, enjoyed the cool, refreshing water as it swished around their calves. They spoke of school, favorite foods, and dreams of the future. Other than an occasional peek at the sun, neither kept track of the lapsing hours.

"How long have we been sitting here?" Adley finally asked.

"I'm not sure." Victor was only mindful of the chat he was having with the pretty brunette.

"I'd better get back," Adley said reluctantly. "If I'm out too late my parents will send a SWAT team to look for me."

"We can sit at the big pine when we get back and talk a while longer," he offered, as if knowing she would rather be anywhere than inside the mansion. "You'll be able to hear when your parents send the cavalry charging up the trail."

It was great having a friend who happened to be an attractive boy who liked her company. It was also great not having to bother with a foreign object picking at her heels. They let their pruney feet air dry and then put on their shoes. Victor untied the patient horse and wedged Greystoke's lead rope through a loop in his jeans.

Adley laughed. "So that's why you don't wear a belt."

"Yeah, but it's embarrassing when he takes off without warning." She laughed. He studied her. "You know, I don't get to hear you laugh very much." He kissed the back of her hand but didn't let it go even when she blushed.

They started their walk back to Grandma Aggie's.

Her smile faded but a hint of it remained. "Not much to laugh about these days."

He diverted the topic yet again. "My mother is a great cook, and one day I'll ask her to make you paella."

"What's pie-ay-ya?" She tried to imitate his accent.

He grinned. "A Spanish dish made with seafood and rice. You should know. That's part of your Spanish heritage," he said.

"I didn't know I had a drop of Spanish blood in me until two days ago," she reflected. "Paella sounds like a good idea. Let's ask your mom to make it as soon as we get rid of that 'grave inconvenience' in my room."

"Okay," Victor said. "But I get the biggest lobster."

"There's lobster in paella?" He laughed and described the contents of the flavorful cuisine as they neared the manor.

No sooner had they arrived at the base of the large tree than Roger Lange called out for his daughter. "Adley!"

"Just a minute, Dad!" she shouted through the trees and shrubbery then spoke more quietly to Victor. "I guess we got back in the nick of time."

"Adley, please. Don't go into your room for any reason."

"I won't. I promise."

"I'm going to keep trying to get hold of my uncle," he told her. "I want you to call me if anything happens today. Or tonight," he added and squeezed her hand.

"Adley!" they heard her father call.

"I'm coming!" she shouted back.

Victor kissed Adley's forehead and watched her shoulders droop as she reluctantly trudged the short distance leading back to Capilla Manor.

"Call me tonight?" he asked not too much louder than a whisper, and she nodded, smiling.

His phone calls, especially his visits, were the only thing she had to look forward to these days. That and being fatally attacked by whatever it was that had the power to kill her the second she turned sixteen.

Thankfully the curse couldn't kill her as long as the hematite handle remained in place. If it wasn't for the handle, according to Victor's great-uncle, at precisely eight o'clock at night on her birthday and for twenty-four hours afterward, she'd be in a world of trouble.

Luckily for her, she at least had the hematite fixture attached to the bedroom door.

Chapter 21

Caroline joined Adley in ripping out clumps of dried grass and healthy weeds the next morning. When she complained of a back ache and the need for a bath, Roger took Caroline's place and helped his daughter create a new garden.

"I'm glad you chose to work out back today," he told Adley.

"I've got the energy for it," she said. It was the first night she slept a little more comfortably. Adley didn't go upstairs at all after her visit with Victor, and she had grown more accustomed to the nighttime noises. "Besides, I think the nicer it looks out here, the more meals we can take outside."

Roger paused briefly. "Does this have anything to do with the problem you're having in your room?"

"It's just nice to eat outside in the cool shade."

"It is," her dad agreed.

He loosened a number of large stepping stones of various sizes and colors. Once Adley pulled up the weeds sprouting around them, Roger embedded the stones back into the ground. He scattered old grass seed he found in the garage on the chance that it might grow in the large area around the patio that they had already cleared.

Her father brought out a glass of iced tea for both of them, and he sat in peaceful silence on the worn patio chairs as Adley watered the yard.

The water fell from the end of the hose like a light rain onto the darkening mulch, and some dripped down from the nozzle, wetting Adley's hand.

"Where's Mom? I thought she was going to come back outside after her shower."

"She had to run some errands."

He chose not to spoil any of Caroline's plans by telling Adley that her mother was shopping for her birthday presents.

His wife had called a few minutes ago from the mall and said that she found the perfect accessories for their daughter's new room. Best of all, she found a door knob on sale that matched the others on the second floor. Now they could replace that troublesome handle that Adley constantly complained about.

Roger remembered that Anne Marie collected an assortment of odds and ends for her pawn shop. The silver handle was probably worth a few dollars, and he might take it over to her after he installed the new one.

Adley finished watering while Roger enjoyed his iced tea. She coiled the hose into a large clay pot. "Thanks for helping, Dad."

"Think nothing of it."

Adley slid her palms back and forth, drying her hands. She scraped the excess dirt off her shoes and picked up her father's empty glass. "Refill?"

"No thanks, honey." Roger closed his eyes and enjoyed the scattered warmth of the sun that sliced through the patio cover, thinking about the newfound peace at Capilla Manor.

☣ ☣ ☣

The time spent outdoors relaxed and satisfied Adley, but she didn't have the nerve to tell her father the real reason why she wanted to be outside. It was better to keep quiet than risk the chance of ruining the one rare, beautiful morning she'd spent at Capilla Manor, next to all the terrific time she had spent with Victor. Too bad she couldn't count on the welcome state of happiness continuing, at least not while the curse was a factor in her life.

Adley entered the French doors to the family room and walked to the formal living room off the foyer where a landline was plugged into the wall. With her father resting on the patio outside, he wouldn't be able to hear her talk to Victor from the other side of the house. Fortunately, he picked up on the second ring.

"Hello?"

"Hi. It's me," Adley said.

"Is everything all right?"

"Yeah. I just needed to hear your voice." Adley thought she could feel his smile across the phone line. "My nerves are shot."

"I have some chores to finish up for now, and then I can come over."

"Then I guess I have to let you go," she said, disheartened.

"Call me later, and we'll try to arrange a visit, okay?"

"Okay." She felt foolish for calling and discouraged because he didn't have the time to talk. "Somehow, just talking to you puts me at ease."

"Um, Adley?"

"So much for being at ease," she inadvertently groaned. "I hate when you have that tone of voice. It isn't good news, is it?"

"Calm down, Adley," Victor said firmly, "and let me tell you before you get all hysterical on me."

"What is it now?" Her high-pitched voice bordered on hysteria, but she managed to keep her volume down. "Is it going to slice my skin off before killing me? Is it going to get my parents first?"

"I've been looking through the gypsy manuscript. I can't read it all, but I was able to make out a few passages. I told you that the families added their own sections to the book. Most of them wrote that the day before killing its victim, there won't be any noise, and there's nothing to be seen at all. None of the creepy hand scratching, crawling, or tapping."

Adley rubbed at the tension that found its way into the back of her neck. "Thanks. I guess that's not bad news. I'll keep an ear out for…nothing. Why won't it make any noise?"

"I'm not sure I interpreted it correctly." He avoided a direct answer. "Traditional Castilian is harder to translate than the Spanish we speak now."

"Victor!" Adley cried impatiently. "I know it's not easy for you to share more bad news, but I want to know what to expect. The more I know, the better my chances of survival."

"I don't mean to irritate you, but the thought of more bad news makes my heart ache for you."

"Oh, Victor," Adley whispered. "Thank you. I mean, really—thank you. Now tell me what I need to know. Why won't I hear anything tonight?"

"The book said it's saving its strength."

No further explanations were needed. Her silence confirmed that Adley clearly understood what he meant. Tomorrow, the skeletal creature would be more powerful than any of them imagined. It was going to be capable of killing her. It had only been cruelly teasing her during the last few days, tormenting her with harrowing tactics and effective promises of more to come. Her fear had grown more each day since she had been at Capilla Manor. The creature did an excellent job of setting the stage for a dreadful final act.

Adley emptied the oxygen from her lungs and, after a couple of normal breaths, she said, "All right. I can deal with silence better than having something try to drag me under the bed."

"With my great-uncle gone, I have to do his work, too, so I won't be able to come by until the early evening. He's trying to get down here, Adley. Call me if something happens before then."

"I don't know if my parents will let me go out on the trail that late.

"Don't worry. We'll talk later. I have to get the horses and other animals fed and watered."

"Life goes on," she murmured.

"It does, Adley, but believe me, I'm not letting you go through this alone. You'll be okay until I get there. Okay?"

"Okay."

They said their reluctant good-byes, and Adley felt better, even after having been reminded that her life might be over by tomorrow night.

☣ ☣ ☣

Caroline's secret shopping trip was a success. She'd found what she felt were wonderful presents for her daughter. She parked the car in the garage and left all the presents in the trunk. Not that she needed to hide them. Apparently Adley had forgotten that her birthday was the following day. With her odd preoccupation, insisting some sort of ghostly villain lurked under her bed, Adley more than likely wasn't giving her sixteenth birthday any thought at all.

When she was out hiking the day before, Roger and

Caroline had gone into her room but didn't find anything alarming. They searched under the bed, in the closet, and behind the dressers. Their daughter was obviously craving their attention again.

They wanted to spend more quality time with her, or at least offer to, but these days she wanted to go on her nature hikes with her new friend. That was likely the reason she was so emotional. Lately, Adley didn't keep friends for very long, and maybe she was nervous with the prospect of losing this one, too.

Caroline was wondering what she should tell Adley if questions came up about her whereabouts or if she had made any purchases. As it turned out, Caroline didn't need to explain. She found Adley asleep on the couch, her face and arms covered in soil. Later that evening while fixing dinner, Caroline described the gifts she bought for Adley to her husband.

"I found some cute clothes and jewelry. And a nice boy at the music store recommended some of the latest CDs that most kids are listening to these days. Say, do you think you can replace the handle tonight?"

"Why not?" Roger replied. "I'll do it before we go to bed. Adley will be hiding out downstairs anyway and will be none the wiser."

Caroline smiled. She could hardly wait for Roger to install the crystal knob she found on sale. Adley's exaggerations and complaints about the freezing touch of the silver handle were about to end.

☣ ☣ ☣

Caroline shook Adley gently on the shoulder and spoke softly. "Dinner's ready. Wash your hands and face."

Adley yawned and stretched. She ate her dinner but

tasted nothing and cleared the dinner table, wiping it down like a robot, mechanically and without thought. Her father said he had to get some tools out of the garage, and Caroline rinsed the dishes as Adley stacked them in the dishwasher.

"Mom, can I sleep downstairs tonight?" Adley asked.

Although her father had moved all of her belongings into the room next to her parents, Adley was determined to stay away from the upper story altogether.

Anywhere in the house was too close to that living nightmare.

"I don't see why not," her mom replied.

"Would you mind going up to my room for me and getting pajamas and a clean change of clothes for tomorrow?"

"For heaven's sakes, Adley!"

The last glass clinked brightly as Adley accidentally knocked it against another in the top rack and closed the machine door.

"Never mind. I can ask Dad." She spoke in the guilt-inducing tone she learned how to master as a small child, determined to pull out all the stops to avoid going into her room.

"Fine," Caroline huffed. "I'll get your things. But just for tonight. For whatever reason, it's a traumatic event for you to step foot into that room, or to go upstairs at all. I'm only doing it because it's your birthday tomorrow."

Adley smiled. "Thanks, Mom. Believe me, I really appreciate it."

Her mother dried her hands on a towel and dropped it on the counter. "I don't understand why you won't go up by yourself tonight when you can't even hear the mice this evening."

Roger walked into the kitchen. "I guess you could say it's as quiet as a mouse."

Caroline moaned as Adley listened intently for any of the noises that had come to plague her peace of mind over the past few days. Her mom and dad were right. There hadn't been a single peep from the upstairs all evening.

Her parents left the room, leaving Adley mute, without any clear words of protest to call them back. She didn't know how to tell them that her world was about to drastically change in the worst way possible.

Caroline sauntered casually out of the kitchen as if it were any other normal evening, following Roger as he carried a small red tool box upstairs.

☣ ☣ ☣

Roger and Caroline climbed the stairs to the second floor. "Can you fix Adley's old bed tomorrow? I think the headboard is damaged. A nail or two should do it."

"I'll have a look at it when I replace that silver handle in a minute," Roger said. "Where's the new knob?"

"Right over here," Caroline answered.

Roger waited at their bedroom door while his wife went through a bag hidden in the back of their walk-in closet.

She was delighted at finally being able to get the worrisome task completed and beamed when she handed her husband the small plastic wrapped package.

He examined the parcel closely. "Are the screws and plate in a separate bag?"

"What plate?" she asked. "And can't you use the same screws that are already on the door?"

"Honey, the old ones are silver," he said. "This one needs brass screws and a brass plate which goes behind the knob."

Caroline tapped her palm against forehead. "I wasn't

thinking! It wasn't packaged in a box. I guess I got a good price on it because it was returned. No wonder it was discounted!"

"Don't worry," Roger assured his wife. "I'm going into town tomorrow morning to take the silver handle to Anne Marie's pawn shop. I can pick up some screws from the hardware store and see if they have the brass plate. Then I'll come home and put the new fixture on the door."

"Well, it's not like it will make too much difference when you install the new knob." Caroline said. "Tomorrow's fine."

☣ ☣ ☣

As promised, Caroline brought down a pair of jeans, a light blouse, cotton socks, underclothing, and pajamas for Adley. She planned to watch TV as long as her eyes stayed open, snuggled beneath cozy blankets on the sofa bed in the den. After two sitcom reruns, her mother called down from the top of the stairs and told her to go to sleep, but Adley merely lowered the volume on the big screen. Forty-five minutes later, at eleven o'clock, well after her parents had been upstairs in bed, she made a quiet phone call from the kitchen.

Victor's voice came on the line before it finished ringing the first time. "Hello?"

"Hi. It's me," she said.

"Hi! I'm sorry I couldn't see you today. There's so much work for one person to do on a ranch."

"Don't worry about it. I know you had to do all that stuff."

"I've been thinking of you. A lot," Victor said.

"Me, too. There's no noise, nothing weird happening just like you said, and I'm more freaked out than ever."

Victor spoke softly, yet firmly. "Just stay out of your room. The handle should hold."

"Should? What do you mean—*should*?" she demanded.

"We didn't have the gypsy writing when my uncle made the handle to capture the demon. Great-Uncle Pablo told me it was a stroke of luck that the fixture kept it in the room. He said we can't predict what will happen at eight o'clock tomorrow night. Maybe if you met me out back tonight you could stay at our house, and we'll know for sure you'll be safe."

"Are you kidding? My parents said I wasn't allowed to hang out with you. They won't even let me spend a day, let alone a night, in your home."

"Then stay all day tomorrow."

"What do I tell my parents, Victor? That I'll be gone all day at the Trumillos?"

"It might be worth getting into trouble to save your life, Adley," Victor offered. "Please, do it for both of us." Adley heard his affection for her in his comforting words.

"Meeting you for a hike is one thing, but sneaking out for the night? I don't think I can get away with it," she said.

"All right then, tomorrow morning, it is. I'll be next to the phone. Call me the moment it starts to turn light. Leave your house fifteen minutes later, and I'll be out at the big pine. We'll ride back to my house to see Great-Uncle Pablo. The truck had other things wrong with it, but he got it fixed and is on his way home right now."

"Finally! I'm so glad." Adley paused a moment. "Victor, I know you're really worried. I can hear it in your voice."

"I was hoping you wouldn't notice."

"It's okay. I mean, it's nice to know someone is looking out for me. That someone cares."

"I care a lot more about you than you may realize."

She gulped. If it took a gruesome generational curse to know that Victor cared about her, Adley would endure the curse a hundred times over.

"Thank you, Victor. I feel the same."

Now if she could only survive her birthday.

Chapter 22

At that moment, Adley heard a noise. Footsteps heading down the stairs. "Someone's coming!" she whispered into the phone. "I'll call you tomorrow."

"Goodnight, babe."

He hung up, and she grinned at the endearment. It took a few seconds to regain her senses and hang up the phone. Padded footfalls neared the kitchen, and a thought occurred to her. What if it wasn't one of her parents walking in the dark hallway that led to the kitchen? The steps drew closer, and a shadow appeared through the crack under the door. Adley held her breath, and the door slowly opened.

Her father stepped into the room, his eyes bloodshot. "What are you doing up?"

"Couldn't sleep," she answered with a sigh of relief. "Is Mom awake?"

He grabbed a carton of milk out of the refrigerator. "No. She went to bed early. Pulling weeds took it out of her." He looked back into the icebox and began to hunt for sandwich fixings, putting sliced turkey, lettuce, a tomato, mayonnaise, and mustard in the crook of his arm. "How about a sandwich and chips? I'm buying."

"No thanks, Dad," Adley said.

In no time, Roger constructed a fair-sized sandwich.

Adley put the remaining ingredients away and wiped down the counter. Anything to keep her mind preoccupied.

"Thanks, Dee—Adley," her father said.

She smiled and sat back down at Grandma Aggie's desk.

Roger ate his sandwich with one hand as he dug through his toolbox that he'd brought downstairs earlier that evening. "How was your hike?" he asked.

"Great! I found a real neat stream. It's so pretty and peaceful. I'd like to go back and see it in the morning," she hinted.

"You must be talking about Riley's Run-off."

She scrunched her brows. "Riley's what?"

Her father smiled as he shared the story. "A man named Thomas Riley owned a huge acreage roughly forty-five years ago. It ran along the wooded hills behind the house, all the way down to the Trumillo's place. He eventually built a small home on the property. When I was a kid, the stream was stocked with fish, and part of it fed into a small pond half a mile northeast of here. My friends and I used to run across the land to fish with strings tied to branches. We didn't have much luck."

"Let me guess," she said. "The owner caught you kids fishing, ran you off his land, and that's why you called it Riley's Run-off."

Roger chuckled and shook his head. "Not exactly," he said after the last nibble on his sandwich and a few corn chips. He continued to search in his tool box. "Mr. Riley said his place was haunted." Had his back not been to his daughter, he might have seen her flinch. "I guess that's a popular notion around these parts. He claimed to see a ghoul of some sort loitering around. Said it started out at the north side of the property then gradually migrated south to this side. Old Riley said that's what ran him off." Adley's breath caught, and Roger briefly glanced at her but missed her blanched complexion. "And *that's* why it's called Riley's Run-off. The old guy didn't have all his marbles. He packed up and shipped out of state."

Roger found a broken screw driver, pursed his mouth, and dropped it back into the red metal box. "The property sat vacant for quite a few years. It wasn't easy finding a buyer, and he ended up selling it for a song."

"What happened to the people who bought it? Did they say it was, haun—haunted?" she stammered.

"No, but then, no one ever moved in." Her father kept to his task of picking through his toolbox. "The people who bought it tore down the dilapidated homestead. They tried to build a new one but had a bad turn of luck. First, it collapsed half-way through completion, and they tried again, but the frame burned down. They ended up selling the land to the state to settle the taxes, and it's been sitting vacant ever since."

"Why didn't anyone else try to buy it?" Adley asked.

"It may have been because of another accident on the property. Your grandmother said a local died there, and apparently that was enough to spook anyone out of buying the land."

Adley swallowed back a lump. "How long ago did it get sold to the state?"

"Oh, I'd say about seven or eight years ago," he answered.

About the time Victor's father was attacked. Her father continued relating the tale as Adley forced herself to appear calm.

"The state wanted to build a solar power plant, but they ran into difficulties from the outset. The circuits kept popping and they heard glass breaking but they never found anything."

"You mean like what we heard the other day?" Adley asked, watching her father's reaction.

He tilted his head and his eyes lingered on something unseen. "Huh. I guess so." He examined the implements inside the toolbox yet again. "Eventually, the engineers determined that the soil was too sandy on that side of the creek to build, which I personally think is nonsense. Why do you ask?"

Adley didn't answer. By the time he turned around, she had already left the room.

She hurried to the den and sat down on the couch before collapsing like a windblown deck of cards. Her desire to learn more had temporarily abandoned her. The skeletal anomaly that was in her room had to be what haunted the property above Grandma Aggie's. How did it get there? That explained why her father never commented on any unusual occurrences growing up. It hadn't gotten inside until the time Victor's father died four years ago, when Grandma Aggie called Mr. Trumillo to tell him she needed to see him in person regarding a mysterious predicament.

Victor said the coroner wrote on the autopsy report that his father's body was full of snake venom yet the reported injury was made by a dog bite. Dogs? Snakes? All Adley had ever seen was that grotesque profile on her wall and that hand...*Wait a minute*!

The first night she slept in her room she thought she saw a shadow of a hunched figure, with fangs, the silhouette of a dog-like skeleton. She'd heard hissing more than once, too, like a snake ready to strike. It had to be an incredible nightmare. How could any of this really be happening?

Emotional exhaustion took hold of Adley. The thing in her room was more powerful than she'd thought possible, yet Victor said it was saving its strength. How much more powerful could it become? The last ounce of strength drained from her body just thinking about it. She was tired and slowly toppled onto her side, falling in and out of a light sleep.

The TV stayed on all night. She had changed the channels once when a trailer for a show called Curse of the Zombies flashed on the screen. Frayed nerves kept a good night's sleep at bay.

During the dark and early morning hours, one of her parents tiptoed through the lower level of the house, not knowing Adley was pretending to be asleep. About thirty minutes later someone came down and poured a glass of water before retreating upstairs. Adley was sure it was to check on her rather than to get a drink. She generally accused her mother and father of insulting her by treating her like a small child, but now she welcomed their concern and their company.

She strained to hear any scraping or tapping noises from the floor above her or the wicked hissing that usually seeped through the air vents. Tonight, however, unsettling stillness pierced the atmosphere. It was definitely not a typical night—living under a haunted roof and in such dangerous conditions. She wished this was the last night she had to sleep in the horrible mansion.

And she realized that it might very well be her last night anywhere.

☣ ☣ ☣

Adley woke up before her parents and waited anxiously for dawn to near, elated when the sun floated above the horizon.

The sky was painted with dramatic streaks of fuchsia slashing into blue but she didn't see it, nor did she take no-

tice of the billowy clouds, typical for a classic desert scene
before a storm.

The vision went unappreciated because Adley couldn't
say she was glad the fateful day had finally arrived. In the
past, she imagined her sixteenth birthday to be a milestone,
but not like this. She made her way to the kitchen and
picked up the phone to call Victor Fortunately, he was
awake and answered on the first ring, as she expected.
Maybe he didn't want the noise to disturb anyone else in
the house. Maybe he was looking forward to hearing from
her.

"H'lo," came the yawn.

"Victor?" Adley asked in a hushed tone.

"Good morning. Happy Birth…" It was too late. Victor
was suddenly wide awake and wisely silenced himself.

Adley already felt the sting of his poorly worded greeting. Tired and irritated from lying awake half the night in
anticipation of unimaginable events of the day yet to come,
she snapped, "Thanks a lot."

"I'm sorry. I can't believe I said that."

Adley didn't want to bite any heads off so early in the
morning, especially Victor's. Besides, after a second of
consideration, she knew his intentions were good. "Is your
great-uncle home yet?" she asked.

"Yes. He arrived earlier this morning."

"Did you tell him what's been going on? Will he help
us—uh, me?" she corrected.

"Yes, of course, but it's complicated. I'm going to take
you back to my house, and he'll tell you all about it. We
stayed up most of the night on the phone as I read the book
to him. And Adley? When my great-uncle got here, he said
he found a way to get rid of the curse once and for all!"

"He did?" It was the first good news Adley heard in a
while.

"I can meet you at the big pine in twenty minutes," Victor said.

"See you then."

Adley hung up the phone, more grateful than ever for Victor's friendship. She never had a more caring and reliable friend. Or a cuter one. And she had never been one herself until her move to the wicked mansion. In a fit of general appreciation, Adley brewed a pot of coffee for her parents and readied the patio table for their breakfast. She had already grabbed a quick bowl of cereal for herself, preparing to leave as soon as her parents sat down for their meal. Just as Adley set the sugar bowl and creamer on the glass-topped table, her parents shuffled outside, onto the large patio.

"I was sound asleep until I smelled something wonderful," her father said.

"Well, someone got up early," her mother said, a cheerful lilt in her voice. Her parents observed the dishes nicely displayed outside on the patio. A few fresh sprigs of rosemary and lavender that grew in shady patches of the yard had been tied together with a ribbon.

"I admit I've become accustomed to you setting the table, but a platter of freshly cut fruit, a pot of hot coffee, and a basket of sweet rolls are really more than we would have expected," Roger said.

Caroline squished her daughter in her arms with an affectionate hug. "Thank you, honey. This is a lovely breakfast, but it's your birthday. I was going to make you some Belgian waffles."

"I don't mind, Mom," Adley wheezed under her mother's vice-like embrace.

"Thanks, Dee—Adley," her father said. "This is really nice of you to go through all this trouble on your birthday," he said, complimenting her as he gave her a gentle hug.

"At least let us clean up," Caroline said.

"Absolutely," her father agreed.

"Sure. Why not?" Adley gushed, genuinely embarrassed by the praise.

They didn't know they gave her great peace of mind by not including her in clean-up duty or making her wait while they finished eating. Today, she wanted to avoid the inside of Grandma Aggie's mansion at all costs.

"We thought you'd like to go into town with us this morning," her mother said. "Maybe we can pick out a couple of presents and have lunch later at a nice restaurant."

"If you don't mind, I'd like to take another hike out back."

"We can join you," her dad happily suggested.

Caroline pressed. "And we can pack a picnic lunch for later."

"Uhm, Dad, Mom? Do you mind if I go alone?"

"Well, no, honey," Roger answered. "It is your special day, after all. But don't you want to be with your family?"

Today she had to leave, not just for the day, but maybe for the night. One plan she devised was to call from the Trumillo ranch and confess to maintaining a friendship with Victor and his family. She'd then ask to stay for dinner and if they refused, remain with them regardless of her parents' wishes. Getting permission to spend the night at Victor's house was a long way from asking to stay for dinner.

A veto was more than likely in order, whether Adley wanted to spend the night with the Trumillos or just stay for dinner. She had developed a last minute back-up plan. For this she had to muster up the audacity to see it through. She hadn't yet concocted a better scheme than running away, preferably without her parents knowing. Perhaps she'd slip outside when they took their regular late afternoon nap. Thankfully, it wasn't a decision she had to make right then.

"That's fine," Caroline said. "After all, Roger, we have things to do." Caroline gave her husband a look, the kind that told Adley her mother wanted her father to go along with her decision. "You can go right after breakfast."

"I already ate. Can I go now?"

Roger shrugged. "Remember to follow the rules."

"Run if I see strangers. Take a bottle of water. Stay within calling distance. Yeah, I know the rules, Dad." After gathering her backpack, she waved to her parents and headed to the corner of the yard to the worn trail leading to the safety of the woods.

But no place would be safe for too much longer.

Chapter 23

Victor sat on the felled tree wearing a new pair of indigo jeans and a black cotton T-shirt with a sports logo. In his hand was a neatly wrapped present. He stood, smiling, as Adley jogged toward him.

"Hi," she said, beaming from ear to ear. "You got all dressed up."

"Yeah," he replied. He seemed uncharacteristically shy. "This is for you." He handed her a lightweight box with a pink bow and kissed her softly on the cheek.

Fire roared under her skin where his lips touched her. Adley gazed down at the present as she felt her face flush.

"Open it!" he said.

"Thank you, Victor." She peeked at him then carefully tugged at the paper. "You didn't have to get me anything."

"It's not much, but we thought you might like it."

"We?" Adley asked as she untied the ribbon, opened the box, and pulled away the tissue paper.

Inside was a hand-woven bowl intertwined with web-like strings from a fibrous plant. An asymmetrical design wound its way from the rim to the bottom of the bowl. Brown and white eagle and red hawk feathers adorned the suede laces that hung from the rim. Hematite and turquoise beads embellished the laces.

Adley held the bowl as if it were made of the thinnest glass. "This is beautiful! I've never seen anything like it!"

"It's Native American," Victor explained. "My mother is part Navajo. This belonged to her great-grandfather. It's handmade and very sacred, over a hundred years old. Place it in your—wherever you sleep and you will receive only good things in your life. We want you to have it."

He knew she liked it because tears dripped down her cheeks to her smile. "I love it, though I'm not sure you should be giving me something so precious to your family."

"We knew you'd appreciate it."

"I've never received a gift more meaningful than this, Victor. I'm glad that you're entrusting me with a family heirloom. I'm grateful, not just because this is such a valuable and sacred artifact, but because it means that people care about me. Thank you, Victor."

They looked into each other's eyes and Victor pressed his lips against hers, a small but meaningful kiss.

Adley rewrapped the beautiful gift and carefully set it into the box. Victor placed a hand on either side of her face and kissed her slowly. Adley felt his tongue part her lips. He tasted sweet, like sugar, cinnamon, and other spices. In seconds, she felt as if they'd lifted into the clouds and swirled in a mass of energy, his mixing with hers. He slowly pulled away and she floated back into her body. Adley swayed and Victor laughed as he held her up by the arms.

"I never felt a kiss like yours before," she said in a near whisper.

"Me, neither," Victor said and hugged her to him.

Her body felt like mush, without any muscles to hold herself up.

"C'mon." He took her hand. "My great-uncle really wants to talk to you. Stand on this tree trunk," he said, jutting his chin toward the place they usually sat.

Adley didn't question the order. She stood obediently on the sizeable horizontal limb. Victor coaxed Greystoke to the edge of it and quickly swung up on the animal's back like an adept gymnast. He took Adley by the hand and helped her up to sit behind him, then clicked his tongue twice.

The massive equine changed directions at the pull of the reins and loped onward, along the track of dried leaves and broken branches. Adley wrapped her arms around Victor's waist, and he held her arm with one hand, holding the reins with the other. Though their chatter was lighthearted, it was overshadowed by the reason for the visit to Victor's house. Today was her sixteenth birthday, and if the legend was true, it could very well be her last day alive.

About thirty minutes later, Victor directed Greystoke down a dirt path, and the Trumillo's ranch came into view. He left the horse untethered beneath a tree closest to the trail. They strolled through a festive patio filled with bright ceramic pots and colorful flowers strategically sprinkling the well-designed respite. Once through the back door off the kitchen, their noses filled with the aroma of freshly baked bread. Adley spied a dining area with a huge table and a tidy living room beyond. An old man with tan skin and white hair stood near the table. Two older women were already seated.

"Adley." Victor gestured toward his uncle with much ceremony. "I'd like you to meet my great-uncle, Pablo Martinez de Cordoba."

The first thing that Adley saw in Victor's great-uncle was the man's amazing midnight blue eyes. It was easy to see how people thought he was magical. The love and admiration Victor had for his great-uncle was profoundly evident.

Adley shook the offered hand. "I'm very pleased to meet you, sir."

Great Uncle Pablo clasped his warm, strong hands lightly over hers. "And we are pleased to have you in our home."

Victor nodded toward the older of the two women sitting at the table and said with the same amount of respect, "And this is Great-Aunt Gloria." They shook hands. Finally he proudly introduced his mother. "This is my mom, Maria Trumillo."

"How do you do?" Adley asked. Victor had obviously inherited his smile from Mrs. Trumillo.

"We're so glad to have you here," Maria said. She held Adley's hand with both of her own, just like Great-Uncle Pablo had.

"And I'm so glad to be here, and I'm grateful to have people willing to help me," Adley said. "Thank you so much for my amazing birthday present."

"We knew you would like it," Great-Aunt Gloria said, and Maria and Pablo nodded.

"Sit, sit," Great-Uncle Pablo instructed, and the formalities abruptly ceased.

Victor and Adley took their seats at the table. Maria served ice-cold lemonade and egg sandwiches with bacon on thick slices of homemade wheat bread, still warm from the oven. They all chatted cordially of how the two teenagers met and briefly commented on the sites in their sleepy southwest community. As Adley waited for the discussion to begin, she noticed the gypsy book on the sideboard, a reminder of their serious agenda.

Great-Uncle Pablo soon cut through the pleasantries and opened the discussion of the unavoidable subject. "It is only right that you know why all of the horrors in your grandmother's mansion have taken place," he said to Adley.

"What I will tell you is a truth that has been handed down from generation to generation."

Adley scooted forward in her seat, having wondered for the past few days about the origins of the curse.

"Your father's great-great-great-grandfather, Hernando Miguel Rodrigues, was a Spanish gypsy who made his money selling glass wares from a cart. One day he traded beautiful crystal goblets for sparkling jewelry from a street vendor. One of those pieces was a gold necklace embedded with gems that the gypsy, Hernando, wore proudly. It so happened that one of these treasures belonged to the deceased mother of one of the king's most ruthless guards, Francisco Del Diego. Francisco recognized the family crest embossed on the gold. He accused Hernando of being a grave robber, an extremely serious offense of that time.

"The two men became embroiled in an argument. Rodrigues denied stealing the necklace and offered to take the guard to the vendor with whom he had traded. When they found the man, the street vendor vehemently denied having sold the jewelry to the gypsy. You see, the vendor was Mario Del Diego, the guard's only brother. Of course, Mario wasn't going to admit to robbing his own mother's grave, so he stuck to his lie, and the guard believed that Rodrigues had stolen the valuable necklace."

Adley was enthralled by Pablo storytelling. In fact, everyone at the table clung to each word as he mesmerized them with the tale of the curse that haunted Capilla Manor.

"Del Diego grabbed Hernando's arm and tried to cut off his hand for robbing his mother's grave, a permissible form of punishment for stealing back then. But Rodrigues struggled and the guard slashed his arm, cutting deep enough to touch the gypsy's bone. Rodrigues became infuriated at the unjust treatment, and a violent fight ensued.

"The men hit each other and smashed into all the goods

that were being sold in the marketplace. They fell onto in-nocent bystanders and knocked over Hernando's cart, filled mostly with glass oil lanterns that exploded everywhere. It was said that shattering glass was heard echoing throughout the village."

Adley remembered the return trip from Minero and her family thinking perhaps a robber was in the house, breaking glass. "That's what we heard at my grandma's!"

Pablo nodded and continued. "The two men fought each other with no regard for the people who were acci-dentally shoved into the piles of splintered crystal. Some-how, Rodrigues managed to unarm Del Diego. The guard had fallen and stumbled to his feet after pulling a sharp dagger from his boot, but Hernando lunged at the guard be-fore he had a chance to slash at him again. The guard reeled backward. He spun in mid-air and held out his arms to break his fall but slammed into the ground and was, some-how, impaled on his own knife.

"Rodrigues knelt beside the dying man and cursed him in a rage. 'As you have cut me to the bone, may all of your first born descendants meet their death by the hand of the bone you have cut, at the time of their sixteenth year.'"

"Why sixteen? Because that's a significant year for a kid, sweet-sixteen and all?"

"As romantic as the notion sounds, no, that's not the reason," Great-Uncle Pablo said. "Rodrigues knew that Del Diego's youngest son was fifteen. It was common knowledge that the boy was a squire to the king, and the gypsy wanted Del Diego's son to die. Unfortunately, the guard died with his eyes open. If Rodrigues had known, he would not have cursed the dying man.

"Now this is very important," Victor's great-uncle em-phasized. "According to gypsy legend, if the person you are cursing dies before your words are finished, that very same curse falls back upon you instead. Rodrigues damned his own family line without realizing it. When he saw that the guard had died, he fled in order to escape the King's death sentence, as well as his own curse. He sold the heirloom jewelry and paid several peasants to quickly pack and deliver belongings to a ship at the dock in Costa del Sol. He booked passage for his wife, Marta, and his two sons and daughter on the next outbound ship, which happened to be sailing for Mexico with a brief stop in Portugal. This is where the manifest records for the gypsy book had been changed, and the book was crossed off."

The old man paused to take a drink. Everyone at the table remained silent, transfixed, waiting to hear the rest of the story. "In his new homeland, Rodrigues mined for gold and came across a few pieces of gold Mayan coins. The small cache, about half a dozen of the ancient pieces, brought them a small fortune.

"Those who failed to discover any gold in the Mexican mines followed Rodrigues to the higher desert, where they heard of mines rich in turquoise, silver, and copper. Capilla Manor was built, but it wasn't given that name until much later. A decade or so after the move, the mines ran dry and the town folded. Only the Rodrigues family and a handful of optimistic or stubborn miners stuck around. The house was handed down to succeeding generations.

"As the family traveled north to Hachita, the oldest son died of a mysterious illness just as he turned sixteen. The boy had many of the same symptoms as snake poisoning but the only markings found on his body were dog bites on his ankle. It was a terrible tragedy, and Rodrigues knew his son's death was just the beginning of the awful curse he had created."

Great-Uncle Pablo gave Adley a moment to catch her breath. Maria gave her a glass of water. Victor and his aunts were grateful for a chance to shake off some of their anxiety.

The old man waited until they were all settled and continued the story of Adley's ancestors.

"Rodrigues purchased hundreds of acres of land and stock with a few pieces of his Mayan gold. He had enough to cover the cost of building the mansion, constructing stables, hiring help, and setting up the household. The following generations let go of the outbuildings and assorted farm animals and sold off bits of the land, but Capilla Manor remained in decent condition.

"His daughter became a nun, scared to death of marrying and bearing children. She secluded herself in a convent for the rest of her life. The younger child was named Antonio, and he eventually married a Spaniard in Yucatán named Rosalia Corres. They had two children. His daughter was named Roberta, and Rosalia then gave birth to a son. Roberta was on her way to market to sell eggs and was run over by an ox cart with a broken brake handle."

"Let me guess," Adley croaked. "She was sixteen?"

The man gestured a yes. "The surviving son, Armando Rodrigues, married an English woman, Sondra Wilkes, who gave birth, first to a son, then to her two daughters. Their son, Rueben, the oldest, was kept like a prisoner in his own home when he became a teenager. In the gypsy's manuscript, the story says that his parents locked him in a room the day of his sixteenth birthday. There were no windows, and the only door was guarded by his father. Armando sat inside the room, blocking the door. At one point, in the dark morning hours, he fell asleep for no more than five minutes. When he woke up, his son was gone. There were no signs of a struggle, except for the rumpled blanket. Rueben was never heard from again."

It was clear that all the mysterious disappearances and

grisly accidents of the previous generations had definitely followed a pattern.

Pablo continued. "One of his daughters contracted tuberculosis when she was twelve and died. The other, Agatha Elizabeth, married Augustus Lange and gave birth to two children, one of whom is your father."

Up until then, Adley didn't grasp that Mr. Cordoba was describing her family tree. "That can't be right! My father was an only child!"

Maria Trumillo unexpectedly spoke up. "While I worked for Aggie, she confided in me that your father had a brother for a very short while. Her older son lived a day and died from a bad heart. She had him a year before your father was born."

Great-Uncle Pablo picked up the story. "That made your father the second son. And he was safe from the curse."

Adley stared off in another direction, open-mouthed, unable to speak a single word. Then absently, she spoke her thoughts. "My dad had an older brother?" Heads nodded all around the table. "It's all true, then. This curse, the monster thing that wants to kill me on my birthday—"

Her eyes sought out Victor's. His concern for her was a painful reflection on his somber face looking back at her, full of as much pity as it was of fear.

"Just how bad is this going to get?" she asked Great-Uncle Pablo.

He shook his head. "I'm sorry, Adley."

Clearly, it was about to get pretty bad.

Chapter 24

Great-Uncle Pablo drank his lemonade as Maria added more to the story. "Four years ago your grandmother called my husband to tell him about a problem she was having. He died before he could help her. We believe that horrible creature was somehow responsible for—" Victor rubbed his mother's shoulders. She sighed and went on recalling the story.

"It was quiet for a very long time, but one afternoon before your grandmother's accident, she called me and asked me to come over, saying she had something to tell me. She said she was afraid that something awful was hiding inside her home. She said she had spoken to Mr. Riley when he sold his land. He was the land owner who at one time owned the property above Capilla Manor."

"My dad told me about it," Adley said. "He said the man sold his land because he claimed his house was haunted."

"Yes, and Agatha felt that whatever it was that tormented the old man had crossed onto her property," Maria said. "She knew my husband had knowledge of the ancient ways and hoped he might be able to find a way to help her get rid of that thing inside her home. Aggie was a dear woman, but she was very old and often forgot things," Maria tearfully recollected. "Such a dear woman. She loved her gardens."

Great-Uncle Pablo sighed, his patience slightly waning. "Just tell her what happened."

Maria composed herself. "Aggie said she was going to give him a special book she found that might help destroy the monster, but by that time, she couldn't remember where she hid it."

"Why didn't my grandma tell anyone what was happening before she fell? She must have heard or seen something like I did," Adley said.

"At first, Aggie felt that because she was feeble, everyone might think she was losing her mind," Maria said. "Later, she decided not to bring harm to those who came into her home."

Maria's eyes filled with tears as she relayed the truth. Apparently she had been very fond of her former employer and friend.

"Aggie said she didn't believe in the curse until she was pushed down the stairs. We searched for the book in every room up to the day she died and for a while after the funeral. I can't believe she hid it in the room with the handle. Obviously, that's the last place I thought to look." She shivered. "I would never set foot in that room."

Adley asked Pablo a nagging question. "Why is it that when I touch the handle on my door it practically freezes my fingers off, but my parents don't say a thing about it? They've opened that door a lot."

"Only you can feel it—"he said reluctantly, "—because you're the next victim."

The remark delivered an unpleasant tingling all over her skin. "But why didn't you try to warn my father before he came out here?"

"We sent him several letters, all saying the same thing."

"Oh! I heard my parents mention some letters." Adley dropped her head into her hands. "They didn't believe what was written."

Great-Uncle Pablo explained. "We told him that Aggie wanted the house destroyed and it was best to keep away, especially for your sake, but we never heard back from him. We assumed he meant to fulfill her wishes, but apparently he didn't believe us."

"How do you know all this?" Adley asked. "About the curse, I mean. Did you read it in the leather-bound manuscript? Are you a gypsy?"

The room filled with chuckles. "No, *señorita*. None of us are gypsies. The guard who mistakenly accused the gypsy of stealing was my great-great-grandfather, Francisco Del Diego. It has been a generational responsibility to see that this curse is ended, but obviously we've not been successful. You are a descendant of the Spanish gypsy, and that is why we are lending you assistance."

"So Victor is a descendant of the Del Diego blood line?"

The old man's head bobbed up and down and he proudly gleamed at his great-nephew. "Yes."

Adley understood all that she had been told, the most important of which was that her ancestor had accidentally killed a man, put a curse on him, and inadvertently brought that curse upon all the following generations, ending with herself. And Victor's relative was the guard who had been originally cursed. The mood in the room was somber. Faces were carved with the same distress that their ancestors probably felt upon hearing the unbelievable narration for the first time.

Adley sat up straighter. "What's needed to break this curse?"

The old man sighed and shook his head. "You are much too young to have to face this kind of danger. "First, you must know that you have to fight for your life. There isn't much choice here. Live or die. It will not stop going after you until you're dead, unless of course, you make it twenty-four hours past the minute of your birth. Victor said today is your birthday and that you were born at precisely eight o'clock at night."

"That's right," Adley confirmed.

"This means the curse cannot affect you one moment after eight o'clock tomorrow night, but from your birth hour tonight until the same time tomorrow night, you will be in the greatest danger of your life." Great-Uncle Pablo glanced at Victor and motioned toward the large gypsy book on the sideboard. Victor dutifully fetched the lettered work and laid it before his uncle.

Adley saw paper markers slipped in at various intervals. Pablo's gnarled hands slowly lifted the decorative cover.

"Victor has told me of the powers of the devilish thing that lives in your room," he said to Adley. "Many of your ancestors recorded similar experiences they endured and witnessed in this." He motioned to the book. "Hernando Rodrigues brought the manuscript from Spain. Apparently, this curse has been used many times before. Your ancestors wrote the names of family members whom they lost and also what they tried to do to destroy the creature or keep it at bay. One thing we know for sure. The curse has taken on a physical form. It grows stronger as it nears the time to kill and with every kill it makes."

"So can the book help us or not?"

Great-Uncle Pablo explained more about the gypsy

manuscript. "The last three generations of your father's family shared all they could of what they experienced, but they couldn't find the counter-curse because it had been hidden. Perhaps someone thought that by hiding it, others would be discouraged from using the curse in the first place."

"No! They hid the counter curse when people needed it the most?" Adley said, and everyone else at the table reacted much the same, in shocked denial.

Unlike the others, Great-uncle Pablo didn't look disturbed.

Ink drawings of calcium structures in grisly phases of growth were scattered throughout the parchment. They saw the outlines of mutated puppets and pieces of bone floating in the air.

The book showed a picture of curled claws on the frame of a deformed canine with huge incisors, large gaping holes, and ragged edges for eyes.

"Unfortunately, yes. But it so happens that in your struggle with the creature to get the book, the vellum parchment on the inside back cover came loose, and it is there I found the counter-curse," Great-Uncle Pablo said, carefully turning to the last page of the manuscript.

A collective release echoed across the room as Victor hugged Adley, and Maria hugged Gloria. Pablo tugged at the corner of a yellow paper that had been tucked under the parchment glued over the back cover. The top corner of the page had been torn in the scuffle when Adley yanked the book from its hiding place.

"Great!" Victor said, and Adley smiled wide and triumphant. "What are the words that have to be spoken?"

"If it were that simple," Great-uncle Pablo said, and the smiles dropped from their faces. "We are faced with a two-fold problem. You—" He tossed a look at Adley. "—are the target of the curse, and you must say the counter-curse scribed here." He gestured to an elaborate calligraphic text written in Spanish a few hundred years before. "I have as yet to fully translate it as the language is quite old and formal, and it's imperative that I have the exact wording."

"Why can't I just say it in Spanish?" Adley asked.

The elderly man smiled. "You're a very smart girl. The book states that any counter-curse must be spoken in the native tongue of the intended victim." Adley and Victor's eyebrows shot up, and Pablo shrugged. "I didn't make the rules."

Pablo tapped on the lovely hand-lettered words. "What is described here is a simple process. You need only to recite the counter-curse while looking into the eyes of the demonic being. However, it is a dangerous thing to do and requires a great amount of courage on your part."

"If it k—killed me," she stuttered, "before I say the counter-curse, will it end? I'm an only child. I know my parents didn't have any other children after me, and I don't think they're planning to have any more. So will people stop getting killed if I'm d—dead?"

Pablo shook his head. "After careful translation, the answer is no. It says that if an only child dies, it will kill the rest of the family before the curse is over."

Adley brushed her hair back with her palm and huffed, frustrated. "So I say the counter-curse, and then it will be destroyed?" Adley asked him.

"According to this," Great-Uncle Pablo explained, "the curse, not the monster, will be destroyed. What I've read says that after you do your part, you and all of your descendants will be safe. However, that thing has grown too powerful and has a life of its own. If it gets much stronger, neither age nor the ancestry of the victims will make any difference. It will be able to kill aimlessly, any time or any place. And if this happens, from then on, no one will be safe."

Adley ran a surveillance of the room, as if the next victim would step forward. Pablo again referred to the large volume and tipped the delicate sheaves of paper to another marker. A drawing displayed a prone man, his arm extended at full length, actually touching a long, curved tooth of a canine skeleton. A snake-like tongue protruded from its mouth, elongated, and wrapped like a noose around the man's neck.

"Now that it has grown so powerful, the only way to destroy it completely is by touching a bone of the monster." A simultaneous gasp filled the room, and the adults gazed upon the children, who in turn stared at each other.

"What if none of us can touch it?" Adley said, her voice raspy.

The gray-haired man leaned forward. He stared at Victor for a moment and then at Adley. His midnight blue eyes penetrated Adley, and she felt her bravado wilt like warm lettuce.

Great-Uncle Pablo examined all the faces waiting expectantly for his answer. "Then we'll all die."

☣ ☣ ☣

Adley studied her surroundings in the Trumillo house, wanting to learn more about Victor before their short existence together might possibly come to an end. The dining room table was situated off the kitchen between the living area and a utility room housing the washer, dryer, portable sink, closet, cupboards, and a back door leading out to a tidy patio and well-kept yard. The decor made their home look like a museum, a display of holy relics, tribal gourds and drums, and other handmade third world art.

Tension stifled the energy in the room. Maria turned an overhead fan on, and the air helped everyone breathe a little easier. Great-Uncle Pablo discussed his translations of the gypsy book that had been crossed off the original manifest records when Hernando Rodrigues fled Spain.

"From what is written," he explained, looking down at the open book, "it is my understanding that this thing thrives off the act of killing as well as absorbing the energy of fear from its victims.

"Once Adley says the counter-curse, she and all of the Lange's descendants thereafter are freed from the curse. However—" Pablo zeroed in on a drawing on the facing page of a black whirlwind that tore across the scene, host to a horrifying bony image proportionately larger than the humans running from it. "As I said, its deadly force has grown immensely and although the curse will be lifted, the entity will still be alive and will kill without discretion. The only way to destroy the monster is by getting close enough to touch it without being killed first."

Gloria wrung her hands. "*Madre de Diós!*" Maria and Gloria both made the sign of the cross over their face and torsos.

"How can I touch it without getting killed?" Adley asked, puzzled.

"I didn't say you were the one to touch it," Pablo patted her hand, and that small touch seemed to calm her down. "No. Your job is simply to recite the counter-curse. Remember, the writings say that a bone must be touched by the youngest Del Diego descendant. It is Victor who is in harm's way from then on."

Adley's quick intake of breath drew Victor's attention, and his muscled arm sprawled across her shoulders.

"He is the only one who can kill it," Pablo continued. "And hopefully he can do so before it kills him."

Maria's hand flew to her mouth.

"*Viejo*, Victor is so young!" Gloria protested.

"He's the only one who can touch it?" Maria asked. She had already lost her husband to the gypsy's despicable wrongdoing.

"It will continue killing if it is not stopped," Pablo said in his soothing voice.

Victor spoke up. "I'm strong and fast. I can do it, Mama," he assured the woman.

"It's not that you can't do it, Victor. It's just too dangerous," Adley said.

Victor looked proud to play such a valiant role in protecting Adley and hitched up his jeans, straightening up and appearing a bit chivalrous. "No more dangerous for me than you staring it in the face and talking to it."

Great-Uncle Pablo ruined the manly exhibition by asking, "Victor, are you prepared for a face-to-face battle with the prospect of dying?"

Reminded of the great danger involved, Victor sank into his chair and spoke more humbly. "I'll do whatever I can to get rid of that demon." He zeroed his eyes in on Adley seated next to him. "Anything to help Adley."

She winced and asked Victor's great-uncle, "Since this is such an evil thing and all, why can't we just call a priest or some holy guy to help us?"

"It's true that man created this, and man must end this," the elderly man said. "But it was a Del Diego who caused the curse to reverse itself in the very beginning, and a Del Diego must end it. That is the way of gypsy curses."

"It's just not safe," Adley argued. "I mean, I'm willing to do what is right, but I want to spare Victor from possible harm."

Victor looked at her. "I have to do this, Adley, with or without anyone's approval." He took her hand. "Neither of us has a choice." He kept hold of Adley's hand and glanced at his mother. "We have no other option. Someone has to take responsibility and try to stop it from killing."

Maria sobbed into Gloria's shoulder, and the elderly woman patted her niece's back.

Great-Uncle Pablo continued. "All the fear and negativity that has fueled it since its creation two centuries ago has served to transform it into a life form. It is here for one reason and will not stop until it accomplishes its task."

"And that is to kill me," Adley stated matter-of-factly. She didn't even flinch at the possibility of her life ending. The nightmare had extended itself to where she just wanted to get it over with.

"Yes," the old man answered, "and until then, all it will seek is power."

"So I have to face it if I want to stop the curse, and Victor has to face it if we want to stop the killing," she said, her voice grim.

Great-Uncle Pablo nodded his head. "Yes. You must decide if you want to put your life in jeopardy to end the curse, Adley. According to the manuscript," He tapped a page of text in the book. "—after it kills your family, it will restart the curse with your next closest kin."

"I wonder if I should try telling my parents one more time about this entire nightmare," Adley said.

"If they believed you, maybe they'll deny letting you do what is necessary to put an end to the curse," Victor said.

Maria added her own concern. "If you don't tell them what you're about to do, they might hold this family responsible for placing you in danger, or worse, causing your death."

"It's a terrible choice," Great-Uncle Pablo said. "But it's necessary for you to face your greatest challenge, and it seems you may have to do so without your parents' knowledge."

"I've never been asked to make such a grown-up decision before," Adley said. "My parents can't make it for me, not when they don't even believe in the curse, and I don't blame them. It sounds crazy. But I've never been responsible for the safety of others, especially with awful consequences to myself and everyone else if I fail."

"I'm certain that Victor feels the same, being asked to potentially sacrifice his life along with yours," Maria said. "It's a tragedy to ask this of either of you when you just started to get to know each other better and have come to care for each other in a short amount of time."

Victor settled his eyes onto Adley again. "I don't mind admitting that I'm starting to have strong feelings for Adley, but I'm more overcome by the heartache I sense she's suffering than having to put my own self at risk."

Adley smiled, touched by his declaration in front of his family.

"We're here for you, Adley. You won't be alone if you choose not to tell your parents about what's going on. This is your decision alone," Great-Uncle Pablo said.

"I don't think it feels awkward for Adley to count on our support," Victor said. "She trusts us."

"Perhaps you should let Adley speak for herself, *mijo*," Great-Aunt Gloria said.

"Victor knows exactly how I feel," Adley said.

She squeezed his hand, and he tenderly pressed his fingers into her palm.

"I have no doubt that Adley's willing to sacrifice her safety for me, and she knows I wouldn't let her suffer," Victor said, staring into her eyes.

"I'm not surprised that you know what I'm thinking and feeling," Adley said, forgetting that there were other people in the room. It was a first for her to feel this way about anyone. Victor's family, total strangers, were willing to help and that gave her an immense feeling of relief, satisfaction, and a feeling of being accepted like no other.

"I guess I have to do this," she said to everyone at the table.

"We are all in terrible danger if we allow this monster to live," Pablo informed them. "Thankfully, we have it imprisoned in one room, but ultimately the hematite handle will be unable to absorb all of the evil. That time is close at hand."

Fierce determination radiated from Adley. "Well then, tell me what to do."

Chapter 25

First off, it is very important not to be afraid, so you will not give it any more power than it already has," Pablo advised. He looked at Victor, then Adley. "Both of you must contain your fear."

"Honestly, I think I already blew that requirement," she said.

"This is how it was able to hurt your grandma. She heard and saw many strange things but was too afraid to ask for help. She waited far too long to acknowledge its presence, and when she was forced to act, it was too late. She had already been injured."

"I don't understand," Adley said. "Why didn't she tell us?"

Pablo smiled wryly. "You attempted to tell your parents when a skeletal hand tried to drag you under your bed, and did they believe you?"

"No," she replied, looking down to her hands. "They said I was hallucinating." Victor grunted as if disgusted at the harm her parents' doubt had caused. "What happened inside of Grandma Aggie's before the hematite handle was installed on the bedroom door? Where did it hide?" she asked the old man.

"I'm not sure. Maria said that after Aggie fell down the

stairs, whenever she cleaned, she felt a horrible presence throughout the entire house."

Maria quickly bobbed her head, tiny movements that hinted at frayed nerves.

"I think it was waiting," Great Uncle Pablo said. "Waiting, living off the fear it created, as the time grew closer to your birthday."

"And only Victor can destroy it?" Adley asked, just double-checking. Pablo nodded once. "That means that Victor and I have to remain together so that once I say the counter-curse, he can touch it?" she guessed.

"Yes. The only way it will get near a Del Diego is if you are there," Pablo explained.

She frowned. "But I'm confused. One thing I don't understand is that if Victor is to touch it, how can he keep from getting hurt in the process?"

Pablo smiled kindly. "I'm glad that you are more interested in saving my great-nephew's life than your own predicament."

Victor smiled proudly and gave Adley's shoulder a quick squeeze.

"Your question has been asked many times." Pablo tilted the manuscript so Adley could get a better look at the grisly images. "It lashes out with fingers like knives and a tongue like a rope made of bone that usually wraps around a person's neck or ankle."

"My husband was bitten by what the coroner said was a dog," Maria said. "I think the creature slid its tongue around Greystoke's hoof which caused the horse to rear. We noticed strange cuts on its hoof when Pablo put him in the stable."

The two women fisted their hands and rapped lightly over their hearts, lamenting the death of Maria's husband.

Great-Uncle Pablo was a patient man and easily waited through the interruptions before he spoke again. "The answer to your question, Adley, is that Victor has to avoid a fatal cut by the talons or being strangled or flailed by the tongue that is used as a whip. He can touch any other part of its body and cause its demise."

Victor jumped from his seat and raised his arms with balled fists like a winning prize fighter. In a low-pitched baritone, he proclaimed, "I have the power!"

Adley giggled, and Pablo rolled his eyes. He stared sternly at Victor and then her. Victor frowned after the admonishment and sat back down.

"We must devise a plan," his great-uncle said. The teenagers leaned forward. "Adley, you must return to your grandmother's home and find a way to get your parents off the property as soon as possible."

"Maybe I can call and ask them to—" Maria offered.

"No!" Victor and Adley shouted simultaneously, startling the woman.

Pablo caught the apologetic look Adley snuck at his great-nephew.

"Adley's parents have forbidden her to associate with us. They don't know that Adley and I are friends," Victor said.

The old man nodded slightly and considered what Victor said. "Still, you must find a reason to get them out of the house."

"I could tell them I want to go out for my birthday," Adley suggested.

Victor refreshed her memory. "You can't leave. You have to be with me."

"Duh," Adley said. "I forgot."

"More like you wished," Victor said, grinning.

The cough from his uncle ended the bantering. "At

least you can laugh about it." The young couple smiled. "For now," he added, and their smiles faded.

"I'll prepare with sacred rituals. I must make a box—" Great-Uncle Pablo was slightly distracted for the merest fraction of a second but a moment later he spoke to Victor. "Take one of the horses and ride back to the mansion with Adley."

Pablo faced Adley. Her expression finally belied the fear beneath the surface, and her confidence developed a very large crack. Victor's great-uncle well understood her not wanting to go near Capilla Manor. "I want you to return home now. You should be safe while the hematite handle is in place. You must stay out of the room at all costs."

"Believe me, that's not a problem," she confidently assured him.

"That gives us a few hours. Call as soon as you find a way to get your parents out of the house, and we will rush over."

"Can't I stay with Adley?" Victor pleaded. "I don't care if her parents get mad at me for being in their house."

"I need to help you prepare for a face-to-face confrontation with that monster. We haven't much time. Neither of you do."

Adley looked from Victor to his uncle. "But what if—

Pablo's arthritic hands waved her off. "Do not concern yourself with any more details. We're running out of time."

"Thank you for helping me, Mr. Cordoba."

He smiled at her and nodded his head.

Victor and Great-Uncle Pablo escorted Adley outside. Pablo whistled, and Greystoke lifted his head. He clopped after the entourage and into the stable. Victor deftly bridled a beautiful palomino he called Miranda.

The old man walked out of a room grappling a worn but beautifully carved saddle and expertly slid it onto the back of the impressive mare. As his great-uncle finished cinching the girth, Victor walked Miranda to a block with two steps. He asked Adley to climb to the top and slide onto the saddled horse, an easy task with the portable stairs.

Victor took his seat behind her without benefit of the mounting block. One hand held onto the reins and his other arm curved around Adley's waist.

"Call as soon as they leave," Pablo unnecessarily reminded the girl. "It is urgent that we act as soon as possible!"

Victor tapped the flanks of the horse, and it trotted away from the barn. Maria and Gloria waved from the service door as the boy and girl set off through the woods.

A lone tear dripped down Maria's face. She was sorry that Adley had to go back to the old mansion, but more worry was directed toward her son. After losing her husband, she didn't think she could stand to lose Victor in the battle against the ancient curse.

☣ ☣ ☣

Adley's confidence eroded bit by bit the farther they rode away from the Trumillo Ranch. Talking and sharing with Victor didn't last long enough. They reached the clearing where Victor met her the first time on the trail. She didn't want to be without his company. If she couldn't convince her parents to leave, she'd have to survive the terrors of the evening all by herself.

The horse was well hidden from view behind the overgrown bushes and shrubs near the big pine tree. Victor dismounted and held his arms up to Adley. She slid easily into his tender embrace, and he helped her find her footing.

As soon as she was balanced on the ground, Victor said his temporary goodbye. "I know you don't like me to tell

you not to worry, Adley, so I'll just say that I'll do all I can
to help you end this terrible curse."

She smiled at him, having no eloquent way to thank
him for his bravery.

Victor stood very close to her and suddenly swept her
into his arms. "It feels like a knot has grown in my stomach," he whispered into her ear. "And I've got these, like,
strong feelings inside. Stuff I've never felt before and only
feel when you're with me. And it's stronger when you're in
my arms."

"Victor," Adley whispered.

He kissed her, a brief but meaningful touch of their lips
"I'll be waiting for your call," he whispered.

Strands of her brunette hair fell through his fingers and
then Victor placed another light kiss on her lips.

Adley's belligerent personality usually incited the boys
at her school to tug hard on her hair or give her a rough
shove into a locker. She never imagined that she could reel
just at the thought of a wonderful and tender kiss from
someone like Victor. She absently touched her lips as she
watched him gracefully mount his horse and sit comfortably
in the saddle.

Victor smiled and dug his thighs into the well-trained
palomino. "Call me soon. C'mon, Miranda," he said to the
horse.

The mare reacted to the sturdy nudge against its sides
and immediately galloped back the way it came.

As she stood poised like a statue with her fingers
drawn to her face where the touch of his mouth lingered, a
small, dreamy sound heaved from her lungs. She marveled
at the little flutter in her chest, a foreign effect, joyfully
welcomed. After she collected her wits and reluctantly
reeled in her emotions, she forced herself to deal with the
problem at hand.

Adley walked along the path leading to Grandma Aggie's backyard, inventing excuses in her mind to get her parents out of the house. The impressive afternoon sunset gave her a bit of joy and shifted her thoughts to how she felt at the Trumillo ranch. It was a challenge to feel relaxed and optimistic these days, but it was a natural occurrence when she was with Victor and his family. Hopefully, the forthcoming confrontation would not be as bad as Pablo Martinez de Cordoba predicted.

Those hopes were instantly crushed when the back doors of the centuries-old manor suddenly burst open, and her parents stampeded outside. Their clothes were rumpled, their hair unkempt, and their eyes bulged. Caroline's cheeks were striped with tears.

"Deedee!" her father screamed. "Thank God!"

"What's wrong?" Adley called. She ran up to her father, meeting him and her mother half-way into the yard. They put Caroline between them and each grabbed an arm, rushing to the back of the yard where Adley had just left Victor. "What's going on?"

An explosion of crystal sounded within the walls of the Spanish mansion, followed by a terrible, high-pitched shriek that echoed throughout the air.

"Run!" Caroline yelled hysterically as the high pitched wailing streamed out the back door. "Run!" she cried again.

Somehow they must have discovered the chilling secret of her room and unleashed the other-worldly animal from its cell.

"Hurry!" she cried. "We need to move faster!"

Now wasn't the time to confess to a visit at the Trumillo's and she opted instead for silence. They'd find out soon enough where she planned to take them.

Adley dragged her mother past the big pine, and her father rushed behind, following the route into the wooded area and beyond into the small clearing of shrubs and brush. Then they all heard the French doors pound backward into the fixed windows on either side. The crash was a sure sign that they'd been demolished. Dry grass crunched loudly under heavy thudding footsteps, and a deafening howl echoed across the backyard. Roger and Caroline had been forced out of their home and they had no idea what was chasing them. But Adley did.

Caroline wept. "I can't believe this is happening! I can't believe it!"

Her husband took his wife's arm and ran, firmly pulling her along with him.

Adley heard the hammering footfalls of the invisible pursuer drawing closer. "We have to run faster!" she warned.

They stepped up the pace as Caroline ranted, "Oh, no! Oh, no!"

The path was a bit bumpy but generally level. As long as they kept their eyes forward and scanned the ground for occasional dips and large stones they made good progress.

Clinging to her mother's arm, Adley shouted above the uproar in as calm a manner as possible, "Dad, what happened?"

Roger threw a couple of suspicious glances at his daughter. Adley wasn't as upset or shocked by her mother's state of despair, and it looked as if he suspected that his daughter knew more than she let on.

"You already know, don't you?" he asked, panting from his rapid gait. Adley didn't answer, and he explained loudly over the uproar. "I was doing some work upstairs and your mom was in the kitchen. I heard someone breaking glass again, like when we came back from town the other day. Your mom heard it, too, and was calling out to me. I ran downstairs, and she was hysterical, crying about something tapping on her back. Then the lights went out—"

"Wait a minute!" Adley panted and slowed down a bit to catch her breath. She peeked quickly behind them and saw nothing amiss. She stopped and hunched over from the pain in her side and stared at her father. "You heard the breaking glass *downstairs*?"

A terrifying howl, like a tortured wolf, stabbed at their ears. Caroline moaned, her nerves shredded, and all their legs shifted into high gear again, moving forward at top speed.

"Yes! And then I ran to your mother." Her father raised his voice to compete with the ominous bedlam. They kept up the pace as he continued shouting. "We heard ear-piercing screeching and this scraping sound. I can't begin to try to describe it!"

"Like fingernails clawing on a chalkboard?" Adley called out. "Like metal scratching into a wooden floor?"

Her parents didn't stop fleeing for their lives, but both looked incredibly stunned that she accurately described the eerie noises. "How did you know?" her father demanded.

"I'll tell you, but first I need to know why the noise was coming from the first story. Was anyone in my room?"

Caroline choked out an unintelligible word, as if startled that Adley had divined the information.

Her father explained what happened. "We thought we'd surprise you and get rid of that old silver handle on your door—"

"No! You took the handle off the door?" she cried in disbelief.

"I put a new one on. For goodness sakes, this isn't the time to be worried about a piece of hardware!" he admonished her.

"Dad, you don't understand! That handle was made out

of a special stone called hematite. It acted as a lid to contain that thing in my room!"

Her mother gaped wildly about the area. "What thing, Adley? What attacked me?"

Before Adley answered, a malicious growl resounded throughout the forested hills behind them. Caroline skidded to a halt. Her heels dug into the ground, rooting them firmly into the soil. Physically immobilized, she insanely ranted. "We're going to die, aren't we, Roger? Adley tried to tell us! She kept trying to tell us, but we wouldn't listen to her!"

Once again, he took Caroline's arm, and Adley held the other. "Let's not psychoanalyze now!"

Father and daughter hauled Caroline as fast as they were able to run, severely encumbered by her lithe but muscular body supported between them.

Squawks of fiendish laughter pursued the trio at a frightening pace.

"Where's the handle, Dad?" Adley yelled above the wicked cacophony as they fled forward.

"It's at the pawn shop in town. I took it over when I went to get a brass plate and screws. Then I came home, started working on the door again and that's when your mother—"

"—the pawn shop?" Adley didn't believe what she was hearing. "Why did you take it there?"

Her father screamed above the unnatural squalling, "When I was in town last I told Anne Marie that I was going to get rid of it and asked if it was worth anything—for gosh sakes, Adley! A supernatural being is chasing us! Who cares about the damn handle?"

It was the first time she heard her father swear, but it wasn't a good time to remind him of his manners.

"It could be the only way to save us!" she yelled above the chaos. "Is the store open?"

"How do I know?" her father blared.

The firm thud of footsteps on the hard-packed earth sounded like the gallop of a very large dog puffing hungrily behind them. Caroline moaned, almost as inhumanly as the monster that stalked them.

Adley looked over her shoulder and skimmed the wooded area, but couldn't see more than a blackened mist a short distance away.

"What is it?" Her mother slowed them down and struggled to see what was behind them, but her husband and daughter dragged her onward. "I don't know—if I can— keep going," Caroline wheezed.

She wasn't the only one. Adley felt the pressure building up in her sides again, as if a spear poked under her ribs with every step. Her throat was dry and her heart thumped as fast as her rapid intakes of breath.

"How much farther?" Roger called out.

Adley pointed. "We're almost at the Trumillos'." Her father glared suspiciously at her. She confidently added, "We'll be safe in their house!"

The family felt like they had been racing for miles instead of the single one that led to their neighbor's ranch. Their surge of adrenaline kept them barely ahead of the rapidly gaining canine imposter.

"How can we be safe there?" he called over the noise. "You said the only way to keep it away was with the handle!"

"I know," she said as they scrambled toward the Trumillo house. "We'll be safe with them, too. I'll explain later. Let's get out of here!"

A raucous snarling resonated through the trees, like a rabid dog ready to slaughter its prey.

"That's where we need to go!" Adley sprinted ahead to the dirt path.

"Thank goodness!" Caroline moaned. They found a spurt of new energy and tore down the passage that led to Victor's backyard. Out of nowhere, a long skeletal arm shot out from the bottom of a shrub and dug into Caroline's ankle. She yelled, falling face first into the dirt with her foot ensnared by the bony tendon. "Roger!" she cried.

Her body slid backward and she raked the ground, carving grooves into the dirt. Roger gasped at the sight of the disfigured structure, an alien hand attached to his wife's foot. He had never seen anything like it.

Caroline screeched in pain, clawing the ground, as Roger gaped open-mouthed at the unbelievable creature that dragged his wife back into the darkened woods. Adley took immediate action. She grabbed her mother's hands and held fast, leaning her body back to counter the pull of the solid skeletal grasp.

"Dad!" Adley shouted.

Her father snapped back to attention and yanked on Caroline's other arm when an earsplitting siren, louder than Caroline's screaming, shuddered through each one of them.

"Stomp on it!" Adley yelled at her father.

Roger shook off his fright and let go of his wife's arm, which made Caroline cry louder.

"Roger! Don't let go! Please don't leave me!"

Her husband leaped on top of the ivory rope. His full weight smashed onto the bones and a "hissssssss!" flew from the bushes as the arm swept away like a retractable cord on a vacuum cleaner. Scattered pebbles of bone scrambled after it.

"Quick, Dad! Get Mom up before it comes back!" Her father did as he was ordered, helping Caroline to her feet. When her mother was standing, Adley urged, "Mom, run!"

"C'mon, baby," Roger said to his horror-stricken wife. "You can do it!"

Caroline regained her stride, and the family bolted through the yard as the menacing predator continued the chase behind them.

"Faster, Deedee!" her father yelled.

They ran right up to the back door of the Trumillo home. Roger was the first to barge unannounced through the back door, hauling his limping wife and exhausted daughter behind him.

Chapter 26

Before their unexpected guests arrived, Pablo and Victor were engaged in a serious discussion at the kitchen table. The older man was showing his great-nephew where to touch the ghoulish creation. The gypsy's manuscript specifically stated to avoid the mouth with the snake-like tongue that could easily strangle him or knock him to the ground.

They heard a loud threatening growl.

"One of the dogs must be out back," Victor said as he rose from the table.

Pablo pulled the boy back into his chair. "We don't have a spare second to pay any mind to the dogs. You know they'll bark if there's a problem." He didn't know that the dogs were as consumed by fear as Adley's family, and Pablo continued coaching the boy. "When we're inside of Aggie's, don't let anything take you by surprise."

At that precise moment their back door flew open and in tumbled the Lange family. A cloud of doom filled the air, and Great-Uncle Pablo instinctively knew that the power of the sinister curse had been unleashed.

"No!" the old man choked.

Adley was the last one in and slammed the screen door shut. She leaned against a wall, breathing in deep pockets

of air as she scanned the hills. The last of the sunlight filtered through the dense brush to illuminate a spot near the
edge of the woods a short distance away. She saw what
looked like a tail made of bones slither back into the dark
shroud of the forest.

Victor's eyes went wide as Adley's family exploded
into the kitchen. The outburst brought Maria and Gloria
scuttling from their bedrooms.

"What happened?" questioned Pablo. He stared at the
profusely bleeding wound on Caroline's ankle.

Roger looked guiltily at his daughter who continued to
gulp for air. Victor guided the girl to the table, and she collapsed onto a chair, as did her parents. Adley was the first
to speak, huffing and puffing between her words. "My parents—got out of the house—all by themselves."

"I'll give you one guess what happened," Victor told
his great-uncle, his arms protectively about Adley. He
glared in disapproval at her parents.

The jarring ordeal left the Langes visibly distressed as
their emotions had been unhinged after their frantic scram-
ble through the woods. Roger's hair stuck out at the sides
and Caroline shivered as she tried to recoup her breath.
Even Adley teetered on the brink of shock.

Maria wrapped an afghan around Caroline's shoulders.
Victor's family politely waited for her to end her furious
protest of any medical attention, whether it was needed or
not. Caroline's exhaustion finally gave way, and she allowed Maria to bandage the lacerations.

Roger told Pablo about the event leading up to their
bursting through the back door. He carefully explained to
the elderly man exactly what had transpired since removing
the silver-colored handle as Gloria served valerian tea to
settle everyone's nerves.

Victor, still angry with Adley's parents for not believing their daughter when she tried to tell them of the night-mare in her room, stared openly at the injury on Caroline's foot. "Looks like carpet burn to me," he said.

He glowered at the woman and then shifted his eyes deliberately onto her husband.

Mrs. Trumillo stopped in the middle of wrapping gauze around the swollen ankle, gasping at Victor's unusual and deliberate rudeness. Before either she or Gloria chastised him, Pablo snapped, "Impertinence is not a kind quality to possess, Victor, especially when our help is so desperately needed. Right now there is strength in numbers." More gently he said, "Restrain your protective nature, *sobrino*." The Spanish word for nephew was an endearment Great-Uncle Pablo rarely used.

Victor hung his head and apologized, almost sincerely. "I'm sorry, Mrs. Lange."

"Perhaps you need a moment to cool off," his great-uncle said. Adley was close enough to hear Great-uncle Pablo whisper to Victor, "At least you have the comfort of knowing that the monster isn't likely to attack Adley while you're around."

Victor nodded, still so angry he could barely speak. He left the house and stomped out the front door breathing through his nose like a bull, kicking at stones around the driveway as he stayed close to the porch.

Adley stood up to follow Victor, but Pablo raised his hand, "Please, let him work it out."

She respected the man and, after all, he was more fa-miliar with the ways of his nephew than she was. Adley sat back down, hoping Victor was not the kind to hold a grudge. She asked Great-Uncle Pablo a question that had been on her mind.

"If that thing couldn't leave my room with the hematite door handle on, why could I see a dark shadow in the hallway right in front of my room? And I heard it call my name when I was downstairs in the maid's quarters, too."

"It can project an aura, which can't harm you, but not knowing that, it built up your fear. I read in the gypsy manual that it can throw its voice, too. That's when a spirit being can create sound and project it to another location."

"It did a great job of scaring me, that's for sure."

"All of us," Roger said.

Within a few minutes Victor entered the house, still upset, but his jaw was no longer clenched, and the intense glare in his eyes had lessened.

Roger spoke to him immediately. "Victor, you're right to be angry." He looked at the haggard appearance of his wife. "We didn't listen to Adley when she told us she was afraid to go into her room. It was too hard to believe that what she described was real."

Caroline visibly relaxed after sipping the hot tea, and the emotional fatigue kept her from speaking too loud. "Yes. We're so sorry, Adley, Victor," she added. "I'm glad it's over."

Although her husband had not been privy to the dialogue regarding the gypsy curse shared in the Trumillo home earlier that day, he knew that it was not over. They all did, except for Caroline, but she read the expressions on everyone's face who stood around her.

"Oh, no!" she whispered. "It's over, isn't it? That thing is gone!" Her voice rose in pitch and grew a bit louder. "It won't try to hurt us anymore. Right, Roger?" She started from her seat, but her husband gently pushed her back down.

Maria brought another cup of the herbal tea to soothe the woman's hysteria and stood like a sentry until it was half finished. She smiled and took the cup out of Caroline's hand and escorted Adley's disheveled mother to Maria's own bedroom. "*Tio*," she said, addressing her uncle, "give us a few minutes, then you can tell them everything."

☣ ☣ ☣

Maria had Caroline sit down on the bed and instructed her to drink more of the soothing natural remedy. Maria watched as Caroline sipped the tea and critically eyed the room. It had a fine touch of femininity, with lace doilies and pink dried flowers in a charming antique glass vase. Dainty fabric with vines and flower accents splashed across the white furniture. On the dressing table was a photo of Grandma Aggie standing happily between Maria and a very handsome man.

Maria noticed what had caught Caroline's attention. "My husband, Frank," she said.

"I remember the name from the letters. That thing killed him, didn't it?"

Maria picked up the picture of her husband and gazed at it a moment before setting it back down. "What chased you here is the same monster that spooked his horse. My husband died from his injuries. That's why it's so hard to let my son do what he must." A tear dripped down one cheek, and she brushed it away.

"What does this have to do with Victor?"

"My uncle will explain. For now, you must know that our children are the only ones who can stop this."

"But why? How? They're just children!" Caroline protested.

Maria was as patient as her uncle, and she saw that Adley's mother was too upset to accept the truth right then. Victor's mother gave a hint of a smile. "It seems my son cares greatly for your daughter. I think they're *novios espiritus*." Caroline shook her head, not understanding. "Some people call it soul mates," Maria explained. "They have connected and bonded in a way only those who knew each other in a previous life could."

"I'm not sure I believe in that, but regardless, what makes you think this?"

"Well, I've only seen them together a couple of times. It's Victor who tells me what their friendship is like. He says they know what the other is thinking and occasionally one finishes the other's sentences. My husband and I used to do that quite often."

"That's nothing," Caroline said. "Roger and I do that all the time."

"But you've been married nearly eighteen years."

At first, Caroline was taken aback by the fact that the woman knew how long she had been married, but of course, the former housekeeper had to know something of their family, being so close to Aggie.

"Victor and Adley haven't known each other for more than a few days," Maria continued. "Already they know what the other is feeling and thinking."

Caroline's shoulders slumped. "I might have seen that if we hadn't told Adley she wasn't allowed to associate with your son. I'm so sorry."

"No need to apologize, Mrs. Lange."

"Please. Call me Caroline."

Maria smiled. "And you must call me Maria."

Caroline remembered a comment from their previous conversation. "Are you going to tell me why you think Victor and Adley are the only ones who can get rid of this thing?"

Maria saw that Caroline's ranting was over. "I think it will be much better to let my uncle explain the details to you."

Caroline was somber. "I appreciate the difficulty in

permitting your son to be deliberately exposed to a life-threatening situation, especially since it was the same creature that led to the untimely passing of your husband."

"Victor is seventeen now, and he's not afraid to prove that he's a man. I won't take that away from him. His father died bravely, like a knight in shining armor. Well, he was on a horse, at least." Maria smiled weakly. "Victor is so like his father. Honorable, and such a gentleman. I trust that he will be protected as he does what is necessary to save your daughter and the rest of us. Most importantly, you must know this. If that thing isn't destroyed, it will go on killing for generations to come and become stronger with every life it takes. It's a very grown-up decision our children have made to confront it."

Caroline sat forward on the bed. "What do you mean—*have made*? Adley's too young to be involved in all of this!"

"If you saw the brave girl my son has told me about, you'd know how courageous and strong your own daughter is."

Caroline's shoulders sagged again. "I thought that as a parent, I'd have to argue Adley's choice of appropriate clothing to wear to school, or what boys to stay away from, like Victor before I realized that he was a good person. I just didn't ever expect a battle with monsters or that I'd have to support a group of ghost hunters that included my own daughter." She turned the teacup in her hand and shook her head. "I'm ashamed to say that I haven't allowed myself to see my daughter in a grown-up light either, at least not until now."

Maria took Caroline's hand and gave her another small smile. "Knowing when to loosen our hold on our children is something they teach us."

"But how could I miss seeing Adley become a young

woman of good character? You should have seen her. She was so brave and determined when that thing chased us in the woods." Caroline shuddered.

Maria appraised the woman. "I'm glad that you are ready to accept the reality that affects us all. If you can stay calm, I'm sure Uncle Pablo will be explaining everything to your husband right now. Come with me."

☣ ☣ ☣

The women returned to the dining area, which served as a central command post of sorts. Caroline appraised the close proximity between Victor and Adley. What Maria said was true. They looked like they belonged together.

Pablo had already made preparations to destroy the gruesome intruder. He had white candles and amber incense burning throughout the house. Well before the Langes burst through the back door, he'd sprinkled salt and sage around the perimeter of his property, keeping the monster at bay. "Ancient but worthy precautions," he'd told Maria and Gloria earlier. From a box, he extracted two good-sized pieces of raw hematite wrapped in leather, gave one to Adley, and one to Victor. "I'd rather be safe than sorry," he said to them.

"Hematite for—" Victor said.

"—protection from the skeleton." Adley finished his sentence.

Caroline easily recognized the undeniable bond Maria had described between the two teens. Two peas in a pod. Soul mates. Interesting.

"Every little bit helps," Great-Uncle Pablo said.

Roger had been patient but he finally spoke his mind. "I'd really appreciate knowing what's going on here."

Caroline stood next to her husband, and he pulled her

close to his side. An insane howl echoed in the hills behind the house, and a collective shiver ran through the group.

Pablo waved Adley's parents to the table. The Langes sat down, and Maria set another cup of tea in front of each of them. In that instant, almost in unison, when Roger draped his arm around his wife, Victor slipped his arm protectively around Adley's shoulders.

Great-Uncle Pablo relayed the story of the gypsy curse.

"After the recent expulsion from my mother's home by that indescribable being, I believe everything you have to say," Roger acknowledged. "And I can accept the fact that I had a brother who died in infancy. But why didn't my mother ever tell me? Why try to protect me from something that wasn't a tormenting memory for me?"

It was Maria who answered Roger's questions. "Because it was so heartbreaking for her. A mother doesn't share unnecessary burdens with her children." She patted her heart. "Aggie simply filed her memory of the infant away."

"All the years I kept away from her, justifying it by saying I was busy working, thinking an occasional phone call was enough," Roger lamented.

"Your mother deliberately tried to make you feel guilty about not coming to live in Capilla Manor or near Hachita," Maria told him. "She knew you'd rebel because she and Augustus were so rigid in their ways. Once she found out about the curse, the idea was to keep you away, and she was able to do exactly that until she died."

"The past is done and cannot be changed," Pablo advised. "Your job now is to help save your family."

Roger signaled his understanding with a slight nod. "So where is this thing now?"

Pablo looked toward the back yard. "Probably in the woods, waiting for a chance to get close to Adley."

"Breathe," Victor whispered to Adley, whose eyes had widened.

"It may be best to lure the creature back to Capilla Manor," Pablo said. "This way, it can be contained within the building, whereas in the forest it has a better chance of staying hidden, away from anything that can destroy it."

"And how exactly are we going to do get it to go back?" Roger asked.

"With bait," Adley supplied.

Roger looked at Great-Uncle Pablo with questions in his eyes. The old man, in turn, slid the heavy brown parcel to Roger—the book that had been hidden in his daughter's room.

As if he were reading braille, Roger ran the pads of his fingers along the embossed jacket. "Las Palabras," he read with an impeccable Spanish accent. Both Adley and her mother raised a brow at the same time. "What does that mean?"

"The Words," Pablo answered. "This is a book of gypsy lore, the only documented writings of authentic gypsy life, including healing remedies, rituals, and curses that account for what you saw earlier. It describes not only the way to end the curse, but how to destroy the energy, now that it has become so powerful," he said, sliding a dilapidated calfskin knapsack over to Roger.

"What's that?" Roger asked.

"Tools that may help us stay alive," Pablo answered.

"Do you have weapons in there? We need to take stock of how many guns, ammo, knives, and—"

Great-Uncle Pablo waved his hand, knowing Roger was too agitated to pay heed to the gypsy guidelines. "Those are useless against the kind of evil we are fighting. As I just told you, generations before you fought foolishly with a variety of weapons, and none lived to see victory."

"Then how are we going to kill it?"

Caroline appeared baffled as her husband. "If guns and knives aren't going to destroy it, what are we going to use?"

Pablo gave one short bob of his head toward his great-nephew, and Victor stood and raised the backs of his hands for all to see the sole weapon that could defeat the curse.

Adley was shaken, hit yet again with the impact of what Victor was willing to sacrifice for others. For her. She objected to his involvement yet again. "Victor—"

He bowed dramatically and his silly gesture had the desired effect. Adley giggled, however nervously, at the gallant boy.

"I don't understand," Roger stated.

Patient as always, Great-Uncle Pablo explained. "We must do two things. The first is to terminate the curse with a counter-curse." He lifted the cover and pulled it open to a purple-ribboned marker. "Adley will say these words, 'I now remove this untrue curse and its hold on me altogether. It is dissolved into a state of nothingness now and forever.' This will render all future Lange descendants safe."

"If these words end the curse, why didn't anyone else say them before?" Adley asked.

"Yeah," Victor agreed. "All those other kids died, even with the book."

Pablo answered. "Remember—the counter-curse was hidden in the back of the book."

"Oh, yeah," Victor and Adley said at the same time.

"I don't know how many went without having access to the counter-curse. Maybe no one since it was leveled on Hernando Rodrigues. Also, from what I've read, they were either caught by surprise or so afraid as to render themselves incapable of speaking and might have been unable to say the counter-curse aloud or in time."

Pablo looked about the room and measured the fear. No one escaped it. "I guess it's hard to recite two lines of a poem when looking into the eyes of death," he said.

Chapter 27

Caroline and Roger held hands, their fingers intertwined and fidgeting. "So once Adley says the counter-curse, this monster can't touch her?" Caroline asked.

The old man's head shook from side to side. "It can't kill her, but it may still cause bodily harm." He pulled up a green ribbon marker and carefully leafed through the parchment pages of the historical gypsy writings. "To destroy the creature entirely, the youngest Del Diego descendant must touch its bones," Pablo explained to Roger and Caroline. His finger indicated a sketchy image of a scared child trying to touch the leg of a severely deformed skeleton.

"This is the only known way to destroy it." He aimed a sad look at Victor, the youngest Trumillo of the line, then he looked at Adley. "But that can only happen after the curse has been successfully removed."

Roger brushed his fingers through his hair and clarified. "So we have to get the kids safely near it, make sure they stay together, and once Adley does her part, Victor can do his."

"According to this, yes. We must go now, before that cursed spirit strays permanently." He drew a small index card from his shirt pocket and handed it to Adley. "I wrote the counter-curse down for you. Don't lose it." Adley took hold of the card and read it a few times before tucking it into her pants pocket.

"Does this thing know that Victor can destroy it?" Roger asked.

"Yes," Pablo answered.

"At the mansion, the way to get it near me is to lure it out," Victor explained.

"I'm the bait," Adley boldly stated. "I'm the one it wants. For now, that is."

"I see." Her father pressed his lips together and looked at his wife. "I'm not sure we can let her do this."

"Adley is right, Mr. Lange," Pablo said.

"Please call me Roger."

"Our opportunity to destroy it is when we can predict where it will strike next, Roger," the weathered man said with great authority. "This wretched creature is too power-ful to die, even when the curse is ended. People everywhere will be in danger because this beast will be free to roam and destroy lives at will unless it is stopped. We can predict where it will be because it can't resist fulfilling its purpose. It wants Adley next."

Roger looked at his daughter, his eyes brimming with love. "I just don't know—"

"He's right, dear." Caroline said.

Adley and Victor each drew an equally surprised look from the other at Caroline's acquiescence. She touched her husband's arm.

"Adley has to do this," Caroline continued. "She's not a little girl anymore." It was as if the sorrow that filled her heart radiated outward and touched everyone in the room, especially Adley.

Roger appraised his daughter. "I guess I still think of

you as too young and easily scared, but you've already survived a few encounters unlike anything any of us have ever
been exposed to. I realize you've been brave enough to
fight for your life when your mom and I weren't there for
you. And you knew what the possibilities were each time
you faced the creature at the height of its power." Roger
rubbed the back of his neck before speaking again. "All
right, Adley. You can do this, but you do exactly as you're
told."

"I will, Dad," she assured him.

"And you!" He pointed to Victor who sat up straighter
in his chair. Roger's index finger bounced up and down as
he lectured the boy. "You take care of my daughter. She's
depending on you!"

Victor hugged Adley tighter. "I will, sir."

"Thank you, Victor," Roger said, stealing a glimpse at
his wife. "We both appreciate it." Next, he addressed the
elderly man. "What now?"

Great-Uncle Pablo took in all the faces at the table.
"We try to stay alive. Be courageous and stay physically
together," he told the two teenagers. "That thing is less likely to harm a Rodrigues descendant with the youngest Trumillo present."

"But if Adley can't say the curse quickly enough, it can
kill her and then it won't do any good for me to touch it,"
Victor said.

Pablo gently placed his hand on Victor's arm. "It's a
lot easier to recite a poem than to touch the devil." He held
up an index finger and spoke to the group. "It will do what
it can to get us all separated. That makes things very dangerous for each of us." He then explained to Roger, "It can
take several shapes and hurt you with its jaw and tongue.
One of the families recorded that when it is extremely powerful, the tongue can be used like a whip so be careful to

watch what comes out of its mouth. That's what grabbed your wife's ankle." Caroline rubbed her leg. "You and I must keep it away from your daughter until she says the counter-curse. Then, Victor, you must touch it on any bone before it finds a way to harm either you or Adley."

Victor nodded. "I understand."

"I can't help settling this question once and for all," Roger said. "So once Victor touches it, it's destroyed forever?"

"The book says it will be. However, it has gained great power during the course of the last century from killing so many victims. If I am to be honest, then my answer is—I'm not sure." Great-Uncle Pablo turned to Victor. "If you can't touch it, throw the hematite at it. That may at least stop it for a while."

No one spoke. There were no questions left, no reason to stall.

"We must go now," Pablo said. He fiercely hugged Gloria, his wife of fifty-seven years, knowing that it was an unfortunate reality that none of them might make it back alive. He ran his knobby hand down her cheek, brushing a tear off her face.

Maria hugged her son and kissed his forehead, whispering a prayer for his safety. She embraced her uncle and shook hands with Roger. "May you be blessed with the light of angels."

Roger thanked her and then looked upon his wife. Caroline wept silently. He kissed her lightly. "I love you, Caroline."

They embraced and he kissed her on the forehead then studied every detail of her face, in case he never saw her again, then he kissed her more passionately on the mouth.

Adley tried to be more optimistic. She hugged her mom. "We'll be back in time for dinner."

Caroline winced. "Next time you tell me there's a ghoul under your bed, I promise I'll believe you." She hugged her daughter and kissed her cheek. "I love you, Adley."

Maria took Adley into her arms and gave her a kindhearted hug. "Remember, you are a strong young lady. You can do anything. Even this." She left a tiny kiss on Adley's forehead and then joined the other women, all of whom were dignified as they stifled their sobs and dabbed at their tears, wearing glum expressions.

Victor and his great-uncle, Adley and her father waved goodbyes as they proceeded out the door. They piled onto the bench seat of the Trumillos' old truck. Pablo started up the vehicle and the engine roared like an agitated lion. He pulled onto the main road, and their bodies jumped occasionally when the tires hit a pothole or fresh road kill.

Victor, whose hand was entwined with Adley's, sat next to the elderly man. Roger rested his arm on the door. Absorbed by the desert view and the colorful fiery sky left in the wake of the sunset, it seemed everyone considered the irony of the contrasting terror they had yet to face.

The truck rumbled onward to its destination, communication nearly impossible above the thunderous engine. Still, the elderly man issued another repetitive warning, shouting into the windy torrent from the open windows. "Remember to stay together!"

"You've told us that a thousand times," Victor said impatiently to his uncle.

"It's easy to forget the minor details when you're scared beyond reason," his great-uncle replied and made certain that Roger was able to hear him.

Adley pulled the index card from her jeans and said into Victor's ear, "I'm going to read this card the second I see that creature." She started to memorize the words.

"And right after that, I'm going to touch the first bone I see and get my part over with," Victor said confidently but, nonetheless, felt for the hematite stone in the zippered pocket of his cargo pants.

Adley held the card in one hand and viewed the other in her lap. She must have been in a fog, unaware that she had been holding Victor's hand so tight. The skin at the tips of his fingers turned crimson, lacking any circulation. Her grip relaxed, but she didn't let go, and Victor squeezed her hand gently. He heaved an exaggerated sign of relief, and she smiled tenderly at him, grateful for his comfort and support.

The truck neared its undesirable destination and the passengers saw one light shining in the entire building. A thick, sallow mist lit up Adley's room. They gawked at the sheer fabric hanging in the windows as a shadow crossed behind one, then the next.

A grossly enlarged head, hunched spine, and a protruding snout lurched to and fro, skulking behind the translucent screen, a horrifying performance before a terrified audience. Adley trembled. Any bravery she had early on remained at the Trumillo Ranch. She wanted more than ever to be far, far away.

They climbed out of the truck, one reluctant foot hitting the driveway and then another, until the passengers formed a human chain in front of the mansion. Adley clutched Victor's hand, and he seized his great-uncle's arm, who in turn gripped Roger's shoulder. They stared wide-eyed at the heart of evil before them, hypnotized by the oddity.

Pablo broke the alarming trance. "We must not fear it!" he said harshly to the others in reproach. "We must be courageous."

The shadowed creature spun quickly toward the window, as if it heard Great-Uncle Pablo admonish the others. It howled, lifting its pointed chin upward. The monster dissolved into the night, and the light disappeared with the creature.

Pablo removed four flashlights from his tool bag and passed them out.

"What's this?" Roger asked, stunned. "This is what we're supposed to defend ourselves with?"

"They have new batteries," the old man said.

"You're sure we can't try to blow it apart with a shotgun or dynamite?"

"There is only one way to fight it, and neither one of us can defeat it." Pablo lectured Roger with patient authority amidst the inhuman wailing emanating from the mansion. "Even if we blew it up, I read in the gypsy manuscript that it has the ability to reconstruct itself. It's entirely up to Victor and Adley to rid us of this unearthly creation. They themselves are the tools with which to fight."

"What exactly does that mean—it can reconstruct itself?" Victor asked.

"I'm not sure," Pablo replied. "But I think we're about to find out."

Adley pictured her father stepping on the bones in the forest and the way they broke into little pebbles. She recalled seeing the broken pieces roll across her bedroom floor and the one time they tumbled inside her headboard. That was how it reconstructed itself, drawing together all its broken pieces and reforming into a different looking creature. Victor pulled on her hand and yanked her out of her thoughts, then they followed the others toward the residence.

Armed with the flashlights, all four nervously converged on the front doors, taken aback by a formidable bellowing that suddenly pierced the silence.

They temporarily lost their nerve and came to an abrupt halt. Mouths dropped open, yet no one uttered a sound. After the momentary lapse it was Victor who found an encouraging remark.

"We can do this." He swallowed hard as the shivering group proceeded forward.

Pablo twisted the knob and prodded the door open with his boot. The wooden barrier creaked slowly open. In the blink of an eye, a blast of icy air assaulted them, and their ears rang with a clamor of crashing glass echoing throughout the first floor. Screeching and hissing greeted them with the loud tapping of fingernails. They froze at the sound of thunderous bedlam until it died down a long minute later.

Adley pointed to the large room to the right of the foyer. "Sounds like it c—came from the liv—living room!"

Finally Roger ventured past the old man and turned the switch to the foyer lights. They didn't come on. He glanced at Pablo who shrugged, and four flashlights instantly sprayed white light onto the walls and floors. But they saw nothing in the entryway and stairwell. The entire mansion was dead silent.

Adley clutched the wrinkled card—their salvation—and the flashlight in one hand and gripped Victor's with the other. The two shuffled closely behind the men. The group cautiously left the main hall and entered the spacious living room to the right.

Victor shook his flashlight as the beam faded. "My light's going out."

Adley panicked. "Mine, too!"

All at once, every flashlight beam dimmed to nothing. Instinctively, they huddled closer together.

"I thought you said they had new batteries!" Adley whined to Great-Uncle Pablo.

Before the man could respond, the flashlights were

ripped from their hands by a furious, invisible force. Each one slammed against the walls, leaving a pile of smashed plastic and glass rubble on the floor. A deafening cackle flooded the room. Adley's legs weakened, and she unintentionally broke contact with Victor, leaning against her father for support. Victor rubbed his hands along his arms, as if wiping off the same chill that enveloped them all.

Without forewarning, the huge fireplace exploded into a fiery storm and a roaring blaze lashed out at them. Giant talons of fire stabbed at their feet, and they jumped back to avoid a scorching. When the flames died down somewhat, the onlookers fixed their eyes on the devilish anatomy that danced before them in the fire.

Orange-red glowed inside two oval cut-outs above dagger-sharp teeth. A rib cage the size of a buffalo sat on thick haunches of bone. Razor sharp scythes protruded from each of its four feet, making any kick or the slightest slash from the beast a lethal hit. The grisly form matched one of the gypsy's drawings depicted in the ancient book, except that it appeared far more terrifying in person.

Skeletal hands leaped from the flames, and the group jumped back even farther.

"Read the card, Adley!" Pablo demanded.

The giant flames lashed out again, and this time they latched aggressively onto Roger's ankles.

"Aaahh!" He gave an agonizing yelp as it knocked him to the ground and dragged him toward the fireplace.

Adley and Victor stood frozen like statues, immobilized by the unbelievable sight. Victor heard Roger begging for help but his shoes, like Adley's, remained rooted to the ground.

She tried to speak but her vocal chords were as petrified as the rest of her body.

It was Great-Uncle Pablo who first reacted and firmly

grasped Roger by his wrists, stretching him like a human rope in a tug of war, an old man on one end and knife-like talons at the other. They all heard a deadly snicker as the Roger writhed, fighting to save his life like an animal in an iron trap.

"Adley!" Pablo ordered. "Read the counter-curse! Victor, help me!"

Both teens were entranced by the horrifying sight, too consumed by fear to take any action.

Adley stuttered over the words. "I—I—remove the curse—"

"—read from the card!" Pablo yelled. "You must say it exactly as it is written!"

Roger's body slid closer to the blazing inferno, dragged by the bony shackles imprisoning his feet, but Pablo kept his hands riveted to the other man's arms. He bravely stared directly into the ever-changing eyes, now ebony, soulless pits that served as a portal to hell.

The demonic eyes slivered into fish-shaped ellipses, then widened back into large gaping holes. The empty cavity where its nose belonged was a black asterisk, splintered on all the edges. It grinned like a devil with sharpened fangs.

The creature deliberately stared with hypnotizing eyes at the old man as pincer-like fingers squeezed into Roger's flesh. Roger wailed in agony and his screams struck terror in the two teens. Cemented in place, they witnessed the razor-sharp bone easily penetrate his leather shoes and thickly padded socks, slicing through to the skin. Great-Uncle Pablo rapidly tired, straining with all the effort his aging body could summon.

The vile monster was too powerful, and inched Roger's body closer to the licking flames. The all too familiar hissing and snickering turned Adley to stone and shook Victor to the core. They were Roger's last hope and had supremely failed him as the skeletal creature dragged him closer to his demise.

"Adley!" Pablo cried to the girl, who stared transfixed at the surreal image of death. He called her again, and she finally snapped to attention. Immediately, she looked down at the card and faltered, mumbling incoherent sounds. Her mouth refused to cooperate. Tears washed her cheeks and she started over, dribbling words like a babbling baby.

Victor had been trance-like as well, but as he recovered from the initial shock, he found a spot of courage and managed to react. Even if Adley read the words on the card, he was too afraid to touch the horrid monster.

He tore at the zipper on his cargo pocket to retrieve his hematite stone, but the pull-tab broke off and the zipper wouldn't open. In a moment of pure instinct, he grabbed at a large table lamp, hoisted it above his head, and hurled it at the spiny torso. Both the lamp and the bones shattered into hundreds of spiked fragments.

The fire immediately went out and the house lights flickered on and off before the entire bottom level of the mansion was immersed in incandescent light. All was eerily quiet. Pablo hoisted Roger up, who quivered in the old man's grasp. Leaning heavily for support against Pablo's aged body, Roger surveyed the damage.

His thick socks acted as temporary bandages on his bleeding cuts, stopping the flow of blood. Shaken beyond measure, the horrified bystanders caught their breath, overwhelmed by the violent attack. The index card with the carefully written counter-curse was crushed in Adley's hand.

Victor kicked at the small, white pieces of bone amidst the shards of the broken china lamp. Razor-sharp fragments lay piled in front of the scorched hearth.

"Is it dead?" he whispered.

"It couldn't be that easy," his great-uncle said.

Roger surveyed his blood-soaked socks. "You call that easy?" he croaked.

"The pain will keep you conscious," Great-Uncle Pablo said. He jolted to attention as if coming to his senses. "Quick, Adley, say the counter-curse, and Victor can pick up a piece of bone. Hurry!"

"But I'm not looking in its eyes anymore!" she protested.

Roger saw that his daughter was in shock and yelled, "Read the paper!"

She fumbled with the index card, flattened it out, and flipped it over.

"Look! Some of the pieces are moving!" Victor said.

As quickly as they had fragmented, the pieces of bone magically began to reassemble themselves, attaching like powerful magnets to other minuscule sections. It was as if they watched a live puzzle complete itself, piece by monstrous piece, into another gruesome form. Everyone had the sense to back away, but not to flee. They stared open-mouthed as the pieces of bone mutated into a wolf-like frame with the features of a skull that conjured a remotely human resemblance.

They remain transfixed, immobile, until the monster snapped it jaws.

Chapter 28

Roger was the first to step out of his fear. "Read the card!" he shouted.

Victor held Adley's hand as the paper shook in her other. She stuttered over the words. "I—I–now—re—release—I mean, remove—"

She and Victor were unaware that they had been backing up to the stairs. When Pablo saw that they had backed out of the room, it was too late. The mosaic of bone had sprung to the entrance of the formal living room, separating the teenagers from the adults.

"You must read the exact words from the card!" Pablo shouted at Adley. "Victor! Don't be afraid! Get ready to touch it!"

The clump of ivory stalked viciously toward the couple, gleaming at its prey.

Adley finally looked down at the paper and rotated it right side up. "I now remove this untrue curse—"

Before she could say the next words, another brilliant explosion of embers burst forth from the fiery pit, and Adley saw her father and Pablo swallowed by a blinding orange light. Victor turned his back and shielded Adley from the eruption.

She crouched next to him, holding his muscled arms to

steady herself. The index card fell out of her hand, unseen, to the first stair behind her.

The blast had propelled the bodies of the two men into the nearest wall, knocking them both unconscious. The skeleton inspected the slumped bodies on the floor then swung its head back to the terrified spectators.

"Say, it, Adley! Say the words!" Victor frantically told her as the hissing freak swayed like a drunkard and ambled toward them.

Adley looked down to the floor, but the card wasn't in sight.

"I dropped the card!" she cried. "Where is it?"

She looked up and saw the cavernous skull sweep from side to side as it advanced, looming forward, straight toward them. Both Adley and Victor had forgotten the many warnings of Great-Uncle Pablo and, instead of overcoming their fear, they gawked at the forbidding image.

Finally, Victor realized how close the horrible thing was to them. "Run!"

His voice boomed. Adley obeyed his command. She tore her vision away from the bony creature and ran down the hall toward the kitchen. Victor darted up the staircase, thinking Adley was right behind him. He heard the clattering of bone on hardwood floor, galloping toward the kitchen, and knew that Adley was in serious trouble.

He raced back down the stairs. "Adley! I'll save you!"

His sentiments were heroic, but his actions weren't. Halfway down the stairs, his shoestring caught on a broken piece of tile. Victor's body plunged over the stairs, belly-flopping onto terra cotta floor of the foyer. The air whooshed out of his lungs, and his cargo pocket popped open. The hematite stone rolled out of the fabric as Victor's head walloped against the floor, and his limbs sprawled clumsily outward. The blow to his head knocked him out.

Now all three men were oblivious to Adley's desperate cries for help.

❦ ❦ ❦

As soon as Victor gave the order to run, Adley did just that. The phantom tore after her, roaring savagely in rapid pursuit.

"Where to?" she shouted to Victor, but heard no reply. She looked left and right and called out again for him over her shoulder. She was afraid to think why Victor wasn't responding. A terrible insight tore through her like a sharp dagger. She was alone, vulnerable, and the only one who had a chance of saving her was nowhere to be seen.

Adley glanced behind her and saw that she was being chased by a new version of the monster. A spindly spider-like skeleton, with long, angled legs and a rope-like antennae attached to a pie-shaped exoskeleton, chased her toward the kitchen. Frantic, she didn't want to remain in the house to confront the inevitable, preferring to find a method of escape outside, in the hopes that the frightening ghoul didn't follow.

Adley barreled past the sturdy kitchen door. Without thinking, she lunged for the heavy oak butcher's block and muscled it against the door, a sufficient but temporary barricade. Her mother prepared meals on the thick wooden surface and probably never imagined that the solid table doubled as a barrier to keep monsters out of the kitchen. Just in case, Adley shoved a metal knife sharpener through the handle of the door and an iron towel hook on the wall.

The predator plowed into the door, intent on finding a way in.

"Victor!" Adley squealed. "Dad!"

She felt every muscle tense as she pushed against the

door, while scouting furiously for a weapon, and spotted a metal hammer-shaped meat tenderizer hanging from the pot rack high above the area where the butcher block had been. Her strength was fast diminishing against the force of her horrid pursuer on the other side of the door. She had to get to the mallet before the monster could attack her.

Suddenly the door gave way a few inches and a whip of rope-thin, fleshless bone swung into the room. Pointed, double-edged fingernails, tapered to thin tips, mercilessly slashed at her hand. Adley screamed at the hostile on-slaught, her skin burning as each vicious nail gouged into her skin. With all the strength she could muster, she slammed the block against the door. The arm severed and she was free of the long, bony tether.

The string of bone fell to the floor, but Adley knew she only had seconds before it repaired itself. Just as quickly, she formulated the semblance of a plan as pieces of the ap-pendage slid back under the door to rejoin the rest of the maniacal force.

The pot rack was securely hung from steel pipe extend-ers which were fastened to a massive beam in the vaulted ceiling, strong enough to support Adley's weight. If she jumped from the block to the tiled counter, she could scale the cabinetry like a ladder, the top of which would put her about eight feet off the ground. With a flying leap a few feet up and over, Adley could perch on top of the steel rack's crossbar, at least two feet higher than the cupboards. With any luck, the demonic entity couldn't reach her. For a few moments, anyway. Maybe by then someone would come to her rescue.

A few seconds felt much longer as Adley mounted the counters and climbed atop the cabinets. She sprang toward the metal bars in the same instant the kitchen door burst open. The sturdy metal rod holding the pot rack felt like heaven in her hands as ravenous jaws opened wide beneath her, roaring and spitting with a hateful vengeance. She clung to the rack as her body dangled wildly in the air.

The creature jumped up and snapped at her outstretched limbs. She pulled her knees up high, narrowly escaping the sharp fangs. The contorted body squirmed in midair then fell back to the floor and immediately prepared to launch itself again.

Adley climbed to the top of the rack, directly above the hellish spectacle, grateful that it held her weight. The creature crouched below, and she knew it was getting ready to jump. The pots and pans were attached to the S-shape at the bottom of the long, straight hooks so one could easily reach them. In a matter of seconds, she lifted the long steel stick off of the rack that held the hammer-like meat tenderizer well below her at the bottom of the hook.

In her hands, the cooking tool appeared small and insignificant next to the size of the wretched monstrosity below, but it was all she had. The long metal stick that once held the tenderizer clattered to the floor. The wolf-like mass dodged it then launched itself like a rocket. Adley hung off the side of the pot rack and hurled the mallet with an impressive effort. The object struck the center of the creature's head as it rose in mid-air. It was a lucky hit that broke the target into a carpet of hundreds of splintery fragments.

Adley knew that, in no time, all the pieces would reform into a more extraordinary shape than the last one. She dropped nimbly to the floor, landing noisily on the wreckage. She kicked at the pile and scattered the pieces, hoping to buy time for a hasty escape, not only from the kitchen, but from Capilla Manor altogether.

She ran over the crumbled bones, and they crunched and cracked sickeningly beneath her as she scrambled out of the kitchen and sprinted back toward the stairs to find Victor.

He had barely come to when he saw Adley charge through the main hall. He groped his forehead, where a huge knot rose under the skin.

"Adley! Are you all right?"

"Yes! Are you?"

"Yeah." He staggered as she helped him to stand upright. "Where is it?"

The kitchen door burst open.

"Right there!" she yelled.

As Adley had predicted, the monster was more ominous than before. It maintained canine features in the skull, but the body was huge and hunched, like a small but hefty dinosaur.

Adley choked, and "Oh, no!" managed to eke out.

The two stood incapacitated as the thing hissed. Nasty pus-colored poison drooled from its mouth, sizzling as it plopped on the floor. The creature headed straight for them like a stalking wildcat set to leap on its prey.

Its eye sockets were bigger since the last morphing. Numerous teeth were cones sharpened to an acute pinpoint. It bit into empty space, and the powerful jaws slammed shut. Two shriveled forearms were shorter than the rear legs, and the claws on each hind foot were as sharp as any blade they had ever seen. A forked tongue, several feel long, whipped out of the colossal jaws and thrashed through the air. The scaly flesh flew directly at Adley.

Victor didn't have a chance to issue a warning. He bravely jumped in front of her and the sinewy rope wrapped itself with impressive speed into a coil around his neck. The demonic creature yanked at the roped tongue, and Victor fell forward, gasping for breath. It reeled him in, wailing in morbid delight.

Adley's protective instincts rose to the surface filling her with renewed strength. She ran past Victor and pummeled the top of the appendage with her boot. It hissed and pulled in its tongue, leaving a slippery gooey mess on Victor's neck.

"Gross!" he choked.

"Get up now," Adley warned and awkwardly assisted him to stand upright as he caught his breath.

"Hurry! Come this way!" Victor directed. The incessant blaring was so loud he had to shout at the top of his lungs to be heard. "Stay with me!"

He tugged on Adley's hand, and they barreled into the living room to rescue the two unconscious men. Towering flames flared out from the fireplace, forcing the terrified couple back to the foot of the stairs, within striking distance of the atrocious creation. It licked its bony lips and crouched, ready to spring.

Adley caught sight of the card Pablo had given her. She snatched it off the bottom stair just as the beast charged. Victor snagged Adley's arm, dragging her up the stairs and away from the lunging skeleton. The massive size of the bony framework forced it to roll past them and hurtle against a wall.

As they flew up the steps Adley wondered if Victor could muster up the courage to touch the menacing thing. It's claws and tongue were deadly, but if it didn't break apart again, how was he going to accomplish the task? He'd missed another opportunity to pick up a bone, but it wasn't exactly a good time to scold him when something wanted to pick them out of its teeth.

They sprinted up the steps and around the curved stairwell to the second story. In the hallway, they staggered left toward the master bedroom, but a thunderous roar from behind the door sent them scuttling in the other direction.

"How did it get into your parents room?" Victor shouted as he grabbed Adley's hand at the top of the stairs.

"It could always do that—send sound to a different room!"

Victor tugged on Adley's arm, but she didn't budge. He looked down the stairs at what caught her attention. She was staring at the mid-way landing, right into the eyes of the evil that hunted them. Victor was stunned by her heroic gesture, but was too afraid to stick around.

"C'mon, it's going to kill us!"

He pulled on her arm but Adley pulled back even harder. She glowered at the sickening stick figure, crouched and ready to catapult itself at them.

She took a quick breath and recited as fast as she could, "I now remove this untrue curse and its hold on me altogether. It is dissolved into a state of nothingness now and forever!"

The other-worldly spirit bawled, a dark cry bellowing from its lungs. The monster convulsed as bones moved from one part of the ivory structure to the other. It shuddered in agony, howling until it finally stilled. Its eyes creased into slashes, and it looked at Adley then at Victor with a new hunger.

"Now you have to touch it!" she said to Victor.

"You want me to touch *that*?" he hollered back.

The terrifying shape-shifter leaped up at them with the force of a volcanic eruption. They barely had a second to bolt toward Adley's former bedroom. The ghoulish creation brushed the back of Adley's hair and she quivered at its vile touch while its momentum carried the monster forward. It plunged into the wall, spraying clusters of bone chips across the hall. A sharp fragment pierced her shoulder, and she ripped it out, throwing it at the dissected fiend.

"No!" Victor shouted. "I need that!"

It was too late when she realized what she had done. Victor could have touched the calcium fragment and ended their problems in an instant.

A muscle-stinging chill coursed down Adley's spine, and Victor braced to break her fall. She collapsed uncontrollably into his hold. He knew he could pick up a fragment and destroy the unworldly being, but he held Adley in his arms.

"Get up!" he yelled at her. "I need to touch one of the bones!"

He helped Adley's dazed form to stand, but by the time they looked back, the shards had already amassed and developed into a hulking torso and a skull resembling a prehistoric alligator with elongated legs. It had claws like a raptor, a thick jaw with shark-like teeth. The two gathered their wits and resumed their race toward the other side of the second story. The distorted monster regained its balance and took off after them.

They ran the length of the corridor, thwarted by the wall at the end of it. When they spun around, Victor gallantly shielded Adley with his arms, watching in horror as the dreadful, clambering bones slowly closed in on them. It hissed and snickered, lumbering purposefully to build their fear.

Poisonous saliva dripped, oily and yellow. The monster licked the rim above its mouth, as if starving for a human meal. Its talons caught on the carpet, easily ripping through the fibers as it moved toward them.

"It can't kill me!" Adley yelled over the incessant screeching of the monster, trying to wrestle free from Victor's hold.

"But it can still hurt you, babe. I'm not going to let anything happen to you!"

She locked fiercely onto his arm, watching in dread as

the sinister pile of bones advanced on them. "What are we going to do?" she cried.

"Don't worry!" he yelled.

She glared at him. It was the worst possible thing he could have said at that moment.

Adley was on the brink of complete hysteria, but before she could scream about his frustrating remark, the devil's servant screeched.

"Eeee-ahhk!"

Adley shielded her ears as Victor searched helplessly for a way out. They had no means of escape, cornered by the hellhound, trapped at the far end of the west wing in what was truly a dead end.

"We have only one place to go!" Victor yelled. He shoved Adley toward her old bedroom.

"Are you crazy?!" Adley struggled against him. "It lives in there! We can't go into that room!"

"It can go anywhere without the handle!" Victor reminded her.

She pressed against him, but he shoved on her back as if she was a human battering ram. With one tremendous push, he heaved her into the room and raced in behind her as the savage hunter pounced, missing them by a split second. The skeleton's momentum carried it forward, and it crashed into the wall at the end of the corridor.

As the door swung shut, they heard bone fragments scatter against the wall and over the carpet, clicking and clacking like a giant rattle.

Frost layered everything in the entire room. Walls and windows were iced over. Their breath misted in little white clouds as they exhaled into the frigid air.

Victor whirled toward the door and yelled, "Shoot! I can touch a broken piece of bone!"

He raced back toward the door as Adley shouted, "Wait! No, Victor!"

Victor ripped the door wide open and stood face to face with black, bottomless eye sockets and teeth as sharp as cactus needles.

It hissed like a cat and whipped its head back, ready to spit out its deadly tongue.

Chapter 29

Victor slammed the door shut and bounded atop Adley's bed, shoving the reluctant girl ahead of him. "That's another chance I missed to destroy that bloody anomaly!"

Adley repeated Pablo's directive in a frail voice thinned by trauma. "You have to touch it, Victor."

They huddled atop the arctic comforter as the creature repeatedly rammed against the door. "I know, I know. I'm going to touch that creep if it's the last thing I do," he muttered while his eyes frantically scoured the room for any type of weapon.

In the kitchen, Adley had fought blindly because she had a reason to escape. She wanted to get to Victor and then flee the mansion. Now that they were trapped, the reality of their ill-fated situation sank in. It could only seriously injure her, but it had the power to kill Victor.

"We have to stay together!" she reminded him, half crazed. Tears carved through her eye make-up and sweat lines streaked down her cheeks.

Adley remained spellbound by the shadow swaying back and forth that she could see under the crack of the door.

It sounded like a brattling pile of carnage sliding up

against the wooden barrier before it started to bulldoze its way in.

Victor saw that Adley was rapidly sinking into shock. Her skin was pale, her face unnaturally tense, and her back was rigid. Her fingers were white, a human vise on his arm, and her body began to tremble. The scraping on the other side of the door told him he had to act fast.

That's when Adley noticed that he was suddenly too quiet. "You're going to say something I don't want to hear, aren't you?"

"Stay here," he ordered. "I have a plan."

"I was right!" she whimpered. "I didn't want to hear that!"

Adley panicked. Hysterically clutching at Victor, she clawed his back and hair, kicking him unintentionally as she tried to climb on top of him. They teetered on the mattress, and Victor struggled to stand upright.

"You're going to make us fall down!" he warned.

"You're not leaving me! You're not going anywhere, Victor Trumillo!"

Her efforts proved futile. Victor managed to shove her away to arm's length. His hands dug into her shoulders and he took her by surprise saying, "I'll never leave you, Adley. You're stuck with me. For life."

He gently brushed his lips over hers then pried her fingers off, pulling away from her brawny grasp. He grimaced at the relief from the searing pain that encompassed his arms and back.

It was outrageous to see him stand on the floor and kneel down, as if he were going to crawl beneath the bed. Victor gazed purposefully at Adley. She felt trepidation etched upon her face, but he didn't pay attention to it or the continuous buckling of the door as their attacker on the other side repeatedly flung itself against it.

"Please! No! Don't leave me here!" Adley begged.

She spread her arms open as if they had the power to magically draw him back, but he deliberately stayed out of her reach.

Strongly composed and entirely too calm, Victor said, "Trust me, Adley," and then he disappeared beneath the bed.

Adley's throat was raw, her vision clouded by tears. It wasn't that she didn't trust Victor. She simply didn't want to be left alone with her worst nightmare.

"I trust you, Victor!" she squawked hysterically through her tears. "Stay here! Please!" She crawled to the edge of the mattress and didn't see a trace of him. "Victor!" she screamed, beckoning his return. But it was too late. He was gone. Maybe forever. Adley whimpered softly, "No. Come back, Victor. Please, come back."

He'd left her right when she needed him the most—right when a deafening uproar blasted from the hallway, and the bedroom door abruptly burst open. Adley convulsed at the physical state of the bizarre skeleton positioned before her. The oversized head on the deformed body bobbed up and down like a demented puppet. It dangled as if on an invisible piece of elastic, bouncing insanely toward her.

Adley crawled back to the headboard and felt the smooth surface. Curved lengths of bones worked into small arches. She finally recognized the familiar pattern that was so contrary in nature to the rest of the room. When they first met in the library Victor told her about the bed made of bones.

Adley touched the remnants of victims past, descendants of the gypsy who had inadvertently put a curse upon innocent children who probably spent every day dreading their bleak futures.

The grotesque monstrosity inched forward, hissing as it

approached closer and closer, until it stood at the foot of the bed. Her eyelids were stuck open, and Adley felt a foreboding hopelessness. Her muscles felt depleted of any strength, and she was unable to run away. She had nothing left to fight for her life. The Grim Reaper stared her in the face, and all she could do was stare right back into the large asterisk edged eyes, black craggy tunnels leading to unending misery.

The monster sneered at her and tilted its head all the way below its shoulder. A low, harsh whisper filled the room. "Aaa! Aaad!" It was on the verge of saying her name. The hissing warped into coherent syllables. "Aaadd—"

"No!" she whimpered aloud. "Don't you dare say my name! I don't want you to say it!"

The abrasive sound it emitted was all the more vulgar when it snarled, "Aaad-leee!"

A seed of anger rose from a hollow pit in her stomach. She steadfastly refused to suffer at the hand of a malignant disfigurement that had the nerve to call her by name. It was too personal an act, an insult she wouldn't allow. She mentally recited the words Victor's mother said to her before they left the safety of Trumillo Ranch.

Maria said Adley was strong and capable of doing anything, even this.

Adley found a new resolve to resist, to combat the awful being, and to take a stand. She anchored her hands solidly onto the headboard.

Her outrage erupted further. If that thing was able to call her by name, then she was able to tell it what she thought of all the killings and violence.

Securely cemented to the headboard she yelled at it. "I'm going to give you a piece of my mind!"

"Yesssss! Piece by piece!" it hissed and grotesquely

bounced all the more, taking perverse pleasure in scaring her to no end.

"That's not what I meant," she said. What possessed her to dialogue with it? Victor might have applauded her for stalling, but that wasn't her intention. She was outraged by the injustice, the unfair destruction of innocents. "You killed children to make this bed! You hurt people who didn't deserve it, you…you sorry waste of energy!"

It bellowed and whooped in wicked delight. "Now you die!" it hissed.

"I said the counter-curse. You can't kill me!" she argued.

"You will wish to die," it gleefully cackled. It wiggled dagger-like fingers at her and sneered with contempt. "You shall die drop by bloody drop!"

She no longer cared how the bed was constructed. Adley seized the headboard for dear life. Her cheek lay flush against the smooth sections of the bones and she prayed for victims past to come to her aide. She crouched in a ball, limbs tucked beneath her while the ghoul hunkered at the edge of the mattress.

Its bony arms abnormally lengthened, stretching longer and longer. Bladed fingers cut through the layers of the mattress, and two thin lines inched their way toward her. Adley sobbed as she realized what the menacing creature was about to do.

Almost as strong as her fear was the disheartening knowledge that her life would end violently, with regret and alone. She should have held tighter to Victor and not let him leave her. Maybe she should have gone with him so they could have spent their last moments alive together. Adley wished she'd had more control over her anger and had put invisible tape over her mouth so she didn't talk back to her parents. None of that mattered now.

"Victor! I need you!" she called. Her outcry went unheeded.

The monster lifted its head in response to her agonizing plea. In a flash, taloned hands leaped out and snared her ankles. Adley cried out through raw vocal chords as the spiky fingers pierced her jeans, jabbing sharp nails into her flesh. The rest of its hideous body slithered beneath the bed. She heard the monster snicker, and Adley tried one last time before completely giving up her fight.

"Dad! Help! It's pulling me under! Daaad!" No reassuring responses came back. No shouts from her father running to her rescue. Nothing from Victor or his great-uncle.

Adley really was going to die alone.

Sapped of her last ounce of strength, unable to maintain contact with the bed, Adley's weakened hands lost their hold from the headboard. Her limbs sailed horizontally onto the mattress. She clutched the comforter but it proved worthless. The skeletal being dragged her toward the foreboding depths below.

"No! No!" she groaned, feebly attempting to latch onto anything to hold onto but to no avail.

The monster drank in her fear and hissed loudly in triumph. Its limb snapped back toward her and paused to run a razored fingernail down her cheek, creating a bloody line to her chin.

Adley twisted onto her back to prevent her legs from breaking in half when she was painfully lurched over the edge of the bed. Her feet reached the floor and she stood, flapping her arms for balance. Another ferocious wrench on her ankles sent her flying forward, and her arms slapped the floor to break her fall. The creature hauled on her weary body, and she slid farther into the black pit beneath the bed, toward the dark abyss where evil lurked and the curse hungered for more victims. One slow cut at a time to bleed her out, it said, and her life in this world would be over.

She wished the last thing she saw could be Victor's face, but instead, a rope-like hand whipped past her, slammed the door closed, and she heard a definitive click of the lock. A wicked screech filled the room, a victorious broadcast of finality, evoking more fear from its next victim. The high-pitched howling continued as the skeletal rope towed the rest of her battered body beneath the bed.

Depleted with all but an ounce of energy, Adley was comforted by the thought of her very last spoken word.

"Victor," she whispered.

☣ ☣ ☣

The two men finally regained consciousness. Pain ensnared Roger's legs yet his desire to find his daughter sent a surge of adrenaline through his veins. He was assisting Pablo off the ground when someone, or something, screeched in earsplitting decibels from the second story.

"It's Adley!" her father shouted.

The men, hunched over and limping, rushed to the stairs as fast as their beaten bodies could manage—Pablo, his old body taxed to its limit, and Roger, barely able to stand on his injured legs. Despite their physical maladies, they scuttled up each step as fast as possible toward the pleas for help, all the way to Adley's old bedroom. They stood in front of the door, and by then, it was hard to distinguish whether the howls were human or otherwise.

The battered door was locked. "Stand back!" Roger said. He rushed the door with all his strength, but hammering the door with his body was futile.

"Let me help you!" Pablo insisted.

Together the men charged, and their shoulders met the wooden barrier simultaneously. The jolt against the solid door threw them both backward. Suddenly, more frightening than the shrill chaotic racket, was the eerie silence that instantly enshrouded the house.

The muted seconds were an eternity to the men who didn't want to imagine what might be happening inside the room. The sound of nails scratching the wood floor inside Adley's old room was followed by another earsplitting screech, a shrieking trumpet, blaring the triumph of the generational curse.

Once more the two men dove forward, tackling the wooden obstacle that caved in under pressure. They landed on the door as it shot into the room and skidded toward the bed.

The only sign of Adley was her white-knuckled fists entwined in the tattered remains of the dust ruffle. When the door slid to a stop, Pablo and Roger scrambled to their feet and firmly grabbed hold of Adley's hands.

"We've got you, Deedee!" her father called.

Just as it felt like the skin over her ankles was peeling off, Adley felt warm, fleshy hands rip her away from the stabbing grasp of spiked nails.

Much to her surprise and relief, the sharp pincers unexpectedly surrendered their bite.

With both men grappling her wrists she flew out from under the mattress, and their combined gravity sent all three bodies soaring backward. They landed in a human pile on top of the door and groaned from the collision of limbs. They quickly untangled themselves, and after Great-Uncle Pablo caught his breath, he ushered them out of the chilled room.

"Where's Victor?" Pablo gasped.

"Under the bed!" Huge drops of tears streamed down Adley's cheeks. "He said he wasn't going to leave me, and that's when I last saw him."

A noise from under the bed jolted their nerves. A loud thump resounded against the wood floor, and the three huddled in the hallway, wide-eyed and gripped with fear.

Chapter 30

A hand, then another, wormed out from under the bed, followed by the rest of Victor's bruised and scraped, but otherwise unharmed, body.

Both men rushed to his side. Adley stayed right behind them, unwilling to be left alone anywhere. The men snatched Victor by his wrists and dragged him out of the room.

Adley and his uncle knelt beside him while Roger glanced at the area under the bed.

"What happened?" they all asked at once.

For a moment, the boy couldn't figure out who was speaking.

"Victor, are you all right?" Adley asked.

His chest heaved as he gulped for oxygen, and sweat dripped down his brow. He dug into his pants pocket and pulled out a handkerchief lightly wrapped about a piece of metal. It was the hematite fixture that had been taken off the bedroom door.

Pablo shook him. "What happened?"

Victor tried to respond to his uncle's question in between gasps and wheezed, "Nothing—I couldn't—handle."

☣ ☣ ☣

The families basked in the soothing warmth of the early morning sun barely starting to stream through the large picture window in the den of Capilla Manor. Cups of freshly brewed coffee dotted the end tables in the room. Victor and Adley were inseparable, except earlier that morning when Victor joined Roger and his great-uncle in dismantling the bed adorned with bones. They burned it a short distance down road on the farthest corner of Grandma Aggie's acreage.

Maria and Gloria busied themselves in the backyard, cutting some of the wildflowers for a table centerpiece. Maria brought in the first bunch and laid them on a flat wicker basket. She smiled like a lotto winner, arranging the flowers in a vase on top of the antique rolling cart.

Caroline stirred creamer into her coffee and looked at Victor. "How exactly did you touch that creature?"

"I didn't have a chance to. I planned to throw the hematite stone at it, but somehow it dropped out of my pocket so I threw the handle at the skeleton instead."

"How in the world did you get the silver handle?" Roger asked, his hands perched on the curve of his walking cane. "I took it to the pawn shop an hour or so before we were run out of the house."

"While Mrs. Lange was having her ankle bandaged and I had to go out front to cool off, Anne Marie drove up. She said you had pawned Grandma Aggie's silver handle and asked if we'd be interested in having it back since she knew my great-uncle was the man who made it. I figured that it wasn't going to work anymore and zipped it into one of my cargo pockets. After we got to talking about going back to Aggie's, I forgot all about it."

"How did you know the skeleton would go under the bed?" Great-Uncle Pablo asked.

Victor smiled. "I didn't. I thought that since we were in

Adley's old room, and it always seemed to crawl in and out from under her bed—"

"You mean you took a chance on leaving me defenseless with the potential of dying before it dragged me under?" Adley was shocked that he had taken such a risk, especially with her life. "I thought we were friends!"

Victor squeezed her hand and shrugged. "I knew it couldn't kill you. I had a feeling and went with it." Then he spoke to the others. "You should have seen it down there. It was really weird. Like a whole other dimension of darkness opened up underneath that old bed. I was in some kind of dark cave but once the handle struck bone, the black folded in on itself, and I was back on the hardwood floor."

"*Ay, Diós!*" Maria said, cupping a hand over her mouth.

"A good thing you threw it," Pablo said, "but now the handle embodies the essence of the skeleton, and we don't know how long it will hold. With the curse ended, a ritual cleansing is needed to destroy its residual power while we still have it trapped inside the handle."

"Why not just destroy the whole thing—the box you put it in and the handle—all at once?" Roger asked, and the others nodded their sentiments.

"One must touch its bones to destroy it completely, but since that didn't happen we must take extra precautions to remove its power once and for all," Pablo said.

Victor hung his head. "I'm sorry. I was so afraid to go near it."

"No one blames you," Pablo assured him. "If you'll remember, we were all afraid. I'll also make certain that the handle is never found, an extra precaution so the monster has no chance of ever regaining its strength if I'm not successful in taking its power away."

"Why don't you just melt down the handle?"

"Destroying the handle will permit its escape, just as much as removing it from the box, which is why we must take its power first.

"Can you do that?" Adley asked.

"A true gypsy can perform a special ritual to send the destructive energy deep into the earth where it will be filtered by the soil and other natural elements," Pablo explained. "When it rises back to the surface, it will no longer have any power."

Maria placed another arrangement of flowers on the low coffee table and sat on the sofa with Victor and Adley. "Enough of this talk of curses and evil." She leaned toward the matching loveseat where Adley's parents sat. "Do you recognize a change for the better in your daughter's temperament now that this curse has ended?"

"Now that you mention it…" Roger gazed at his daughter a moment. "You mean that thing actually influenced Adley's attitude?"

"Gloria and I found hidden text in pictures of the manuscript," Maria said. "It said an intended victim became irritable and unreasonable months before the attack, some over a year. The agitation grew the closer they came to their sixteenth birthday."

"And it said that just being in the presence of a Del Diego descendant would help to ease those bad feelings," Pablo added.

Adley playfully elbowed Victor. "That's why I like being around you," and Victor gently shouldered her back.

Pablo looked approvingly at Adley. "I'm sure that what Adley has gone through has made her appreciate her family more than she ever imagined," he said to her parents.

Adley overheard and agreed. "It really has."

She stood up and made her way around the table to enthusiastically hug each of her parents.

"I'm glad to hear that, honey." Her father lovingly embraced her. "You know, after that mile run to Trumillo Ranch, I think we'll take a family membership at the nearest gym."

Adley and Caroline frowned, as if the man had suggested scuba diving in the sewer.

"Dad, can't we find a different way of spending family time together?"

Laughter filled the room. Adley took her place next to Victor, but he interrupted the lighthearted bantering. "Sorry, but I can't seem to take my mind off the nightmares of the past week. Uh, *tío*, remember that awful monster in the handle?" he asked his great-uncle. "You said a true gypsy has to perform the ritual, but where are we going to find a gypsy around here?"

"We have a Rodrigues descendant amongst us," Pablo said and gestured to Adley's father.

Roger smiled but then turned sober. "You're serious?"

Pablo nodded.

"After what I've seen and heard these last few days, I guess I'd believe anything," Roger said. "I'll be glad to perform any ritual necessary to rid us of that repulsive creature once and for all."

"Hey! That means I'm a gypsy, too. Why can't I do it?" Adley suggested.

Great-Uncle Pablo smiled at Adley. "You continue to show how brave you've become. However, the victim of the curse cannot be the one to destroy it after it manifested into physical form. Gypsy rules." He shrugged. "I'll make the preparations and tell you all the details tonight. We can complete the ceremony tomorrow," he said to Roger.

Pablo spoke again to Adley. "Exactly one day after your birth hour, after eight o'clock tonight, you will be safe forever, whether that monster is destroyed or not. It won't be able to even tap you with the tip of a bone, but as a preventative measure—" He carefully placed a silk-wrapped parcel in her hand. "Here is a vial of holy water. I had it blessed by many spiritual people throughout the globe during my travels in younger days. A drop or two will protect you if the demon is able to escape the confines of the handle. I will prepare a vial for each of us," he said to the others in the room."

Adley glanced at the clock. "That's about nine more hours from now." She looked squarely at Victor. "If you aren't planning on crawling into any dark pits this morning, maybe we can spend some time together."

Nervous chuckles spread through the room, but it was a good release of anxiety. Victor assisted Adley in opening the vial of holy water while Great-Uncle Pablo addressed the adults.

"Meanwhile, I am keeping the handle encased in a small wooden box filled with sea salt. That monster will remain in the hematite as long as it is packed away with the proper protective qualities of the pure, un-iodized salt and kept in a container made of natural material."

"How did the handle work on my door?" Adley said.

Pablo's patience seemed inexhaustible. "The handle alone should have held, but as a preventative measure I poured sea salt through the hole where the fixture goes before I installed it."

"But why wait another day to get rid of it?" Caroline asked.

"Because there will be a new moon tomorrow night," Pablo said. "The gypsy manuscript said that will increase the power of the cleansing process."

Adley still had reservations. "How do you know it will work?"

His mystical eyes were captivating and practically

hypnotized Adley as he spoke softly to her. "I don't know, but why find out the hard way?"

Adley instinctively palmed the hematite stone that Pablo had given her the day before. "I don't know about the rest of you, but what I want to know is where's the handle at now?"

Everyone nodded their agreement.

"The box is in the back of my truck," Great-Uncle Pablo said. "Tonight I'll wrap it in leather with several different stones, mostly turquoise, which will also help to keep its energy to a minimum. Any negativity that tries to escape, or enter, will be stopped. This evening, I'll bury the box outside in a shallow hole filled with salt. Tomorrow morning after the ritual, I'll move it to a very remote location."

"I have to admit that I never gave credence to any such ritualistic nonsense, but now we're believers," Roger said as he patted Caroline's arm, and she nodded.

"Don't worry," the old man said, and Adley's eyes flew open at the words that stopped reassuring her days ago. "By tomorrow our troubles will be over."

Gloria came into the house through the back French doors carrying a small bouquet of brightly colored flowers and a trampled, white package. Somewhere between receiving the gift and nearly being stampeded by her parents, Adley had dropped her only birthday present. Gloria handed the box to the girl.

"My abundance bowl! Thank you." Adley removed the beautiful Indian artifact from the box. She lifted the gift for her parents to see, and the feathered suede strap dangled at the side of the woven dish. "Mom, Dad. Look what Victor and his family gave me for my birthday. It will bring me goodness in all things."

"It's beautiful," her father said, with an eyeful of appreciation for the heirloom.

Adley looked about the room, resting her eyes upon Victor. "I think it's already working."

"With all that's happened, we never even celebrated your birthday," Caroline said.

"Let's wait until tonight, Mom," Adley said, "after eight o'clock."

"Perhaps you can all join us for an early dinner?" her mother asked Victor's family.

Smiles were exchanged. "That's a great idea. I'll make paella," Maria said.

Victor nudged Adley with his elbow and teased, "Remember, I get the biggest lobster."

"I'm shocked at the difference in the way it feels inside the house now that the creature is gone," Caroline said.

"Yes, it's amazing," Maria said. "Aunt Gloria and I visited Aggie quite often, and Capilla Manor never was this comfortable."

"It hasn't felt this good in years," Gloria added.

Adley chimed in. "I feel it, too. It's as if this were my first time here."

Her parents nodded and, for a few moments, the group quietly basked in the welcoming peace enveloping the residence.

"I know it feels different, Caroline, Deedee. But are you both sure you want to live here after all that went on?" Roger asked. He explained to the other adults, "I have to admit that earlier this morning I was fairly surprised when Caroline suggested we stay at Capilla Manor. Even Adley seconded the motion, but I'm sure she has other motives."

Victor laughed as Adley had been admiring his dark chocolate colored eyes. She looked about the room, embarrassed when she noticed everyone smiling at her. "What?" she asked a bit self-consciously.

"They were just wondering why you don't mind staying at Capilla Manor after all that's happened," Victor told her.

"Duh," Adley said, raising her hand as Victor continued to hold it.

All she wanted in that moment was to be close to Victor and the Trumillos for years to come. The future was a long way off, and she had no idea that one day she'd be living elsewhere, going to college, and living in her own home. Nor did she once consider the possibility that she might ever have to face the wicked demon again.

"It wasn't my room that was the problem, Dad. It was what lived inside it. I actually sensed its evilness like I can sense complete safety now. Without the skeleton, the handle, or that bed in the house, everything feels so much lighter."

"And you're lighter in the head," her father joked. "The last few times I called you Deedee, you didn't even lose your temper!"

"Dad, after hearing that thing say my name, Deedee sounds like heaven!"

Everyone laughed.

"By the way, Deedee," Caroline grinned as she enunciated her daughter's nick-name, "since we're redecorating your room, what color do you want to paint it?"

Adley immediately looked at the old relic given to her from the Trumillos. She admired the basket in her hand and watched the eagle feathers swing on the leather straps. "I think I'd like to go with Navajo White."

Adley was happier than she had ever been in her life. And like she told her father, it really did feel better inside the aged mansion. Without a doubt, the removal of the fiendish presence positively affected every space in their home and every cell of her body.

She recognized a change in her personality, too. She was at peace. Without fear, she possessed a new self-confidence and inner strength that she wanted to last forever. Adley experienced gratitude in droves. She'd learned how to appreciate others and the meaning of real friendship, especially the one she shared with Victor.

For the first time that she could remember, Adley liked herself.

She'd experienced an insane amount of growing up in the past few days. Maybe it was because like Maria said, Adley was no longer under the influence of the gypsy curse. Or maybe she grew up because she was simply another year older. Or maybe it was because Victor was holding her hand, and in front of her parents, at that.

Roger and Great-Uncle Pablo walked out to the patio and discussed the pleasant topic of restoring the estate. The women retired to the kitchen and compiled a dinner menu and shopping list. Adley and Victor sat in the living room, snuggled in the corner of the sofa group, as a black and white movie ran silently on the flat screen. They spoke quietly, rarely taking their eyes off each other.

Victor kissed Adley and she cherished the feel of his soft lips on her own.

"If your parents change their minds and decide to move back to your old home, do you think you'd still like to keep in touch?"

"We're not leaving."

"You're sure about that?"

Adley graced him with a tender smile and whispered back, "Trust me, Victor."

Epilogue

Outside, a sudden chilly breeze kicked up in the front yard, despite the sweltering summer heat. A frenetic whirlwind shrouded in an imposing gray mist, spun steadily in the front yard of Capilla Manor. Dust and dead leaves rose up into a miniature, ebony funnel. The undersized but foreboding cyclone whirled through the dry grass in dizzying spirals. It drew a crooked line to the edge of the woods, the boundary on the east side of the Lange property.

From out of nowhere, a massive black dog, with extraordinarily long canine teeth and eyes the color of blood, sneaked unnoticed into the yard. It skulked about and sniffed at the ground, following the whirlwind trail on a crooked path to Great-Uncle Pablo's old truck. The tip of the whirlwind landed on top of the wooden box and suddenly died out.

Without effort, the animal hopped into the worn bed of the truck, thickly shaded by the sweeping trees next to the mansion and a somber cloud of predestination. The dog whined a bit before easily biting into the wooden container, puncturing two holes with its sharp incisors. Salt spilled out like grains of sand.

The canine jumped down to the hard-packed earth

without making a sound and trotted out of the yard. It carried the box farther down the road and then proceeded to the edge of the woods. With its treasure firmly implanted between its teeth, it slipped unseen into the gloomy mist of the wooded landscape.

Many years later and many miles away, a contractor, hired by a lovely young couple building their first home, supervised his men while they were digging a hole for the swimming pool. A hand-carved wooden box was discovered in the dirt. The small crowd of workers gathered round in anticipation as one of the owners pried open the hardwood container. They all gaped at the beautiful silver handle inside.

Everyone thought it was a good omen to have unearthed the wonderful treasure, and it was proudly installed on the front door.

About the Author

Carole Avila is an award-winning writer, poet, playwright, and self-help author. Since reading the epic story *Go, Dog, Go!* at age three, she knew she was destined to write. "My stories are generally inspired—I dream them or they come to me at the keyboard." In a rare moment when she's not writing, she enjoys reading, sipping chai tea, hiking, and long walks on the beach.

Avila writes several different genres, including young adult, new adult, romance, children's books, paranormal romance, and literary fiction. A number of her short stories, poetry, and brief memoirs have been published, and her play, *Maria's Tortillas*, has been produced. Her paranormal, time-travel romance, *Eve's Amulet ~ Book 1*, is also published by Black Opal Books. She is also under contract with Spout Hill Press on her creative non-fiction work, *The Long Term Effects of Sexual Abuse*, based on her personal and life coaching experiences.

Contact Carole Avila at info@caroleavila.com. Subscribe to her writing blog at https://caroleavilablog.wordpress.com. Her self-improvement blog, *Healing Through Awareness and Self-Expression*, can be found at https://htase.wordpress.com.